CRITICS ARE CHARMED BY LISA COOKE!

"Cooke pens a winning debut. . . . It's a luscious, fast-paced adventure with appealing characters and great scenery."
—*RT Book Reviews*

"The novel is a well-crafted balance between amusing banter, suspenseful plot, and sexual and romantic tension. Minor characters, friendly or not, add interest to the whole. With this debut as a sample of her talent, Lisa Cooke is on the way to success, so take a cruise up the Mighty Mississippi with Lottie, Dyer, and the rest. You'll have a fine time."

—Romance Reviews Today

"Lisa Cooke writes a wonderful post–Civil War game of chance in which the stakes are love and broken hearts."
—*Midwest Book Review*

"[A] very talented, imaginative and enchanting author who knows how to grip a reader and [leave] her wanting more."

—Night Owl Romance

"[B]y page 40 I was hooked . . . an amazing sense of humor and wit . . . Easily one of the most entertaining reads in a long time."

—Fresh Fiction

It's In His Kiss

"How's it coming with the fiancé choosing?" John asked.

Katie set a stack of books on a table and frowned. "Not well, I'm afraid."

"What's wrong?"

"I'm not sure what a good husband should be like. I've never had one."

"Neither have I," he said, hoping she'd leave him out of this.

"No, but you've been married. What's most important?"

Love? Trust? Sex? Hell, he couldn't point out the last one. "I think that changes depending on the person. You'll have to decide for yourself what's important."

She lowered her gaze to her paper, her cheeks suddenly turning pink. "I think he'll have to be a good kisser."

His eyes riveted to her mouth as he thought of kissing her full, soft lips. Her tongue darted out to moisten the lower one, and he felt it in his gut . . . or maybe a little lower. Would she like his kiss? He suspected he would like hers very much. Squeezing his eyes shut, he attempted to jerk his mind back from its sidetrack. He had no business even thinking about kissing Katie Napier, but for some reason he was incapable of thinking about anything else.

Other *Leisure* books by Lisa Cooke:

TEXAS HOLD HIM

A
Midwife Crisis

Lisa Cooke

LEISURE BOOKS NEW YORK CITY

A LEISURE BOOK®

February 2010

Published by

Dorchester Publishing Co., Inc.
200 Madison Avenue
New York, NY 10016

ISBN 10: 0-8439-6362-X
ISBN 13: 978-0-8439-6362-5
E-ISBN: 978-1-4285-0795-1

The name "Leisure Books" and the stylized "L" with design are
trademarks of Dorchester Publishing Co., Inc.

Printed in the United States of America.

10 9 8 7 6 5 4 3 2 1

Visit us online at www.dorchesterpub.com.

To my wonderful children, Gus and Bethany;
you've made your momma very proud.

Acknowledgments
A special thanks to the midwives who gave technical advice for this story and all those who have brought millions of babies into this world, safe and sound. And to Diane, Erin, and Leah—the cool kids at Dorchester who make their authors feel very special.

A
Midwife Crisis

Chapter One

Wayne County, West Virginia, 1898

Grandma Cole was as good at dying as anyone Katie Napier knew. Always careful to grimace only slightly or to moan with the tiniest inflection, she had the art of suffering down pat.

"Katie?" her grandma called from the back room.

Unfortunately, she also had the uncanny ability to waylay Katie's plans, sight unseen. Katie rolled her eyes and set down her reticule. Her trip into town was about to be postponed.

"Yes, Grandma?" she yelled from the kitchen.

"Do you have anything for my rheumatism? It's hurting something fierce today."

"I'll fix you some willow tea," she answered, already stoking the fire in the old stove.

The large cast-iron contraption took up most of the corner in the little kitchen in the log cabin, and this time of year the fire stayed burning even if it was just a low sizzle. The stove heated the one-story cabin better than the fireplace, and it required less fuel. A definite benefit considering her pa never seemed to get around to chopping firewood.

Katie set the kettle on the stove and adjusted the

damper in the blackened flue. A quick gust of cold air swooshed under the kitchen door, lifting the edge of the rag rug near the sink. She took a moment to tuck the rug into the threshold before returning to the cupboard to find her willow tea. That threshold had needed to be replaced for months now, but as with everything else around here, if Katie didn't do it, it wasn't going to get done

The kettle steamed as though it read her mind. No sense in getting worked up about the chores that needed to be done. None of the others seemed to care whether the cabin fell in around their heads.

"Katie?" Grandma yelled. "Is that the kettle I hear?"

"Yes'm," Katie answered, pouring the hot water into a cup and placing the tea ball in to steep. "It'll be ready shortly."

If she hurried, she should be able to grab her coat, take the tea to Grandma, and get out the door before anyone else could postpone her trip.

The front door opened, and a rustle of dried leaves swept in with Grandpa. "Mornin', Katie girl." He attempted to hang his jacket on a peg by the door, but he missed, and like the leaves, he left it to lie as he ambled off to rest by the fire. She wasn't sure exactly what he did in the course of a day, but whatever it was, it required a lot of resting.

"Anything to eat?" he asked, stretching out in a chair by the hearth. Yawning, he scratched his belly in preparation for his morning nap. Not too unlike the coonhound already curled up by the fire, except Ol'

Blue had chased some critters that morning and actually had a reason to rest.

Katie sighed. "Can't you fix it yourself?"

She grabbed a broom, hung his jacket on the peg, and opened the door to sweep the forest back out to the porch. She was careful not to step on the rotted board by the door. If she fell through and broke her leg, they'd all starve to death before they found the kitchen.

"Now, Katie, you know I would if I could," Grandpa said, sounding even more forlorn than Ol' Blue.

Returning inside the cabin, she set the broom by the door and grabbed her cloak from its peg. "There's bread in the Hoosier, but be sure to rewrap it so it won't get stale."

She pulled on her cloak and stepped out the door, closing it as Grandpa whined, "But, Katie—"

Her family hadn't intentionally set out to ruin her day; they just didn't like it whenever she went to town. The three-mile walk into Kenova would take most of the morning, and while she was gone they had to fend for themselves. Not that they were lazy . . . overly . . . it was just that their health plagued them.

Overly.

Pa had a bad back, though how he got it was a mystery. One day he just declared he had one, and there it was. Grandma Cole had been afflicted by a similar unknown malady soon after Ma died. Grandma took to her bed to die too, declaring that life without her baby girl was too hard to bear and she'd just as soon go home to the Lord. Of course, that had been more than four

years ago, and the Lord still hadn't seen fit to take her.
Maybe He didn't want to have to fix willow tea every
whipstitch.

Grandpa Cole was a different story. Actually, he had
a different story about every time anyone asked. His
current one involved something bad with his knee, or
was it his foot? Didn't matter, whatever it was, it was
bad and required a lot of resting.

But despite everything, Katie loved them dearly.
They were all she had, and from the looks of things, all
she was ever going to get.

The crunching of fallen leaves underfoot was the
only sound as she walked down the path through the
woods toward town. As usual, the crisp fall air lifted
her spirits and relaxed the knotted muscles in her neck.
So relaxed, in fact that she'd made it to the bottom of
the hill before she realized she hadn't taken Grandma
her tea.

Oh well. Grandma would live, despite her earnest
efforts.

Truth be known, Katie really didn't need to make
this trip into Kenova, but it was the only time she
didn't have to care for anyone but herself. Besides, one
of her dresses needed a new button. The old one
was . . . scratched . . . probably.

It felt good to get out of the log cabin and into the
sunshine, if only for a few hours. Tomorrow she had to
gather herbs and begin fixing teas and poultices for winter. A lot of people depended on her for medicines and
such, and she couldn't let them down. But today was for
Katie, and she intended to enjoy every minute of it.

She patted the book of Shakespeare's plays tucked

inside her winter coat. It was time to return it to Frank Davis. He had an extensive collection of books, and he'd allowed Katie to borrow them ever since she could read. Unfortunately, she had read all he had, most of them more than once. She hugged her beloved tome once more. Parting was such sweet sorrow.

Dr. John Keffer adjusted the diploma hanging on the wall in his office for the tenth time. It wasn't that it kept tipping; he just didn't have anything else to do. In the two weeks since he'd set up practice in this little town, he'd had fewer than five patients, and two of those were afflicted with nothing more serious than curiosity. Either these people were extremely healthy or they didn't realize a genuine doctor now lived in their midst.

Not a backwoods hoyden with a bag of herbs or some smelly poultice, but a doctor with a medical degree from Harvard University. They should be pleased, honored in fact. But instead they were conspicuously absent.

"Daddy?" his daughter called from the doorway.

"Julia, you know you aren't to be in here when Daddy's working." Sounding curt even to his ears, he tried to soften his response with a smile. He hoped her five-year-old mind wouldn't realize it was forced.

Large blue eyes widened as she cocked her head to search for something in the room. Tiptoeing to the window, she opened the window seat, then shook her head so deliberately that her copper-colored ringlets bounced. Then she stooped down to look under a table and shook her head, obviously failing again.

"What are you looking for?" he asked, when his curiosity finally overcame his impatience.

She brought her finger to her lips and made a tiny shushing sound. "Sick people," she whispered.

Sick people.

He'd been looking for those himself. "Evidently, the people in this part of the country are very healthy." Or couldn't read the sign outside his door that said *Doctor*. That possibility seemed more plausible. ·

"Oh," she said, before her dimples flashed around her smile. "Can we go home, then? Maybe Mommy would come back if we go home."

"I've told you a thousand times," he snapped, "your mother can't come home." John clamped shut his mouth, forcing his gaze away from the hurt in his daughter's eyes. She was only a child. How could he expect her to understand something that was beyond his grasp as well?

"Julia?" Mrs. Adkins stepped into the room. The old housekeeper reached her hand toward Julia before glancing nervously at John. "I'm sorry, Dr. Keffer. I was making biscuits, and the next thing I knew, she'd took off."

He nodded curtly, then walked to his desk and picked up a piece of paper he pretended to read. "Yes, well, be sure to keep her out of here when I'm working."

Mrs. Adkins took Julia and hurried from the room as though she expected him to bite. Probably wise. He'd never been known to have a biting problem, but lately anything was possible.

He pitched the paper back on the desk and walked

to the window. There were no patients lining up outside his home or any ambling toward the downstairs
room he used as his office. Looked like another day of
adjusting the frames on his wall. He frowned. Waiting
around for something to happen hadn't been productive to this point. Maybe it was time to take matters
into his own hands.

Leaving the sanctuary of his office, he ventured to
the kitchen. It was rare for him to enter that part of the
house, and the coziness he encountered surprised him.
A fire burned in the fireplace, and the smell of beef
stew filled the air.

Mrs. Adkins had her biscuit dough rolled out on the
counter, and Julia sat on a tall stool cutting circles in
the dough with a tin cutter. Flour covered both the
counter and Julia as Mrs. Adkins sang quietly under
her breath. A pang of a memory caused his throat to
constrict.

Lois used to sing like that.

"Mrs. Adkins?"

She gasped and spun toward him. "I'm sorry, Dr.
Keffer, I didn't hear you call for me. Do you need
something?"

"I didn't call for you."

"Oh." She nodded, then waited for him to explain
his sudden and unusual appearance in the kitchen.
And for a brief moment, intense loneliness wrapped
around his heart.

"I wondered if I could ask you a question," he said,
forcing his mind back from its darkness.

She smiled in relief as though she'd expected him to
lash into her. Had he been that difficult? "I was won-

dering if you had an opinion as to why I've had so few patients."

Her smile faltered, then returned with no small effort on her part. "Maybe nobody's ailin'."

"Mrs. Adkins, you and I both know that is not the case."

Her round cheeks flushed as she glanced toward the floor and cleared her throat—an obvious delay tactic. "Maybe it's just because nobody knows you. Folk are kind of shy around outsiders."

"But I'm not truly an outsider. This was my grandfather's home."

"Yes, but you never lived here, and folk don't remember you visiting as a child."

What she said was true. Even he remembered very little about his visits to this town. "Thank you. I shall remedy that immediately." He turned to leave, then realized he didn't know where to remedy it. "Where should I go to meet the locals?"

She wiped her hands against her apron and wrinkled her gray eyebrows in thought. "Lots of folk visit down at the store, and of course, everybody goes to church on Sunday. If you was to go there, you'd get to meet 'bout everyone sooner or later."

The store he could deal with. Church? He hadn't been on speaking terms with God for some time now, but if it would help these simple people trust him, maybe he could tolerate it.

"I'm going out for a while. I'll be back for dinner."

Trust was an important thing. How stupid for him not to realize it had been the cause of his problem. Luckily, it would be easy to fix. After the people met him, they would realize he was an intelligent, highly educated man, more than capable of tending to their medical needs. Once he got past this obstacle, he would probably need an assistant to help with the throngs who would seek his help.

Right.

Grabbing his coat from the hall closet, he stepped out into the clear fall day. The bright oranges and reds of the maple trees contrasted sharply against the brilliant blue of the sky. As if an overzealous artist had painted the hills around town, stopping just short of the river as it snaked its way past.

The bright colors irritated him more than pleased him. The world had no right to be anything other than gray. It didn't fit.

Nothing did.

Picking up his pace, he headed for the store Mrs. Adkins felt would be the bastion of the local populace. He'd only visited the establishment once, when he'd first arrived in town. Mrs. Adkins had taken care of the purchases after she was employed, but perhaps he needed to take over that duty until he was no longer considered a stranger.

A bell jingled at the top of the door when he pulled it open to enter. The smell of tobacco and freshly ground coffee met him as he walked into the store.

A potbellied stove sat in the corner, its heat filling the interior as well as providing a central area for customers to sit and chat. Five men occupied an assortment of rocking chairs and benches around the stove, their conversation stopping abruptly when they noticed him.

"Gentlemen," he said in a form of greeting.

"Mornin'," a few of the men answered.

He nodded and walked around the store, pretending to look for things.

"Can I help you?" An older man ambled over behind the counter. His red bow tie and matching suspenders stood out starkly against the white of his shirt. Curious blue eyes looked at John over the top of a pair of glasses perched on the end of his nose.

"I'm Dr. John Keffer." He held out his hand. "I've just set up practice here in town."

"Frank Davis." The man shook John's hand. "I seen your sign out at the old Myers house. Wondered who you was."

"Robert Myers was my grandfather."

"You Julia's boy?"

John nodded. "I named my daughter after her."

"I remember when your ma got married and moved away. What brings you to these parts?"

Good question. How could he explain to him it was because New York had become unbearable and there was nowhere else to run? He couldn't, at least not now in Frank Davis's store with several men listening while they pretended real hard not to.

"I decided this would be a great place to raise my daughter." He forced another smile. He was getting pretty good at that. "It's beautiful here, and there are no other doctors around. Right?"

"Well, we don't have no real doctors, I don't suppose. But we got Katie."

"Katie?"

"Katie Napier. She takes care of what ails us. Knows her herbs and such real good, and she's delivered more babies than I can count."

The door jingled again.

"Mornin', Frank."

John turned toward the door and the woman who had spoken. Clear gray eyes flashed quickly at him, then smiled. The lips smiled with a little less enthusiasm, but then, it would have been inappropriate for a lady to smile at a man she didn't know. A tiny freckle marked the top of one cheek, providing the only imperfection he could find in her otherwise flawless complexion. She wasn't classically pretty like the debutantes of New York, but there was a wholesomeness about her that seemed to fit with this place.

"You're in luck, Doc. This here's our Katie," Frank said.

Katie allowed her smile to warm, and a tiny dimple made an appearance at one side of her mouth. "Did Frank say you're a doctor?"

"Yes. Keffer. John Keffer." He wasn't sure what to do or why he was at a sudden loss for words. No bigger than a minute, in her worn coat, her dark hair pulled back in a simple bun—she wasn't someone he'd normally give a second glance, but her presence was imposing for some reason. Probably because Frank had said her name like she belonged to them.

"I'm Katie Napier." She offered her hand, and he wished she hadn't. This tiny woman was the local healer and chances were they were going to do battle. Touching her made it more personal somehow. He

shook her hand feeling like a boxer who'd just entered
the ring. Only his opponent didn't realize that a battle
had been joined.

"Pleased to meet you," he said, but time would tell
on that.

"Katie?" One of the men by the stove spoke to her.
"You got anything for a cough? My boy's been coughin'
somethin' fierce."

"Sure, Tom. Just come up to the house, and I'll give
you some comfrey."

Another jumped in, "Ida's due any day now. You going to be around? I don't want to deliver that baby myself."

The other men laughed.

"I don't think she'd want that either, though with
this being her ninth child, she could probably deliver it
herself," Katie said with a smile.

John listened, unable to believe his ears. The men
were firing questions at Katie, asking for help with him
standing right there. Hadn't these people been paying
attention?

"I'm a doctor," he said, raising his voice above the
din.

The room suddenly went silent. All eyes shifted to
him as if he'd just turned purple. "I have an office
down the street, and I'd be happy to help any of you."

He faced Katie. "Not saying that you don't do a fine
job. I'm sure you do, but I'm a trained medical doctor."
He looked back at the men. "From Harvard."

Still silent.

Finally the one she'd called Tom cleared his throat.
"I'm sure you're a fine doctor." The other men mum-

bled agreeing comments, nodding their heads with much more zeal than the situation merited.

"Well," he said, hoping for a brilliant comment to suddenly pop into his head. "I'll look forward to seeing your son in my office." It wasn't brilliant, but it would do.

"Sure, Doc." Tom nodded and John felt better about his situation.

Coming to the store had been a good idea, and now that he was no longer a stranger, the recent lack of patients should end. Obviously the people around here were in need of medical attention or they wouldn't be relying on a countrywoman and her bag of voodoo medicine. He'd better return to his office and prepare for his new patients . . . or adjust another diploma. At least he could be assured there were plenty of those.

Chapter Two

"What do you think is wrong?" Grandpa didn't like the turn this conversation had taken. Grandma had that look in her eye like something needed done, and the last thing he wanted to do was something.

"I think Katie's getting tired of doing all the work around here," Grandma said, settling into her rocker by the fireside.

"What makes you think that?" His son-in-law, Katie's pa, propped his feet up on the hearth, his large belly rolling over the top of his pants as he scratched his chin whiskers. Gil wasn't a bad sort, and when it came to being worthless, none was better, but solving problems wasn't one of his gifts.

"Well . . ." Grandma set her rocker in motion while she contemplated the question. "Haven't you noticed lately how she's gettin' behind on her chores? The laundry's piling up, she ain't canned near enough to last through the winter, and this morning, she didn't even bring me my tea." She harrumphed. "A woman on her deathbed can't even get tea."

"You ain't in your bed. Can't you get your own tea?" Gil asked, proving Katie had gotten her brains from her mother.

The rocker stopped and Grandma glared. "I can't

be expected to stay in bed *all* the time. Even a dying woman needs to get up now and agin'."

Grandpa threw a glance in Gil's direction. He'd better shut up now before Grandma skinned him. She'd worked real hard at dyin' these last four years, and nothing riled her more than to point out she hadn't done it yet.

"I don't know what we can do," Grandpa said, hoping to save Gil's hide. "I don't know nobody who could come out to help her. Leastwise, not without payin' them."

The rocker started back up. Gil was saved.

"I've been thinkin' about that," Grandma said. "Katie will be thirty years old come Thanksgiving, and she still don't have a husband."

"Husband?" Gil chuckled. "She don't even have a beau."

"That's my point. She needs a man."

"Whatever for?" The rocker stopped again, only this time her gaze leveled on Grandpa. He didn't think his question was *that* stupid.

"For younguns."

Oh. Maybe it was.

"Besides," Grandma continued, "if she marries, we'll have another hand to help out around here, and once the younguns are growed, they can help out too."

"What makes you think she'll want to stay here if she marries?" Gil asked with a frown. "Her new husband might want to move away."

Grandma smiled. Heaven help them. Her smile rarely was a good sign. "That's why it's important that *we* pick Katie's husband."

* * *

The walk back to the cabin was more interesting this afternoon than usual. Katie's mind couldn't seem to let go of her meeting with Dr. John Keffer. Such a big man. Of course, next to Katie, about everyone seemed big.

He was handsome enough with his broad shoulders and dark hair, but when his green eyes had looked into hers, they were empty inside. Like some of the life had been sucked out of him.

Katie stomped her feet against the sandstone stoop that led to the front porch of the cabin. No sense in carrying in any more dirt than necessary. The rest of her family had probably added more than their share while she was in town this morning, and far be it from any of them to sweep it back out again.

She opened the door and froze. Everyone sat in the front room, staring at her as though she might fly away. And no one immediately asked her to do anything. Something was amiss.

Grandma sat in her rocker by the fire, evidently done with dying for the day. Grandpa had a smile on his face, despite the fact that he had no food in front of him, and Pa looked as though he had no idea what was going on. Well, at least *that* part was still normal.

"Good afternoon, Katie," Grandma said with a smile.

Uh-oh.

Katie removed her coat, hung it on a peg by the door, and debated whether to run while she had the chance. They probably wanted her to put a new roof on the cabin or clear forty acres of land, and her feet were too tired for her to contemplate that at the moment.

"We was just talking about you," Grandma said.

Really? Katie never would've guessed. "Do I want to know why?"

"Katie," Grandma said with a shake of her head. Her admonishing tone was no doubt intended to make Katie feel guilty. It didn't . . . much.

"We were talking about you because we're worried." Grandma sighed a little to emphasize how worried she was, before she continued. "You'll be turning thirty next month, and we think it's time you got yourself hitched."

Katie's brows shot up with enough force to spring the hairpins from her bun. "*Married?* You can't be serious!"

She looked at Grandpa. He nodded in agreement, but most likely because he feared for his life if he didn't. Grandma was wiry but fierce, dying or not.

"Pa?"

Pa shrugged and glanced at Grandma. He didn't like to be put between a rock and a hard place. "Don't you *want* a husband, Katie girl?"

Another man to cook for and clean up after didn't sound all that appealing. "I've done just fine up to now. I don't see the need."

She headed to the kitchen. With all the thinking they'd evidently done in her absence, they were going to be hungrier than usual tonight, and supper wouldn't cook by itself.

The fire in the stove had almost burned out, and the wood bin in the kitchen was empty, as usual. Katie stepped out the back door, and darted to the pitifully low woodpile to grab some small logs for the fire. She returned shivering and mad, though she didn't know why. This was the way her life had been for years and nothing had changed. Then again, maybe that was why she was mad.

"Pa?" she yelled. "We need firewood soon or we're going to freeze to death."

Pa ambled into the kitchen and opened the stove with a grunt. "That's why you need a husband. There's only so much I can do, with my back and all." He straightened with a grimace and rubbed his back to bring home his point. "Another man would come in handy around here."

If that other man knew which end of an ax to use.

Katie harrumphed. She wasn't as good at it as Grandma, but she was learning. Pa left, which was a good thing. The temptation to fix his back with the log she held was too strong to be healthy—at least for Pa.

Grabbing her mixing bowl out of the cupboard, she plopped it onto the table with more force than needed. But mixing bowls didn't talk back, and the sound it made helped ease her ire somewhat.

Grandpa limped into the kitchen as she opened the Hoosier door to get some flour for biscuits. His knee must be hurting. Or was it his foot? It was hard to keep up with his ailments. They changed more often than he changed his socks.

"You know, Katie, a husband would be a fine addition around here."

Must be his turn.

She worked the tin sifter of the flour bin for a moment before she realized only a fine fluff sprinkled into her cup. Dragging a stool over to look into the top of the bin, she harrumphed again. It was practically empty.

"We're out of flour," she grumbled to no one in particular, but since Grandpa was there, he decided to respond.

"Why didn't you buy some when you were in town?"

"Because we're also out of money." She would have to gather eggs to sell so she could get money for flour. At least it allowed for another trip to town.

"You see?" Grandpa grinned. "You need a husband."

She didn't want to ask, but couldn't stop herself. "How would that help?"

"If you marry a man with means, you'll always have money for flour and such."

"Then I can cook all the time?"

"Exactly!"

Grandpa had better leave. That empty bowl would look mighty good turned over his bald head right now. "Would you mind fetching me some more firewood?"

"Sure, but I won't be able to get much. My knee's acting up today." He hobbled out the back door with such effort that Katie would've felt sorry for him, if he hadn't been limping on the other leg a moment before.

Grandma entered the kitchen, a blue shawl wrapped pitifully around her thin shoulders, and an expression so pious the angels themselves should be weeping. She dragged a chair out at the table and lowered herself into it with a heavy sigh, hooking her cane on the edge of the table. Grandma never used her cane, but she carried it with her wherever she went, just in case she might need it.

Katie steeled herself. The first two pleas, though heartfelt, would pale in comparison to this one. The queen bee was about to make her move.

"You know, Katie, when your mama died, my heart broke in two."

Katie softened. Grandma wasn't fibbing about this. "So did mine."

Grandma nodded. "She was as good a woman as ever was." She looked up with genuine sorrow in her tired eyes. "You're a good woman too, and I'm proud to call you my granddaughter."

A tear stung the corner of Katie's eye. Even though she knew her grandma loved her, it was something that was never said. Grandma hadn't used those exact words, but it was as close as Katie would likely come to hearing it.

"You're all the joy that's left to me now," Grandma continued, "and I can't die easy till I know you've got younguns of your own to give you that joy in return."

Babies.

She had to give it to her. Grandma had managed to find the one thing that would make Katie take a husband. Every time she delivered a new baby, her heart cried, first for joy, then for sadness because she had no little ones of her own. For a while she pushed it away, promising herself that she had plenty of time to have children. But lately the feelings wouldn't leave no matter how hard she shoved.

Time was passing and God help her, but Grandma was right. "I don't know anyone who'd want to marry me," Katie muttered, suddenly feeling ancient.

Grandma laid a frail hand against her heart and patted with the utmost of efforts. "No need to worry, Katie girl. Grandma will take care of that for you."

Chapter Three

"Pa, if you don't hurry, we're going to be late." Katie could hear the church bell pealing as they rushed down the street to the old frame building, but the sight of children laughing and playing in the yard allowed Katie to slow down a bit. The service hadn't started yet.

"I don't know why you're in such a hurry." Pa huffed and puffed as he walked. "We could be an hour late, and there'd still be plenty of sermon left. That man likes to hear himself talk."

Katie secretly agreed with her father's opinion of Reverend Stoker, but church was important to her for many reasons. It was one of the few opportunities she had to visit with the other women in the area, and once winter hit, she would be cut off from the outside world for weeks at a time. Her trips into town would be few and only be made on days when the stores were open.

"He's just doing the Lord's work, Pa."

"Looks like he could do it with a few less words."

Grandpa chuckled. "Which would you rather listen to, him or Grandma?"

Pa snorted. "I'm here, ain't I?"

Grandma hadn't made a trip into town since she'd started dying, and though Katie hated to admit it, it was one of the reasons she looked forward to the trip so much herself. Grandma's heart was in the right place, but Katie only knew that because she had the habit of clutching it whenever it looked like things weren't going the way she'd planned.

"Katie?" Oh no, Eunice Kopp was heading her way. The old woman was as wide as she was tall, and if ever there was a walking maelstrom of disasters, it was Eunice.

"Good morning, Eunice. How are you?"

She took the polite greeting as a genuine invitation to list her maladies. "Oh, I've been better. My knees are giving me fits this morning." She stopped in front of Katie and panted for a moment. "And my stomach is hurting somethin' fierce. I don't know if I ate some bad pork or if my liver's needin' cleaning. Would you have something for my liver?"

"Did you eat some sauerkraut?"

"Yep, but it didn't help." Eunice rubbed her belly to drive home her point.

"If you want to come up to the house tomorrow, I can give you some calamus root. That ought to help."

"That'd be good. I need some more willow tea for my rheumatism, and I'd like to visit with your grandma anyway. How is Mable doin'?"

"Well, she still isn't dead, but she's working real hard at it."

Eunice chuckled. "If anybody can do it, it's your grandma."

Turning toward the church entrance, Katie took the brief pause in conversation as an opportunity to head into the sanctuary. Eunice hadn't started on her family yet, but it was only a matter of time.

"By the way . . ."

Oops, Katie'd waited too long.

"I was wondering if you'd pray for Tim's mother. She's having spells now, and it looks like her heart is 'bout to give out. His pa ain't much better," she added with a shake of her head over her in-laws' distresses. Unfortunately, Eunice had a large family, and Katie knew her well enough to know she was just warming up.

"Of course I will." Katie continued walking, praying as she went, but she'd pray about Eunice's family later. Right now she prayed for divine intervention.

"Katie?" Rebecca Fisher called to her when she stepped into the sanctuary. Katie hurried over to speak to her as Eunice waddled on down the aisle. *Thank you, Jesus.*

"How are you today, Rebecca?"

Rebecca smiled and patted her tummy. The babe inside would be making its exit soon. "We're doing good." Rebecca already had three children, and Katie had delivered them all.

"I'm finishing up a quilt to give you for delivering this one, and I've got some apple butter in the wagon for Davy's poultice. It worked real good. His coughin' has all but stopped."

"Glad to hear it. Another quilt will come in handy with winter coming." The quilts and apple butter *did* come in handy, though Katie wished at least some of the people she doctored had money to pay with. Frank Davis wouldn't trade apple butter for things like flour or buttons.

"Holler when you need me," Katie said to Rebecca

as she headed toward her pew, where Pa and Grandpa had already settled in.

She'd just lowered herself when Pa looked behind him and frowned. "Who's that feller?"

Turning toward the entrance, she spied the tall, broad-shouldered form of Dr. John Keffer. "He's the new doctor in town," she said, trying not to appear too interested, though the same could not be said for the rest of the congregation. A host of shoulder poking and whispers rolled across the room as all eyes riveted on the newcomer.

"He stands out like manure on a white horse, don't he?" Grandpa said, and Katie had to agree.

No one she knew had the expensive clothing or the regal bearing that practically screamed "Big City" the way John's did. And to make matters worse, he was alone. Or was he? A tiny hand slipped into John's from behind, and a child hurried to meet his step.

He appeared about as comfortable as a sinner in hell, but the little angel holding his hand was already in heaven. Too far away for Katie to hear, the child gabbed a mile a minute and smiled at everybody she passed. A halo of copper curls bounced on her head as she tugged John down the aisle, searching for the perfect seat. She all but shouted when she found one.

Oh dear. Not only was that *not* the perfect seat, but it was the Pennington pew, and Gloria didn't look too pleased about the possible intrusion. Katie hurried down the aisle to intercept, before he committed the only truly unpardonable sin . . . taking someone else's pew.

"Dr. Keffer?" she said, saving his soul from hellfire, or at least from Gloria. "How good to see you again."

John wished he could've said the same thing. But finding Katie Napier standing before him, all primped and polished for church, didn't set well with his already soured morning. He hadn't intended to bring Julia along—was determined not to, in fact—but when he'd mentioned going, she beamed and squealed for joy.

She wanted to make friends. That's what she'd said, and John felt like a bastard for not realizing she hadn't. So he'd endured countless questions and endless giggles as they walked to the church in hopes of making friends.

Friends.

As though that would fix anything.

"Who's the pretty lady, Daddy?"

Pretty lady? "This is Miss Napier, Julia."

Julia held out the sides of her pinafore and curtsied like a princess. "Pleased to meet you, Miss Napier. Are you Daddy's girlfriend?"

Katie's cheeks flamed pink. "I—um—"

Could this morning get any worse? "Miss Napier and I only just met," John said, trying to remove at least some of Katie's discomfort. His own seemed to be a permanent fixture.

"That's right. Your father and I met the other day at the store."

Julia wrinkled her brow in earnest thought. "Are you Daddy's friend?"

Katie glanced at him before she smiled at Julia. "I hope so."

"You're a girl, right?"

"Usually." A glint of humor twinkled in Katie's eye.

"Then you're his girlfriend." Julia said it as though it was the most logical and wonderful conclusion, and if it had been anyone other than Katie Napier, maybe it would've been. But he was about to take Katie's place as the local healer, and he doubted she would use the word "friend" to describe him after that.

An uncomfortable silence filled the air as Katie searched for an appropriate response. Luckily, Julia could fill silence better than anyone. "Miss Napier?"

"Yes?" Katie answered.

"Could I be your friend too?"

The dimple by Katie's mouth winked as she bestowed a smile on his daughter. "I'd like that very much. Maybe you two could sit with me, if that's all right by your pa." She glanced up at John for approval, as though he could refuse.

"Could we, Daddy?"

John gave his polite smile. "Of course."

Julia's tiny hand clutched Katie's as the three made their way toward the front of the church and Katie's waiting seat. A quick introduction to Katie's father and grandfather finally left John sitting in a place he'd never expected to be again. Hypocrisy didn't set well with him. Yet here he was, about to worship a God who'd done nothing for John except turn His back when he'd needed Him the most.

A tiny, gray-headed woman, so frail a puff of wind could swoosh her away, took her seat at the old piano at the front corner of the church. She closed her eyes, and just when John thought she'd died, she attacked the keyboard, filling the sanctuary with music . . . or some approximation thereof.

Soon the congregation was singing along with the unidentifiable tune, which turned out to be a rendering of "Rock of Ages." Even though John knew the song, he remained silent—mostly because he didn't feel like singing but partly because of Katie.

Her lilting voice drifted around him, surprising him with its purity. Not the trained vibrato of a New York opera singer, but a sweet, simple tone, void of pretense, replete with gentleness. Simultaneously soothing and aggravating him, it brushed against feelings he'd rather have left alone.

He should've stayed home.

The reverend stepped to the pulpit as the last note rang out in the sanctuary. Ruddy faced, and with a few extra chins, he hooked his thumbs in the pockets of his black vest and glared at the congregation.

"Brothers and sisters," he said, chins bouncing, "there have been a few issues brought to my attention that need a fixin'. Some of the boards at the back of the sanctuary are rotting, and if we don't fix this rot-ation soon, someone's going to fall through."

Rot-ation?

"I also have discovered a polecat holed up behind the privy. Took a while to notice, seein' as how the smell kind of blended in, but I think that varmint needs removin' before he makes his mark on our congregation."

A few chuckles and murmurs rumbled through the room before the preacher regained their attention and warmed up for his sermon. "But now for the more serious matters." Leaning across his pulpit, he made an arching sweep with his hand. "There are sinners amongst us that need a-savin', and we best pray for their souls."

All heads bowed and eyes closed, except John's. He bowed his head, but closing his eyes seemed like an open invitation for a sneak attack. So while the others prayed for sinners, he took the opportunity to study those around him, in particular, Katie.

She was the closest, sitting just on the other side of Julia. Her lashes fringed against her cheeks like dark feathers, and the skin beneath the feathers looked as creamy as satin. Most of the women he knew *wore* satin. None of them actually resembled it.

"Amen," the preacher said, and John jerked his gaze away from Katie's face.

He hadn't intended to study her so closely, but she was an enigma, and he'd always been mighty curious. Of course if he remembered correctly, curiosity had been known to kill a few cats.

"Today's sermon is from the book of Genesis." The preacher held up his Bible as though the followers wouldn't know to what book he was referring.

Bibles flipped open around the room, and pages rustled to the right passage. John checked his watch. Ten o'clock, and the sermon had already started. Not bad. At this rate, he should be home before eleven. Settling into the old oak pew, he carefully schooled his face to appear rapt with interest.

The minister rambled on about Sodom and Gomorrah, and how Lot pitched his tent toward Sodom. For some reason, the tent pitching raised his fervor, and along with it came his voice. He shouted about the wrath of God and the vengeance meted out on the sinners in Sodom. And just when John thought he could get no louder, the preacher slammed his fist against the pulpit and yelled, "*Lot pinched his tit!*"

Suddenly the congregation quieted. Then a nervous twitter—or should that be titter?—fluttered across the room along with coughing and a blurted giggle or two.

The minister cleared his voice and said, "Lot *pitched* his *tent*." But the damage was already done, not only to Sodom and Gomorrah, but to Lot's tit as well.

Grandpa hurried out of the sanctuary and across the churchyard to catch Harold Crowley before he could get away. It wasn't a difficult task—Harold and Grandpa were old friends, and *old* friends didn't move too fast.

"How you doing this morning, Harold?" Grandpa slowed down to shake Harold's hand.

"I'm good. Yourself?"

"Good," Grandpa said, careful not to sound too anxious with the rest of his conversation. Harold had a big house and more money than he knew what to do with. Grandpa had thought about it for days, and if all went the way he hoped, he'd never have to work again in his life.

"I was just wondering how you're doing, living on your own and all. It's got to be hard without Matilda." He shook his head with so much pity it almost brought tears to his eyes.

Rubbing his hand across his scruffy chin, Harold grunted. "It ain't easy, but Tildy's been gone for three years now, and I reckon I'm used to it."

"You hire someone to do your cookin' and cleanin', right?"

Harold nodded.

Grandpa sighed. "What you need is a wife to tend to those things for you."

"I don't need no wife."

"But if you had a wife, you wouldn't have to pay for cookin' and such."

Harold frowned. "Why do you care all of a sudden if I have a wife?"

Uh-oh, Harold was getting suspicious. "I'm not saying I care, it just hit me the other day." He pulled Harold away from the others and lowered his voice. "Don't say nothing to nobody, but Katie's looking to get hitched."

"What's that got to do with me?"

"I think you should marry up with her."

At first, Harold stood in total silence; then he blurted out a laugh and a half. "I'm old enough to be her grandpa! You of all people know that."

"Katie ain't no spring chicken herself, and she ain't looking for some randy pup to keep her up all night. She wants a good man who can provide for her, and one that'll treat her right."

Harold shook his head. "That's foolish."

"You sayin' you ain't man enough for her?" He'd known Harold a long time, and if that didn't raise his dander, nothing would.

"I'm man enough for any woman, but what makes you think Katie'd want to marry me?"

Heh, heh. Got him. "I know for a fact Katie would marry up with you. She all but told me so herself." Or she would once he explained it to her, but that was just a detail.

"I don't know . . ."

"She's a good woman, fine cook, and can whip up anything you need to fix what ails you." Grandpa watched Harold's eyes for a sign of agreement. It was close.

"That *would* come in handy."

Real close. "What do you say? Are you up to it?"

"If you're sure she's willin' . . ."

He smacked Harold on the back and grinned. "Come on out Saturday, and we'll set a date."

Gil Napier knew he wasn't good with book learning and such, but he also knew he wasn't a bad sort. Grandma, Grandpa, and sometimes even Katie seemed to forget that fact. Now with Katie fixing to marry up, there was too much of a chance for another to find him lacking . . . unless Gil found Katie's husband first.

He had to be a good man, one who would take care of Katie and agree to stay in the cabin to help out. He couldn't be too smart or too dumb, just somewhere in between, like Gil. And he knew exactly who that man was.

Freddie Powell fit all the guidelines and, as luck would have it, was coming Gil's way. Granted, he wasn't much to look at, a little skinny, and his hair did some wild curling, but he was a good kid mostly, and he'd been sweet on Katie for years.

"Freddie?" Gil hiked his pants up, as much as his belly would permit, and sauntered over to talk to his future son-in-law.

"How you doin', Mr. Napier?"

Gil liked that *mister* part. Showed the boy was respectful. "I'm doin' good, Freddie." So much for the polite talk, now it was time to get serious. "I was thinking about you in church this morning, and I wondered if you're still livin' with your ma."

Looking at his feet, Freddie cleared his throat and nodded. "Yeah, I ain't got nowhere else to go right now. Why?"

"Your ma ain't too easy to live with, is she?"

Freddie flushed, then grinned. "She can be a bit bossy."

"You know, what you need to do is get married so you can be your own boss."

"*Married?* I ain't even got a girl!"

"A fine feller like you don't got a girl? You've got to be joshing me."

"No, sir, I ain't joshin'."

Rubbing his hand across his chin, Gil frowned real hard to show he was thinking. Then he snapped his fingers. "I got it! Katie's lookin' to get married, maybe you could marry up with her."

"*K-Katie?*" Freddie stammered, and for a moment, Gil expected the boy to swoon. "Katie would never marry up with me."

"I happen to know for a fact she would. She knows what a fine man you are, and I suspect she's always been sweet on you."

"*Me?*" Freddie gulped. "Are you sure?"

"She ain't said so right out, but I seen her looking at you." Sort of.

"*Me?*"

Freddie was going to have to learn to say more than "me" if he planned on keeping a girl like Katie interested. "Katie knows a good man when she sees one. Why, I'm sure if you'd like to marry her, she'd be pleased as punch."

"I—I don't know."

Gil'd better help the boy out. If Freddie turned any redder, his face might explode. "Katie's a fine girl and marryin' her would give you a chance to leave your ma's and start a family of your own. You want to do that, don't you?"

"Sure, but *Katie*? I don't think she's ever even talked to me."

"She just don't like to come across as forward. You know how women are." Gil nodded and winked a conspiratorial wink. "She's going to marry up with someone. You gonna let her get away?"

"I don't want to let her get away." Freddie didn't sound real convinced, but Gil knew the boy would cotton up to it soon enough.

"Course you don't, son." Gil patted him on the shoulder. "I'll take care of everything, just come on out Saturday, and we'll set a date."

Who would ever have thought Reverend Stoker could preach for two hours? John knew it now and so did his backside. Julia wasn't as tired, but then, she'd fallen asleep soon after the tit pinching and hadn't awakened until the last amen. Lucky child. Careful to watch for rot-ation in the church floor, John stepped out into the afternoon sun.

Most of the parishioners stood in the yard, gabbing

about one thing or another. And try though he might, he couldn't stop his gaze from seeking out Katie, not that it wasn't easy to find her. She stood surrounded by people, all talking and laughing, and no doubt asking her for medical advice.

A pregnant woman gave Katie a jar of something and another handed her a shawl. Two children tugged on her skirts, impatient for their chance to speak with her, and all the while, John felt invisible. None spoke to him, none smiled his way, and for all the good it'd done to come to church, he might as well have stayed home and adjusted diplomas.

"Daddy?" Julia tugged his hand. "Did you have fun at church?"

To answer that question properly, he would need words a child her age should not be exposed to, so instead, he glanced down at Julia and shrugged. "I suppose. Did you enjoy it?"

"Oh yes! It was the most fun I've had in the longest time, and now I have a new friend!" She bounced with excitement while she giggled. "Can she come over for dinner? Can she please, Daddy?"

Even his own daughter had been enthralled by the ever-popular Katie Napier. "I'm sure Miss Napier is very busy."

"Oh no, Daddy. She wouldn't be too busy for me."

Who would have thought a person with such short legs could move so quickly? In a flash, Julia raced across the churchyard toward Katie and her throng of worshipers.

"Hell," he mumbled. Now not only would he have to fetch his daughter, but by the time he did, she would have invited Katie to dinner, if not to move in with them.

He hurried across the yard; the dinner invitation was probably already set, but he might be able to keep the spare room empty.

"Julia?" John used a stern "Father" voice that usually captured his daughter's attention, but evidently his daughter had gone deaf. Lucky for her, she was already clutching the hand of the great healer.

Katie threw her head back, laughing at something Julia said, and the sound of it stopped John in his tracks just a few feet from his destination. He cleared his throat. "Julia? You mustn't bother Miss Napier." He hesitantly closed the distance. "I'm sure she has plenty to do."

Katie turned to him with eyes sparkling and a smile still wide and inviting. Then quickly her smile lessened, and she lowered her gaze to Julia. "She's no bother, Dr. Keffer."

Julia tugged on Katie's skirt like the other urchins had done. "Can you, Katie? Can you come to dinner?"

An embarrassed expression crossed her features before Katie smiled again. "I can't today, but thank you for the invitation."

"But you can come sometime, can't you?"

John would need to talk to his daughter as soon as they returned home. Though he didn't know what to say. Don't be hospitable? Maybe he could inform her that it was wrong to make friends, at least with these people. They were different.

"Well . . ." Katie's voice sounded unsure, and now

he knew what to tell Julia. It was wrong to make people feel uncomfortable, especially her father.

John reached for Julia's hand. "I'm sure Miss Napier has more important things to tend to."

Julia's lip trembled as she looked up at Katie. "Are you too busy for me too?"

His heart fell.

Kneeling down to Julia's level, Katie gave her a hug. "I'm never too busy for a friend."

"Julia and I would love to have you to dinner some time, Miss Napier."

Who said that?

Well, maybe John *couldn't* blame that on a stranger passing by, but he could and would blame it on temporary insanity . . . and on his daughter's trembling lip. If having Katie to the house *once* would make Julia happy, then it could be arranged. Of course if there really were a God, and the jury was still out on that, Katie would be unable to attend, ever.

"Thank you," Katie said. "That would be nice."

"Yeay!" Julia clapped her hands. "I'll tell Mrs. Adkins as soon as we get home. I'll make the biscuits."

Katie smiled again as John took Julia's hand and led her away. He'd intended to take Julia's hand but not Katie's smile, yet oddly enough, it stayed with him as he walked down the street toward his home.

Chapter Four

As if dying wasn't bad enough, now it appeared as though Grandma was going to have to endure a visit from Eunice Kopp.

"Well, Mable," Eunice said, after she plopped her ample bottom into a chair by the bed, "How are you doing today?"

Grandma harrumphed. "I'm dying, Eunice. How do you think I am?" That would shut up a normal person, but Eunice wasn't normal, so she giggled instead.

"I suppose dying would get tiresome after a while, though of course, I'm envious of you sometimes. My family has gone through so much, I think sometimes dyin' would be easier than living through all this."

Oh Lord, now it was time for Eunice to bemoan her family's ills, as though she were the only one with difficulties to endure. Grandma allowed her mind to wander to more important things, like finding Katie a man. It was going to be hard to do since all this dying made it difficult to get around. If only she had someone to do the legwork for her.

Hmmm. She glanced back at Eunice, still rambling about her infirmed. "Eunice?" Grandma said as soon as Eunice stopped for a breath. "I was wondering if you could help me out."

Eunice blinked in surprise and leaned closer with intense seriousness. "Of course I would, Mable. You and me go back a ways. What do you need?"

Sighing deeply, Grandma laid her hand against her heart. "I'm worried for my Katie."

"What's wrong?"

"Oh, there ain't nothing wrong with her directly, but she's turning thirty soon, and she still don't have a husband. I'm afraid she's too busy to look, and I can't get around much to find her one."

"Is she *wantin'* to get hitched?"

"Of course she does!" Grandma snapped before she remembered she wanted Eunice's help, not her anger. "She wants younguns," she added with as much humility as she could muster.

"What do you want me to do?"

"Who are some of the eligible men around here now? I ain't been out for a while."

Eunice wrinkled her brow in thought. "Well, I can't think of too many the right age except my Randy."

"Randy?"

"My grandson. He just moved back here from Williamson."

"How old is he?"

"Twenty-six."

That was close enough. "Is he handsome?" Grandma didn't want any ugly grandkids.

Eunice giggled. "That's his biggest problem. All the girls down there set their cap for him and chased him something awful." She leaned forward to whisper, "A couple of them actually claimed he'd got them with child." She sat back and shook her head. "Of course, that's ridiculous. He wouldn't do such a thing. They just wanted to force him into marriage."

"Why didn't he marry one of them?"

"None of them girls were good enough for him. That's why he come on home."

"My Katie is too good for most anybody. I don't know if she'd want him."

Eunice bristled. "Randy's a handsome young man, strong and virile. If Katie's wantin' strapping young-uns, my Randy can give them to her."

Strong, good-looking grandkids were appealing, but that would make Eunice family. Grandma glanced askance at Eunice. The woman *was* a fine cook, and if her grandson was as robust as she made him sound, he could do quite a bit of work around the cabin. With any luck at all, Eunice wouldn't live much longer anyway. She was an old bag and as unhealthy as they come.

"Have him come on out on Saturday, and if I—I mean if *Katie* approves—we'll get 'em hitched."

Chapter Five

Drumming his fingers on the desktop wasn't very productive, but he'd adjusted the damn diplomas so many times, there was a danger of wearing holes in the wall.

John shoved away from his desk and paced across the room to the window. The street was just as empty as it had been five minutes ago. He could go to the store again, but he'd been there every day this week since Monday and still no one had come to him for treatment. At this rate he didn't need a medical degree . . . he needed a hobby.

His nose caught the whiff of something wonderful drifting from the kitchen. John knew if he went there he'd find Julia elbow deep in biscuit dough and Mrs. Adkins humming while she cooked. Domestic pleasures weren't important in the large scheme of things, but he *was* a little hungry. Maybe there was a muffin left over from breakfast.

"Tell me about the baby," Julia was saying, as John stepped into the room.

"What baby?" He only asked the question out of politeness, so why did Mrs. Adkins suddenly seem uncomfortable?

"I have a new grandbaby. He was born just last

night. I was hoping after I got dinner started I could go to Sally's home to help her tend to him."

"She lives nearby?"

"Yes." Mrs. Adkins set a kettle on the stove. "He's a dandy, but the delivery was tough. Katie had to work real hard . . ." She froze and the look on her face would have been comical if it had been put there under other circumstances.

"Katie?" Was he doomed to be in that woman's shadow even in his own home?

"Sally's known Katie most her life, and I knew you was busy . . ." Mrs. Adkins continued to work, rattling pans in an attempt to hide her answers. "It was just a baby after all."

But it wasn't just a baby. It was the final straw. His own housekeeper's daughter had gone to Katie instead of him.

He left the kitchen, no longer interested in muffins or domestic bliss. Something had to be done, but what? He couldn't force the people to come to him any more than he could force Katie to stop tending to them.

Hiding in the bushes to tackle the infirmed as they sought Katie's help was tempting, though not practical. Perhaps he could tie Katie on the end of a stick, like the proverbial carrot, and dangle her in front of the ill until they followed her to his home.

Shaking his head, he returned to his office in hopes of finding a better solution. There was no way Katie would stay on the end of a stick, leastwise not without paying her.

Then it hit him.

A beautiful solution flashed in his mind, like the

brilliant light of a divine revelation. He smiled, refusing to feel guilty for his planned deception. After all, what harm could come of it? The sick would receive real medical care. Katie would be compensated financially, and as for John?

Well . . .

Perhaps he would get the chance to finally put his demons to rest.

Chapter Six

"Do you think that's enough taters and beans?" Grandpa asked, poking his nose over Katie's shoulder while she added onions to the sizzling skillet.

"It's the same amount I always fix, why?"

"I sort of invited someone over for supper."

"Sort of?" She didn't really care about guests for supper, but a little warning would've been nice. "Who?"

"Harold."

"Oh." Katie added a dash of salt to the potatoes and onions, before she gave the beans a quick stir in the kettle. Mr. Crowley was an old friend of Grandpa's, but she couldn't remember him coming to supper before.

"Uh, there's something I been meanin' to tell you—"

"Make sure you fix plenty tonight, Katie," Pa said, interrupting Grandpa's confession, as he ambled his way into the kitchen. "I've invited some company."

"Who did *you* invite?" She hoped whoever it was didn't eat much. Two extra guests might stretch dinner a little thin.

"Freddie Powell."

Good. As skinny as Freddie was, he wouldn't eat more than a sparrow.

"Freddie's a fine young man," Pa said, hiking up his britches as he walked to the stove to taste the potatoes. "Real respectful and politelike."

"That's nice," Katie replied hesitantly. "But why did you invite him to dinner?"

"Uh, you see—"

"Katie?" Here came Grandma dressed in her Sunday best. "Is that what you're wearin' for supper?"

Katie glanced down at her brown everyday dress and shrugged. "I always wear this dress."

"That's my point. We're having special company tonight, and I think you ought to pretty up a little."

Oh no. Grandma must have invited a suitor.

Muffled voices from the front porch stopped Katie's attempt to find out more. Pa, Grandpa, and Grandma hurried from the room, each struggling to reach the door first. She wasn't sure, but she could have sworn Grandma tripped Grandpa with her cane.

Katie stood in the kitchen, debating whether she should "pretty up" or run for the hills. Evidently her family had been busy this week.

Sighing, she dried her hands on her apron before untying it and laying it across the back of a chair. She couldn't get too mad at Grandma since she *had* agreed to let her find a match. But it would have been nice if she'd had some warning that a prospective husband would be arriving tonight.

She stepped into the front room amongst the commotion of two guests arriving at once.

"Katie, dear," Grandma said, ushering a handsome young man in her direction. "This here is Randy Kopp. He's Eunice's grandson, and he's just moved back from Williamson."

Thick, dark hair brushed over the man's forehead, drawing attention to bright blue eyes. One of which, winked at her as he reached his hand out in greeting.

"Pleased to meet you, Katie."

She shook his hand and smiled, finding it impossible not to respond to the sparkling, white teeth flashing at her, complete with a rather attractive set of dimples.

"Yes, I—"

Grandpa grabbed her shoulders and spun her around where she almost collided with Harold Crowley.

"You remember Harold, don't you Katie?"

Harold cleared his throat. She shook his hand, wondering why Grandpa had invited Harold out on the same night she was to meet her prospective husband.

"Good to see you again, Katie." Harold turned and glared at Grandpa. "I thought you said Katie and me were getting hitched." He jerked his head toward Randy. "Who's this pup?"

Married? *To Harold?*

"Wait just a minute!" Pa said, wading into the middle of the pack. "I done found Katie a beau, and he'll be here any minute now. You other fellers can go on home."

A knock on the door gave Katie a second to catch her breath. Pa hurried to let in yet another intended suitor.

"Katie," Pa said, hurrying his choice to stand before her. "You remember Freddie Powell, don't you?"

She remembered Freddie, but she didn't think she'd ever had a conversation with him. Mostly because he always looked like he was about to swoon. "Hello, Freddie," she said, and his face turned scarlet.

"Good evening, Katie." A cracking voice and bobbing Adam's apple added the final touch to Freddie's expression of total terror.

Freddie's hair was slicked with enough pomade to slide him through a gopher hole. And like the others, he was dressed either for courtin' or for a funeral. In Freddie's case, the funeral could be his own. She couldn't recall ever seeing a young man look so scared.

"Now, this is the feller you need to marry," Pa said, grabbing Freddie's shoulders and giving a good-natured shake. "He's hardworkin' and respectful—"

"He ain't no more respectful than Harold!" Grandpa interrupted. "This young generation don't know nothing about respect."

By the time Grandma jumped into the fray, Katie thought her head was going to explode. They were all talking at once, each touting the good qualities of their suitors, though they seemed more intent on convincing each other than Katie. Their dedication was so focused, in fact, they failed to notice when she left the cabin for the relative quiet of the front porch.

The huge autumn moon loomed just above the horizon, and the brisk night air cooled her heated skin, if not her temper. They could have warned her. Three beaus, each as different as night was to day, each with good qualities, she was sure. But how was she supposed to make a decision when she didn't really know any of them?

Maybe marrying wasn't such a good idea after all.

"Katie?" Pa stepped out onto the porch. "What you doing out here?"

"Hidin'."

"Now, Katie, there's no reason for you to sound so forlorn. You're wantin' to get hitched, aren't you?"

"I thought so, but I figured I'd have some say in who I was going to marry."

"You *do* get a say in it, but you'd be crazy not to pick Freddie. He's a good boy, and he'd work real hard at tryin' to please you."

Shrugging, she kept her focus on the moon. "I can't marry a man I don't know."

"I wouldn't expect you to, but you can give Freddie a chance, can't you?"

Katie didn't answer. She was still peeved and didn't really know what to say anyway. Pa took the hint and slipped back into the cabin. She wondered who'd be next, but she didn't have to wonder for long.

The door creaked as the next of her family members came to convince Katie of his or her choice.

"Katie?" Grandpa called to her from behind.

She groaned. "What do you want, Grandpa?"

He hobbled closer, wearing the expression he always wore when attempting to give sage advice. "I know you probably think Harold's a mite old for you, but that's what makes him the perfect match."

This should be interesting. "How?"

"He's got a boatload of money and that big old

house in town. Why, he'd spoil you rotten and then make you a wealthy widow to boot."

Katie's jaw dropped. "You want me to marry him, then hope he dies?"

"Now, now, I didn't say that."

Pursing her lips, she glared at him. "I think you need to go back inside and send Grandma out for her turn."

"Her turn?"

"To convince me that Randy is the best match. I must admit I'd love to know her reasons, though I suspect I already do."

Grandpa nodded, then headed back into the cabin. In a blink, Grandma was on the porch.

"All right," she said tugging her shawl around her shoulders, her cane dangling from the crook of her arm. "I'll tell you why you want Randy."

Katie folded her arms across her chest and raised her brow.

"A man like that will keep a smile on your face."

Her mouth gaped again. *"Grandma!"*

Grandma harrumphed. "Don't *grandma* me. You think I was always this old? You said you were wantin' younguns, and I can't imagine a feller that would be more fun to make 'em with. If you've got any sense at all, you'll marry Randy and whelp lots of little ones, all with dimples."

With that bit of advice, Grandma returned to the cabin, leaving Katie fanning the cool air against her face. Randy was handsome, but there was more to a good husband than just looks, wasn't there?

Of course it might not matter anyway. Apparently none of her suitors had been aware that others were going to show up. They might have all changed their minds by now, leaving her just as much of an old maid as she was when this evening began.

With resignation, she left the privacy of the porch—it wasn't very private anyway—and returned to the lion's den. The chattering stopped as soon as she entered the cabin. Her three intendeds stood with their perspective champions, each facing her as though they expected an answer on the spot.

Harold's face was red, and the fists clenched at his sides led her to believe he was about to hit someone. Freddie's face was also red, imagine that, but it appeared to be caused by a lack of air. Maybe Pa ought to remind the boy to breathe every once in a while. And then there was Randy. Confident, a casual grin turning up one side of his mouth, he winked again as though he already had this contest won.

"Gentlemen," she said, "I want to apologize for the confusion. It appears as though my family has decided to take my future into their hands without filling me in on the details."

"Now, Katie—"

She held up her hand to stop her grandpa from interrupting her. "*If* any of you would like to go on home, I understand and there'd be no hard feelings." She waited for the men to respond, but all stood their ground silently, darting glances at each other, then back to her.

"Well, in that case, I reckon I'm going to have to make a decision."

With a cock of his handsome head, Randy chuckled. "Come on, Katie. Do you really have to think about this?" He raised his brow and glanced at the other two men. His expression indicated he clearly felt she would be a fool not to choose him. Which might have been the case, but fools rush in, and after waiting nearly thirty years, rushing at this point seemed more than foolish.

"Yes, Randy, I certainly need to think about this. I don't know any of you gentlemen, and I have no intention of marrying a man until I'm sure I want to live with him the rest of my life."

"How—how are you going to pick?" Freddie finally gulped enough air to speak.

Good question. "I'm not sure just yet. I'm going to need some time."

Harold puffed up his chest and cleared his throat. "I think you should pick the man who can provide for you the best."

"That's a fine idea," Grandpa said, immediately throwing in his opinion.

Pa stepped forward. "I think respect and a good heart should be the most important thing." He smacked Freddie on the shoulder, nearly sending him to the floor.

Randy snorted. "She don't need none of that. She needs a man that can protect her and work hard. I think we should fight it out, and the last one standing, wins her hand."

He took the opportunity to flex his arm, patting the muscle that bulged beneath his shirtsleeve. His gesture triggered another eruption of opinions and arguments, all six talking and pointing fingers at each other.

"Just a minute," Katie said, but she might as well have been talking to the wall.

"If y'all will get quiet . . ." A deaf wall, at that.

She took a deep breath. *"Quiet!"* she shouted, and all eyes riveted to her, with brows raised in surprise. "I have no intention of using fighting or bribes or any other lamebrained ideas to pick my husband." She lifted her hand again to cut off the protests from each mouth currently gaping at her.

"I will pick my husband based on my own reasons."

It was a fine speech, and she was proud of it as she marched from the room with the pretense of setting supper on the table. Truth of the matter was, she wanted to leave before any of them asked her for more details.

She didn't have details.

She only had beans and potatoes.

And sometimes a woman simply has to go with what she has.

Church again. It seemed as though the only chance John had to interact with the locals was at the store and church. But he'd endure it for the chance to approach Katie. She'd be here, singing like an angel and basking in the adoration of her following. They would all clamor around her, begging for medical help as though John were nothing but a lawn ornament.

That was about to change, assuming John could survive another of Reverend Stoker's marathon sermons and Julia's bouncing excitement. Bringing his daughter probably qualified as manipulation, since he did it knowing full well Julia wouldn't leave without talking to Katie. But desperate men take desperate measures, and Julia loved the crowd anyway.

"Can we sit with Katie, Daddy?" Bless the child. She already knew her lines.

"I suppose it would be all right, as long as Miss Napier doesn't mind."

"Oh, she won't mind," she said, smiling with delight. "She's my friend."

Pulling away from John's grasp, Julia directed her bounce down the aisle straight for Katie's pew. He watched as Katie turned to smile at his daughter, giving her a hug in welcome.

John was surprised to realize he had grinned in response. He sobered immediately. His daughter's excitement over seeing Katie again was the only explanation he could find for his odd reaction. It certainly wasn't because *he*'d looked forward to seeing her. A business proposition was all he intended to offer, and once he no longer needed her, he planned to sever their association posthaste.

"Good morning, Dr. Keffer." Katie turned her smile on him, causing his step to falter slightly. He hadn't expected her to look so genuinely pleased to see him.

"Good morning. I trust Julia isn't being a bother."

"Of course not."

"I told you, Daddy. Katie's my friend." Julia turned back to look at Katie. "Can we sit with you?"

Katie's gray eyes twinkled as she scooted aside to make room. "I'd like that very much."

Julia giggled, then did something totally unexpected. She darted around Katie's knees and took a seat on the other side, leaving John no option but to sit beside Katie. Thankfully, there was plenty of room. At least there was until her father and grandfather slid into the pew from the other end.

By the time all the scooting and adjusting had taken place, there wasn't a scant inch between the side of his leg and Katie's blue skirts. She moved and the inch disappeared, making him painfully aware that his thigh brushed hers.

Correction, there were layers of petticoats and other fabrics between the two, and he was acting ridiculous. Forcing his attention to the front of the church, he prayed for the first time in years. Granted, he only prayed the piano player would tackle the cantankerous contraption so they could stand to sing, and he could regain his inch when they sat back down. But it qualified as a prayer nonetheless.

As though she had been eavesdropping on his thoughts, the little old lady teetered to the piano and started a painfully out-of-tune melody. Everyone stood to sing, affording John a second to relax. Until Katie offered to share a hymnal with him. He glanced down at her, surprised again at her small stature. He'd bet he could lift her in his arms and not even notice the load.

Not that he ever would do such a thing.

Her slender hand turned the page, and the congregation began to sing. Reluctantly, he held his half of the hymnal and sang along quietly. Katie's clear voice was more pleasant to listen to than his anyway.

The song ended too quickly and when they returned to sitting, his inch appeared to be gone forever. John tried to concentrate on everything except Katie, but a whiff of vanilla pulled him back into her realm. Must just be hungry.

"Brothers and sisters."

Thank God, Reverend Stoker took the pulpit. Was that another prayer? Perhaps he was becoming a fanatic.

"Today's sermon is from the book of Ephesians," the reverend said, pausing a moment to allow the congregation to find the scripture. "Chapter six, verse sixteen." He cleared his throat then began, "'Above all, taking the shield of faith, wherewith ye shall be able to quench all the fiery darts of the wicked.'"

John settled back to pretend to listen. He had more important things to think about, like why Katie's vanilla scent should matter to him or why the thought of her thigh next to his made him as nervous as a young boy. He wondered if his thigh made her nervous.

Ridiculous.

He didn't smell like vanilla or have skin like satin. He wasn't even pretty.

Where in the hell had those thoughts come from?

". . . and sinners surround us all . . ." Reverend Stoker's voice pierced through John's thoughts, which was a good thing. The last thoughts were disconcerting at best.

Fidgeting, John tried to move his leg away, but the inch was gone permanently, and his movement only managed to allow him to feel the side of her thigh more clearly.

He glanced at her to see if she was as uncomfortable as he was, but she sat, stoic and unaffected, captivated by the reverend's sermon. Maybe he should try that approach. Furrowing his brows, he forced his attention to Reverend Stoker and his fiery darts. Based on the reverend's fervor, the wicked in this community must be very busy.

"You must arm yourselves!" he shouted, slamming his fist against the pulpit. "Surround yourselves so you will be protected from the wiry farts of the dicked!"

The reverend had done John a great service. He was no longer concerned about Katie's thigh or the scent of vanilla. He was too busy wondering what exactly wiry farts were, and if the dicked often had trouble with them. Perhaps they came from eating barbed wire and beans.

He would have handled the wiry farts with much more aplomb had he not felt Katie's shoulders shake beside him. Looking down at her was his fatal mistake. She had raised her hand to cover her mouth, but her dimple could not be hidden so easily.

A smile tugged the corner of his mouth.

He coughed, but it did no good. A laugh bubbled up his throat, where he tried to squelch it despite its uncontrollable desire to escape.

Cough again.

Katie giggled softly, then covered it with her own cough, one he could feel more than hear.

Folding his arms across his chest, he rubbed his hand over his chin in an attempt to relax his face muscles. He couldn't give in or the laugh would blurt out, embarrassing himself and all around him.

Should he concentrate on the sermon? Not likely.

That was what had started this dilemma to begin with.

She cleared her throat again. Good idea. It seemed to be the plan of action for most in the congregation. He hadn't heard that much throat clearing since the last flu outbreak.

Chapter Seven

Katie saw the muscle twitching in John's cheek. Like the rest of the congregation, she had developed ways to restrain herself during Reverend Stoker's *accidents*, but today's was threatening to undo her—most likely due to her nerves being on edge. John sat so closely beside her.

She could feel the heat from his body and smell the bay rum he'd used after shaving. Though none of that affected her as much as the feel of his leg against hers. She'd tried not to move in the crowded pew, but he was fidgety today and every time he shifted, his thigh brushed hers. It was all she could do not to gasp in response.

It'd been a week since she'd last seen him, and despite the fact that she'd tried not to think about him, he had occupied more than his share of her thoughts. Even here in church, it was think about either him or wiry farts.

Oops. She giggled.

John's shoulders began shaking, so he moved, and that thigh of his seared her from knee to hip.

"Turn in your hymnals to page four hundred thirty-two," Reverend Stoker said, and Katie couldn't have been more relieved.

Flipping to the right page, she bolted to her feet. John reached to share the hymnal with her and for some reason, his hand on the book drew her attention more than a hand should. Strong square fingers with neatly trimmed nails, a smattering of dark hair brushed his wrist. The only adornment was a thin gold band. A wedding ring implied a wedding, so where was the wife?

"Amen," the congregation sang, and she realized with a jolt she'd missed the hymn. It seemed appropriate considering she'd missed most of the service altogether.

The crowd dispersed quickly with the women making their way out of the sanctuary first. Today was Homecoming and that meant a meal had to be laid out, eaten, and cleaned up before they could go home.

"Are you going to stay and eat?" Katie asked John as she stepped into the aisle. "There'll be plenty."

John smiled the empty, tight-lipped smile he seemed fond of and said, "I suppose we could stay for a bite. I need to speak with you about something anyway."

Something else to add to her curiosity quotient.

"Katie?" Oh dear, Randy Kopp had spied her in the aisle and was heading her way, glaring at John.

"I'm Randy Kopp." He stuck out his hand toward John, but Katie had the feeling it was more of a challenge than a greeting.

"John Keffer," John said, returning the glare, much to Katie's surprise.

He shook Randy's hand, and Katie knew knuckles must have been crunching. Each man stood toe-to-toe, neither breaking the grip or the eye contact, until Katie couldn't take it any longer.

"Randy? Did you need a word with me?"

Finally hands dropped, and the duel ceased. Randy turned toward her, grinning. Such a charmer.

"I was wondering if you'd let me sit with you at dinner today"—he leaned closer, lowering his voice—"so we can get to know each other better."

"Wait just a pea-pickin' minute." Harold Crowley stormed toward them with determination and a scowl. "You can't hog her all to yourself."

Freddie's flushed face appeared around Harold's shoulder, though instead of speaking, he simply nodded in agreement.

She couldn't let all three sit beside her. She only had two sides. Not only that, but just the thought of keeping those three from attacking each other all afternoon left her tired.

"I'm sorry, gentlemen. I've already asked Dr. Keffer and Julia to join me for dinner."

John must have sensed her distress, for as soon as she finished speaking, he did the strangest thing. He placed his hand on her back, low like a man does to escort a lady friend from the room. If she didn't know he was married, she'd have sworn he was marking his territory.

"If you gentlemen will excuse us," he said, gently directing her down the aisle with Julia following behind.

The warmth of his hand on her waist felt oddly intimate as they left the sanctuary to head for the tables set up in the side yard. Several of the women had slipped out of the service early to set up the meal, leaving Katie nothing to do except help John find his way around.

Pine boards set on sawhorses provided a long make-shift table for the forty or fifty parishioners staying for lunch. Tablecloths, in an array of colors and prints, covered the boards and brightened the side yard, as though the maples in their fall foliage weren't enough.

A few of the children darted around the food table, giggling as Rebecca Fisher threatened with a large wooden spoon. Pa and Grandpa were already at the front of the line.

"Can I go play with them, Daddy? Can I, please?" Julia tugged on John's sleeve.

"You should probably eat first," he said before adding, "Shouldn't she?"

Katie glanced up from Julia, surprised to see John had directed the question toward her. At first she thought he was teasing, but the look in her eye told her otherwise. He truly didn't know.

"I think your pa is right," Katie said, stepping in where she had no right to. Where was his wife? "Let's eat our lunch and then maybe you can play for a spell."

Julia's tiny lip only pouted a second before she grabbed her plate and hurried down the food table. Katie followed behind, helping place food on Julia's plate until they reached the end, and the three found a spot at the picnic table to sit and eat.

No sooner had she picked up her fork than Harold Crowley came hustling across the yard. "I brung you something to drink," he said, plopping a cup of water in front of her, then scooting onto the bench opposite them.

"Why, thank you, Harold—"

"This here was the last piece of Mrs. Pennington's apple pie." Freddie set the pie in front of her, taking a seat beside Harold, where the two began some sort of elbow duel as they vied for room for their plates.

"That was nice of you, Freddie. Gloria makes the best apple pie in these parts."

John cleared his throat. "There are plenty of other seats, if you gentlemen are crowded."

Harold harrumphed. "So you can have her all to yourself?" Harrumph number two. "That ain't goin' to happen."

Good grief, here came Randy, carrying his plate. He took the seat beside Freddie.

"Well?" John asked Randy. "What did you bring for Miss Napier?"

"I brung her water," Harold bragged.

"I brung her pie," Freddie added, a little more humbly.

Randy grinned. "I brung her scenery." He winked at Katie, and she had to admit he was pretty.

Harold groaned. "You are so danged full of yourself—"

"Listen, you old fart—"

"Gentlemen!" John stopped Randy before things got any uglier. "There's a woman and a child present."

Julia tugged on Katie's sleeve, pulling her down to

whisper in her ear, "Is he the wiry fart we're supposed to stay away from?"

It probably wasn't an appropriate time to laugh, but Katie couldn't help it. Harold *was* wiry and as for the other part, well . . .

"No, honey," she said, as soon as she could talk. "Reverend Stoker didn't mean . . ." What *did* Reverend Stoker mean? Oh dear. She glanced at Julia's plate. "Why, look, you've eaten your lunch. Maybe it would be all right with your pa if you want to play now."

John didn't respond, but his response wasn't necessary. Julia had bounded away before Katie even managed to put the period at the end of her sentence.

She returned her attention to the men, only to find Harold seething, Freddie blushing, and John glaring. As for Randy? He was grinning, but then, he did that a lot.

Was that his foot brushing against hers under the table? Surely not. She tucked her feet under her bench, not daring a peek in his direction.

They ate in uncomfortable silence until finally all three men blurted at once, "Katie, I was wondering," and from there the sentences jumbled around each other, as they each asked to walk her home. She tried to answer over the din, but gave up as their bickering overcame their desire to walk with her.

Sighing, she picked up her plate and left the group, not caring if her sudden exit was rude. They were becoming more irritating than wool under britches.

"Miss Napier?" John hurried to catch up with her.

"I'm sorry, Dr. Keffer. I guess I'd just had all I could take."

"That's understandable." He stood with her while she scraped her dinner remains into the slop pail, then rinsed her plate in a bucket of water.

"Are they always like that?" He gestured toward her suitors, still arguing away at the table.

"No." She took his plate and proceeded to clean it. "It just started when I agreed to marry them."

John's brows rose, and then frowned. "*All* of them?"

"Sort of." She dried their plates and returned them to her basket.

"How can you 'sort of' have three fiancés?"

"It was an accident." And one she didn't want to talk about just now, at least not with John. "What was it you wanted to ask me?"

He hesitated for a moment, probably wondering about her abrupt change of subject, but being the gentleman he was, he didn't ask any more questions on the matter.

"I was hoping I could convince you to help me."

She hadn't expected that. "How?"

"I would like to employ you to work with me in my office. I need some help learning the area and organizing my equipment. Two or three days a week, you decide. You could tell your friends where you are so that if any need to see you, they could stop by there."

He paused, then added, "I'll pay you well."

Money. She could actually earn a little money for such things as flour and ribbons. But working in town would mean being away from home part of the week.

"*Katie?*" Grandpa yelled across the yard. He sat under a big shade tree with enough food in front of him to feed Wayne County. "Can you fetch me some dessert? My knee's a-hurtin'."

"I'd like some too, Katie girl," Pa chimed in, scratching his belly.

Katie looked up at John and smiled. "When can I start?"

Chapter Eight

John hadn't expected Katie to be so easily convinced to work for him. Of course now he was faced with the small dilemma of what to do with her once she arrived. His plan had been to use her as bait for the ill, but she probably wouldn't agree to sitting on the front porch with a sign around her neck. He needed something legitimate for her to do.

Pacing around his office, he studied the immaculate shelves, all his equipment neatly organized and his medical books in their alphabetical order.

"Damn," he muttered, quickly jerking the books onto the floor, before collecting his instruments and laying them in a pile.

It wasn't enough. That small mess could be organized in a matter of minutes, not days. Rushing to the basement, he retrieved some of the smaller crates that had been used to ship his possessions from New York. He returned to his office and stuffed everything he could into the crates. Emptying drawers, pulling pictures from the walls, he managed to achieve his desired results. The room was in shambles and not a moment too soon.

The clanging of the brass bell on his front door announced the arrival of a guest. Peeking through the curtains, he saw Katie standing on the porch. Her dark cloak pulled closely to ward off the chill, the handle of a basket looped through the crook of her arm. He took the time to regain his breath as Mrs. Adkins answered the door.

"Dr. Keffer?" Mrs. Adkins said. "Katie Napier is here." She stepped through the doorway of his office, and her mouth gaped open.

Don't say anything, Mrs. Adkins, he willed, knowing the state of his office surprised her. Hell, it surprised him.

"Miss Napier," he said, walking toward Katie in hopes of stopping Mrs. Adkins from exposing his charade. "I'm so glad you agreed to help me. As you can see, I need it."

He glanced at Mrs. Adkins, and the twinkle in her eyes told him his secret was safe with her. "I'll leave you two to work," she said, pulling the door closed behind her.

"My, oh my," Katie said, turning a small circle as she removed her gloves and eyed the pandemonium around them.

"I've been occupied," he lied, "and I just haven't had the chance to organize things since I've moved in."

"Well"—she allowed him to remove her cloak—"we'd best get busy."

He laid her cloak across the back of the only accessible chair in the room, then picked his way through the chaos to his medical instruments. Those were the first things he had to get off the floor; the thought of one of them breaking under foot sent a shudder through him.

"Did you get a chance to tell your friends they could contact you here if they need you?" Was that too obvious? He glanced askance, but she didn't seem suspicious.

"Yes, I told several people at church yesterday." She dug through his box of diplomas. "As a matter of fact, Eunice Kopp is stopping by after a while for some goldenseal root. Her stomach is actin' up again." She smiled before continuing. "Of course, by the time she gets here she could have six or eight other things actin' up."

She lifted his medical diploma with its ornately carved wooden frame from the crate. "Do you know where you'd like to hang this?"

"Hmmm." He pretended to think. "How about the wall behind my desk?"

She crossed the room and hung the picture on the nail it had occupied until fifteen minutes before. "Why, that's perfect." Standing back to admire her work, she made a quick adjustment to the frame. "And the nail was already there."

"What luck," he mumbled, taking as much time as he could to place his stethoscope in the cabinet, scooting it a few inches to the left, then back to the right. This disaster needed to last a few days, or at least until he had the chance to create another. "So when is Mrs. Kopp coming by?"

"This afternoon."

He kept his back to her with the pretense of putting away his instruments, but the truth was, he found deception more difficult than he'd anticipated. "Does Mrs. Kopp have a large family?"

"Yes, and all of them sick with one thing or another."

"Good. Not that they're ill, of course, but good that they can come here—or to you—for help." Could he have bumbled that any more?

Silence.

Great. Katie was already on to him. Slowly he turned toward her, expecting a knowing, if not rebuking, expression on her face. Instead, he found her kneeling on the floor beside his medical books, touching the leather bindings as though they were gold.

"Do you read, Miss Napier?"

"*An Elementary Treatise on Human Anatomy*," she read from the cover of the top book on the stack. "I don't read books like these, but I read most anything I can get a hold of."

"And what is your favorite?"

A wistful smile flitted across her lips as she carried Leidy's anatomy book to the shelf. "Shakespeare."

She could not have surprised him more if she'd spoken in Chinese. "You—you can read Shakespeare?"

He hadn't intended his response to be condescending, but the spark in her eye and the pink flush to her cheek told him he'd offended.

"Yes, Dr. Keffer," she responded, her voice cool as a frosty windowpane. "I can read Shakespeare."

"I'm sorry, I didn't mean to imply . . . it's just that most people find Shakespeare tedious."

She carried a few more books to the bookcase. "I guess I'm not most people."

And a truer statement was never made.

At least now he understood why her speech was more educated than that of the others. Returning his attention to his instruments, he moved the stethoscope back to the place he'd had it before he'd stuck his foot in his mouth. The ticking of the mantel clock made the only sound in a room that was far too quiet.

"*Othello?*" he asked, when he could bear the silence no longer.

"*Romeo and Juliet.*"

"That's my favorite too."

Glancing at her from the corner of his eye, he caught her glancing back with a wry smile, subtle but enough to melt some of the frost. "So tell me, Miss Napier, how did you manage to end up with three fiancés?"

"I made the mistake of agreeing with my family when they decided it was time I got hitched."

He turned his attention to his syringe, the stethoscope finally landing in the correct spot. "Don't most people marry only one at a time?"

She chuckled softly, and the frost melted completely. "I only intend to marry one of them, but I'm having a horrible time deciding which one. Every time I'm around them, they fight and bicker with each other so that I can't get a word in edgewise."

"Perhaps it would work better if you saw them separately."

"How would I manage that?" She seemed genuinely interested in his opinion, and genuine interest should never go unrequited.

"You could give each of them a different day of the week to do their calling. That way you'd get to know them without the interference of the others."

"That's a good idea. Now, can I ask you a question?"

"I believe you just did."

She smiled, and the sun broke through. "You know what I mean."

He returned her smile, unable to do otherwise. "Ask away."

"Will your wife be joining you any time soon?"

He froze. It took a second before his mind allowed him to remember that none of the people here knew what had happened. It was only natural for Katie to assume Julia's mother would be following from New York. He turned back toward his cabinet, finding it easier to say what he had to if he wasn't looking at her.

"My wife is dead."

"I'm sorry." Her voice was hushed and tinged with the uncomfortable realization she'd opened a painful wound.

"No need to apologize, Miss Napier." He fought down the paralyzing guilt, threatening to choke him. "You didn't kill Lois . . . I did."

Chapter Nine

The jingling bell at the top of Frank Davis's door sounded far too chipper, given Katie's frame of mind.

"Mornin', Katie." A chorus of greetings met Katie from the men sitting around the potbellied stove.

"Mornin'," she responded, barely looking up from her reticule.

John had given her money to buy some ink for his office, even though Katie had seen a full bottle in one of the crates. Didn't matter. She'd gladly jumped on the excuse to make a quick trip to Frank's store. John's startling revelation had left them both too rattled for polite conversation.

Katie didn't believe for one minute he'd murdered his wife, but the pain in his voice left no room for questions.

He'd talk when he felt like it.

"Katie?" Harold said, separating himself from the gang around the stove.

"Oh, good morning." In her frazzled state, she'd failed to notice him.

"I heard you was working down at the doc's office now."

"Yes, but just a few days a week."

"If'n you was to marry me, you wouldn't have to work nowhere."

Except in his kitchen? "I'm working because I want to."

He snorted. "Ain't proper for you to work so much alone with that man."

"Dr. Keffer is a respectable gentleman, and his daughter and housekeeper are there at all times." Her response probably sounded defensive, but Harold hadn't heard the pain in John's voice. Defending him seemed natural at the moment.

The bell at Frank's door jingled again, causing Harold to glare at the person entering behind her. She sighed. That could only mean one thing.

"Mornin', Katie."

"Mornin', Randy," she answered before she even saw his face. She didn't need to. She'd seen Harold's.

"Dagnabbit!" Harold fumed. "Do you have to be everywhere I am?"

"Listen, you old coot—"

"Gentlemen!" Katie interrupted before they came to blows. "It's actually good that you are both here." She waited, hands lifted to keep them apart, until they relaxed and faced her. "This arguing and bickering is keeping me from getting to know any of you."

"He started it," Randy said, pointing an accusing finger at Harold.

"*You* started it when you walked in the door," Harold answered, and the hackles rose again.

"Hush!" Both sets of eyes rolled toward her sheepishly. "I have decided the only way to solve this problem is to separate the three of you when it comes to seein' me. Harold"—she tipped her head in his direction—"you get Mondays. You're welcome to come out to the cabin on Monday evenings for dinner, if you'd like, and we can get a chance to talk a little."

Turning toward Randy, she said, "And you can have Wednesdays. Freddie gets Fridays."

"And the doc gets the others?" Harold asked in a tone Katie was beginning to find annoying.

"The doc isn't courting me."

"Ain't the doc married?" Randy asked, his ire suddenly directed away from Harold.

"He's a widower," she murmured, digging into her reticule for her money. Time to get ink and get out before she had to defend John to Randy too.

"So you're workin' alone with the doc, and he ain't married?"

Too late. His tone matched Harold's, and she'd had about enough of both of them. "I'll work with whoever I've a mind to, and if you two don't like it, I'll just marry Freddie."

Whipping around to the counter, she slammed the coins on the top with more force than she'd intended. Poor Frank jumped, knocking his glasses sideways on the end of his nose.

"I need a bottle of ink, Frank."

Frank hurried to retrieve a bottle from the shelf behind the counter and hand it to Katie. It wasn't like her to raise her voice or slam her hand on countertops. It felt pretty good, despite the fact Randy, Harold, Frank, and the gang around the potbellied stove stared at her in disbelief.

She stuffed the bottle into her reticule and walked to the door, head held high. If they didn't like this side of Katie Napier, so be it. She liked it fine.

The trip to the store had been the perfect remedy for the tension that had built between her and John. By the time she returned, he was back to normal, smiling his tight-lipped smile and rearranging the instruments in his medical cabinet with the speed of a snail. No wonder his office was still a mess. The man couldn't even put away a bandage without moving it ten or eleven times.

They talked of nonpersonal things, such as Shakespeare and the weather, until it was time for her to take the three-mile hike back to her cabin. Her mind whirled through a thousand possible reasons why John would say such a thing about his wife's death, while she traipsed down the wagon road and across the creek to her home.

That whirling mind was the only explanation she could give for why, until Harold thumped on their door precisely at dinnertime, she'd forgotten it was Monday. And she had promised Harold Mondays.

Grandpa beamed as he hurried over to shake his hand. "Katie, why didn't you tell us Harold was coming over for supper?"

"I wasn't sure he'd be able to make it." She quickly pulled more bread out of the Hoosier and set another plate at the table, hoping her excuse sounded reasonable.

Harold barely nodded in her direction before Grandpa dragged him to the hearth to warm up and chat. Her irritation at basically being ignored only escalated when immediately after dinner Grandpa and Harold dove into a game of checkers that lasted long after Grandma and Pa had already gone to bed.

Katie darned socks while the two laughed, goaded, and bickered away the evening, leaving her knowing no more about Harold when he left than when he came. Except that he wasn't as good at checkers as Grandpa and occasionally, according to Grandpa, he cheated.

"You're just mad 'cause I beat you," Harold said, pulling on his coat and hat.

Grandpa hooked his thumbs into his suspenders with a snort. "We'll just see about that next time you come."

It was all Katie could do not to roll her eyes. Another evening of those two carryin' on was not something she looked forward to.

"Harold, can I ask you a question?"

"Of course you can, Katie." His surprised expression made her wonder if he'd forgotten about her existence until that moment.

Lifting her cloak from the peg by the door, she gestured for Harold to join her on the porch. Getting away from Grandpa was the only way she'd get a private word with her would-be husband.

They stepped into the cold night and across the creaky porch boards to a pair of rocking chairs where Katie took a seat. She waited while Harold creaked into the other one.

"Why do you want to marry me?" she asked, once all the creaking was done.

"I, uh . . ." He stopped to think, which was probably a good thing. "You're a fine cook and a good woman."

Not a ringing endorsement for a marriage proposal, but it was no doubt honest. "That all?"

"Course not." He chuckled and suddenly she felt herself blush. "A man my age needs a woman what's good with herbs and such."

"Oh."

"My bowels ain't what they used to be."

"Oh." Again, but then what else could a woman say after something like that? "Well, I'm glad we had this little chat," she said, wishing she'd stayed in the house with her darned socks.

Harold bid her good night, then walked down the hill to his waiting wagon. His old horse was standing patiently in the same spot he'd left him, the only evidence of passing time being the pile of manure on the ground behind the animal. Evidently, the horse's bowels worked just fine.

Chapter Ten

Katie hurried down the wagon road, hugging her cloak against the chill of the brisk morning. Her breath came out in wispy feathers, reminding her that winter was just around the corner as a stiff breeze sent the fall leaves raining around her in a cascade of colors. Soon the color would be gone, leaving the gray of winter to accompany her on her walks.

She doubted John had made any progress in his office after she'd left the day before. The pace he set wasn't exactly breakneck speed, unlike the pace she was setting now. She had an eerie feeling something was watching her from the woods. Silly, she was sure, but she still took a moment to find a stout stick before continuing on to town.

Grandma's mood had been nothing short of grumpy when Katie had left. Evidently, fixing her own lunch greatly interfered with her plans for the day, though it seemed to Katie that dying could be worked around lunch as easy as not. Her unsympathetic thoughts kept her company the rest of her journey and didn't fully go away until she found herself standing on John's front porch.

Should she knock or just walk in? It was the door to his office as well as his home, but so far she hadn't seen any patients, so she wasn't sure if they walked in or rang the bell. Luckily she didn't have to ponder long before John opened the door. He must have seen her walk up to the house.

"Good morning." He smiled, and for the first time since she'd met him, it went clear to his eyes.

"Mornin'." She returned his smile, relieved that the tension of the day before was gone.

He directed her into his office. "I haven't accomplished much since you left, I'm afraid."

Imagine that. "That's all right. I'm sure today we'll make great headway."

What an odd expression on his face. Almost as though he didn't want to make headway. Maybe he dreaded the task of organizing since he did it so poorly.

"I've asked Mrs. Adkins to bring you some hot tea, and I've built a fire. I thought you might be cold from your walk."

"It is a little chilly this mornin'." She allowed John to take her cloak before she made her way to the fireplace to warm up. How nice of him to think of her comfort, unlike Harold, who had forgotten her entirely until his checkers game was over.

The hot tea did wonders in fighting the chill, but unfortunately, the reprieve didn't last long. Someone rang the door chime and in a moment, Mrs. Adkins was ushering Rebecca Fisher's father into the office. "Katie?" Bruce said. "I's hopin' you could come with me. It's time for Rebecca's birthin'." He gestured toward the street. "I brung the wagon."

"Of course." Katie grabbed her cloak and headed

toward the door, making it into the hallway before she remembered John. "I'm sorry, Dr. Keffer. This will probably take much of the day, but I can come back tomorrow to help."

"Of course. Mrs. Fisher's birthing takes priority, but . . ." He hesitated. "I was wondering if I could come with you."

Katie glanced at Bruce, who shrugged as though he was leaving that up to her. "Come along, if you'd like, but I'm warning you, the road to the Fishers' isn't the best."

John hurried to grab his coat and a small leather bag that she assumed had medical supplies, and followed Katie outside to Bruce's wagon.

The bench up front was only large enough for Katie and Bruce, leaving John no choice but to sit in the back. There was nothing for him to sit on except the hard wooden floor planks, which explained why John winced when he finally climbed out at Rebecca's cabin.

"I told you the road was rough," she whispered, hurrying past him while he retrieved his bag. His only response was a grunt, but she didn't have time to wait for more. This was Rebecca's fourth child and chances were he'd be quick making his way into the world.

Rebecca's husband met Katie at the door, a frightened expression on his face. "Somethin's wrong, Katie."

"Why do you think so?" She continued past Paul over to where Rebecca stood clutching the back of a chair, stoic but white lipped as the pains shot through her body.

"Somethin' ain't right," Rebecca muttered, echoing Paul's concerns. "My water's broke, but the baby ain't comin' yet."

Katie motioned to the bed. "Let me see what's going on."

She helped Rebecca walk to the small bed in the corner of the cabin, where she reclined slowly on the quilt. "All men out," Katie ordered, waiting until the cabin was cleared. She lifted Rebecca's nightgown and checked for the baby's head. A quick internal exam confirmed Katie's fear. The baby wasn't lined up for birthing.

"Rebecca," Katie said, using a calm, controlled voice. Panic wouldn't help anyone right now. "We're going to have to turn the baby."

Rebecca nodded, despite the fear that flashed in her eyes. "What do you want me to do?"

Katie waited a moment while a contraction racked Rebecca's body. "I want you to try to relax your belly while I push."

She placed her hands against Rebecca's belly and waited for another contraction to lessen. Then she shoved with all her might. The baby moved a little, but the next contraction shoved him back where he'd been. This would've been so much easier if she could have turned him earlier in labor. As it was, every time she pushed on Rebecca's belly, it contracted with a vengeance. She needed help.

"I'll be right back," Katie said, hurrying to the front door.

All the men and Rebecca's other children stood on the front porch, waiting for the wail of a new child.

"Dr. Keffer?"

John crossed the porch. "Yes?"

"I need your help."

"Wait a minute." Paul grabbed John's arm. "I don't want no man touchin' my wife. Katie can do this."

"Paul." She leveled her gaze at him. "He's a good man, and I'm right here. I need his help to move the baby."

Paul shook his head again.

"Listen." She leaned closely to him so Rebecca couldn't hear. "If we can't move this baby, Rebecca could die. Please let him help me."

Rebecca yelled as a contraction ripped through her, leaving her panting and white in its aftermath. Paul blanched, nodding reluctantly in agreement to Katie's request.

John wasted no time hurrying to Katie's side, getting ready for the next relaxation of Rebecca's abdomen. He jerked off his coat and rolled up his shirtsleeves before placing his hands beside Katie's and waiting. As soon as the belly softened, he shoved with Katie, and the baby moved considerably.

"Don't let up," Katie instructed, fully aware that he probably knew what he was doing, but she didn't have time to find out for sure.

They held pressure through the following contraction, then shoved again as soon as the next break came. Katie felt the perspiration bead on her upper lip as they worked to move the child into the proper position.

After about an hour of pushing, the baby slipped to the canal and Rebecca yelled, "He's comin'!"

"I know he is," Katie answered, moving around to

help with the final part of delivery. She lifted Rebecca's nightgown.

Paul stuck his head in the cabin door. "You can come out with me to the porch now," he said to John. "Katie can take it from here, cain't you, Katie?"

Most men were funny about another man doing what they considered woman things, and evidently Paul was no different. Katie guessed she should just be grateful he'd allowed John to help turn the baby.

"Sure," she answered briefly, having no more time for talking. A tiny head was making its way from Rebecca's body.

Katie was aware John had stepped from the cabin with Paul, and she knew he had to be upset, but she'd think about that later. For now, one more push against Rebecca's belly freed a small shoulder, and the fourth little Fisher slid into the world. Wet and wiggly, she let out a cry while Katie tied the umbilical cord and cut it.

She wrapped the child in a blanket and handed her to Rebecca. "It's a girl."

Rebecca smiled through tears of relief and exhaustion, reaching for her baby to place her on her breast. Katie loved this moment. The pain was over, for the most part, and both mother and child had made it. That wasn't always the case and had it not been for John, Katie feared it wouldn't have been the case this time either.

"Thank you," Rebecca said, tired but happy.

"You're welcome," Katie said, and she meant it. She would smile for days because of this.

As soon as the afterbirth was delivered, she cleaned

up Rebecca and stepped out to the porch for a breath of cool air. John stood rooted to the spot, while Paul, Rebecca's father, and her other children hurried inside to see the new baby. He was still clearly angry for being sent from the cabin.

"Thank you for your help," she said, because she didn't know what else to say.

"I'm a doctor. I should be the one thanking you for *your* help."

Even though his anger wasn't directed toward her, she wasn't about to apologize for something she'd been doing for nearly fifteen years. "I don't know how it is in New York, Dr. Keffer, but around here, menfolk don't like it when another man touches their wives."

"I'm not 'another man.' I'm a doctor."

"But you're a handsome one." She regretted her words as soon as they left her mouth. She'd intended to point out the reason a man might be jealous of him, but instead, the statement hung in the air as his gaze locked on hers and suddenly she forgot her original intention.

He *was* handsome.

Terribly so.

"Well . . ." he finally said, before lowering his eyes, apparently at a loss for words.

So she took over. "Well . . ." It seemed to be the only word not lost at the moment.

Luckily, Rebecca's father stepped onto the porch. "Y'all ready to go back to town?"

"Yes," they both answered, a little too quickly, as Katie darted to the wagon.

Chapter Eleven

"How do I look?" Grandma asked, sashaying into the kitchen like a young girl on her first date. Her gray hair was combed and twisted into a bun at the base of her neck, and she'd put on her blue Sunday dress complete with a brooch pinned at the neck. Her cane dangled from her wrist like a bracelet as she crossed the kitchen to sample Katie's cooking.

"Why are you so dolled up this evening?" Katie asked, as though she didn't already know the answer. Today was Wednesday, and Randy Kopp was coming to dinner.

"Shoot, this old thing?" Grandma scoffed, with a wave of her hand. "I just thought I'd clean up a little for dinner." She tasted Katie's chicken noodles, then added salt. Grandma added salt to everything. Katie was just glad she wasn't baking a cake.

She couldn't blame Grandma for having interest in tonight's guest. She'd gussied up a little more than usual herself, but what girl didn't want to look her best when a handsome man came calling? A flutter landed in her belly, not because of Randy's visit, but because of the brief memory of John's face when she'd blurted that he was handsome on Rebecca Fisher's porch.

Uncomfortable? Maybe.

Surprised? Definitely.

Pleased? Now, that's where the flutters came in. A fleeting look in his green eyes had actually seemed pleased.

That, of course, was *not* the reason she'd decided not to go in and work this morning. Laundry needed doing. Noodles needed cooking.

And, maybe, bellies needed to de-flutter. Some.

A knock on the front door had Grandma moving faster than she'd moved in years. "I'll get it," she hollered, wielding her cane as though she'd conk anyone who got in her way.

Katie wiped her hands on her apron before removing it to drape across the back of a chair. She surely hoped Randy didn't play checkers.

She stepped into the front room just as Randy was removing his coat. He gave Grandma a kiss on the cheek, causing her to giggle like a schoolgirl, and then turned his considerable charm on Katie.

Spit and polished, all dressed for courting, he was a sight to behold. "I brung you some apples," he said, handing Katie a basketful of fruit. "Grandma's tree done real good this year, and I thought you might like to bake a pie."

"Why, thank you, Randy."

She felt her face flush as deep a red as the apples when he winked and added, "You're looking mighty pretty tonight, Katie."

"Ain't he sweet?" Grandma gushed as though Randy had spoken to her, just before she grabbed his arm and ushered him to the fireplace.

Grandpa's snort drew Katie's attention to the fact

that he'd stepped up beside her. "She's actin' like a danged fool. The floozy."

Katie was used to Grandpa complaining about Grandma and visa versa, for that matter. It seemed they rarely had anything good to say about each other. But for some reason, tonight his comment made her stop and think. "Grandpa?"

"Huh?" he asked, still glaring at his errant wife.

"Why did you marry Grandma?" She suddenly had a need to know if the love had gone away or if there never had been any to begin with.

"Why did I marry her?" he asked, clearly surprised by her question.

She nodded. "Why did you vow to stay with her 'until death do you part'?"

"Because I didn't figure I'd live this long." He grunted, then walked away, leaving Katie no clearer on her question than before the grunt, but she didn't miss the way his eyes never left his floozy-fied wife. The love was still there, just a tad rusty.

"Supper's on, everybody," Katie said, returning to the kitchen and her salty noodles.

She set the kettle on the table and proceeded to dish out a bowl of green beans and boiled potatoes. A pan of warm corn bread finished the setting, just in time for Grandpa to say grace. Randy had taken the seat beside her, which probably was fitting. The brush of his foot against hers during grace probably was not.

He wasn't even fazed by the look of censure she threw his way, a look she about wore plumb out by the end of the meal. If it wasn't his foot, it was his knee or a slight brush of his hand against hers. Each chastising glance she gave him was met with a wry grin or the slight wiggle of his eyebrow. She was beginning to wonder if Randy was his name or a description of his constant condition, when Grandma hailed him to join her on the settee by the fire so they could chat.

Ever the charmer, he couldn't refuse. But when the evening came to an end, Grandma was still chatting. Katie couldn't help feeling a little sorry for him.

"Katie?" he asked, as he pulled on his coat. "Can you step out on the porch for a spell and say good night?"

He looked so forlorn she couldn't refuse. Besides, refusing to be alone with a man she was considering marrying seemed silly. Grabbing her coat from the peg, she stepped out behind him onto the porch. The door barely closed behind her before he pulled her into his arms.

"Randy!" She shoved against his chest, but he only chuckled. The boy was strong as well as pretty.

"Come on, Katie. How are we supposed to get to know each other if we don't have a little kiss or two?"

She turned her head quickly, causing his lips to land on her cheek instead of their intended destination.

"Randy, we don't know each other well enough for that." She pushed harder, and he released his grip.

"Katie—"

She held her hand up to stop him midsentence, then pointed to the rocking chairs. Grinning, he followed her unspoken instructions and crossed the porch to a chair. Oddly enough, the boards didn't creak as much as they had with Harold.

"I want to know why you want to marry me," she said, taking the chair beside him.

His silence told her he really hadn't thought about it before.

"Um . . ." He paused. "You're a pretty woman and a good cook."

"And?" If he said anything about his bowels . . .

"And I ain't never lost a woman to no man. I ain't goin' to lose to them other two now."

Competition. Suddenly she felt like a prize calf he was trying to win at the county fair. "That's not a good reason to marry a woman."

"That ain't all," he said, his lip curving up in his most devilish grin. "That just makes it more fun."

And then he showed her why he had women falling all over themselves over half of West Virginia. He dropped his smile and took her hand, looking her squarely in the eye. "It's time I settled down, and you're a fine woman, Katie Napier. A man could do much worse for a wife."

With that, he kissed the back of her hand and bid her good night, leaving her to stare out into the darkness, contemplating her alternatives. At this point, she could serve her purpose as either a trophy calf or a laxative. As if that wasn't enough, Freddie had yet to make his bid. How was that poor boy going to top those?

Chapter Twelve

Would Katie notice he'd undone some of the work they had finished the other day? John hoped not as he removed a few books from his lower shelf and carried them across the room. Since he had painstakingly placed those on the shelf originally, maybe she wouldn't realize they'd been unplaced. But regardless of his sabotage, the office would be finished today, and Katie would need another task if he was going to keep her. Hmmm.

The clanging of the door chime told him Katie had arrived. The woman was nothing if not punctual. "I'll get it, Mrs. Adkins!" he shouted, running his hand back through his hair.

He opened the door and Katie threw him a smile that made her eyes sparkle. Though now that he thought about it, all her smiles made her eyes sparkle.

"Come in." He motioned for her to enter and stepped back to allow her to do so. "I'm not sure we can finish in the office today, but we can try."

"If we work a little faster, I imagine we might."

The look she gave him left no doubt as to whom she thought was slowing down the process. Choosing to remain silent instead of attempting to deny the truth, he followed her into the office. Her focus immediately landed on the shelf he'd just emptied, before she sighed and removed her cloak. Not only was the woman punctual, but apparently she was also observant.

"You know, Dr. Keffer, this would go much more quickly if you didn't undo what we've already done."

"Whatever do you mean?" He took her cloak, immediately turning his back so she couldn't watch his face. For some reason, he was convinced she'd know his lie if she saw his eyes.

"I feel sure those books were already put away when I left."

He shrugged, then walked to the pile of books he'd carted across the room. "Julia must have been playing in here." He carried them back and set them on the floor by the bookcase. "I'll talk to her about it later."

Kneeling, he began placing each book on the shelf, reading every spine as though he couldn't decide where exactly it should go. The quiet room was too conducive to working. He'd noticed Katie often stopped her tasks when she answered questions, particularly when those questions involved her. "So, what made you suddenly decide to get married?"

She stopped digging through the crate on his desk and looked off to think. He grinned to himself over his own genius.

"What woman doesn't want a husband?" She returned to her digging.

"Forgive me for saying so, but I would think, had you wanted a husband, you could've had one long before now."

"Why, Dr. Keffer, are you calling me an old maid?"

"No," he answered quickly, feeling a bit foolish

when the twinkle in her eye told him she'd been teasing. "But you must admit," he said, moving a book a few inches to the left, "most women are married by your age."

"I suppose." She picked up a paperweight and set it on his desk before she stopped to elaborate. "I had a few beaus years ago, but when my ma got sick, I knew I was the only one who could help her. There was a woman who lived near here who was a good healer but too old to get out and help people anymore, so I started going to her to learn all I could to help my ma."

Katie fell silent and maybe it was none of his business, but now he actually wanted to know more. "What happened?" he asked.

"Hattie was good but not good enough. Neither was I, I guess, 'cause after years of trying, Ma died." Her voice had dropped to the point he could barely hear her.

The mantel clock ticked five times before he finally said, "I'm sure you did your best."

She looked at him and for a brief moment he felt her despair. An emotion he recognized, as it had been his constant companion for some time now.

But as suddenly as her mood had darkened, she smiled, though wanly. "Anyways, after Ma passed, finding a man didn't seem all that important anymore."

"Until now?"

"Until now."

"Why the sudden change?" And why his sudden interest? He *wasn't* interested, of course. He only needed to keep her from working.

She shrugged. "I guess I'm like most women, and I want to have children."

"So you're not looking for love?"

She blushed prettily, and he realized too late that his question had been far too intimate. Whether this woman was looking for love was none of his business—again.

"I'm sorry, perhaps I overstepped."

"Oh no. It's all right," Katie answered, even though it wasn't. John's question had knocked the wind out of her, and now she felt as though she had to answer. "I guess everyone hopes for love, but I don't need to love a man to marry him."

"Ah," he said, nodding and returning to his books. She suspected he wanted to ask more, but dared not, and far be it from her to encourage him. That man had the uncanny ability to throw her off guard better than anyone she'd ever met.

Time to change the subject. "What made you decide to move here from New York?"

"I, uh, thought it would be a good place to raise Julia."

"She's a lovely child."

He nodded, then moved another one of his books. If he didn't quit scooting them around, he was going to wear out the bindings.

"Sometimes," he said, "I don't know exactly what to do for her."

Katie stopped sorting the items in John's desk drawer and raised her eyes to him. He sat on the floor near the bookcase, staring off in some unknown thought or maybe a memory, a black book forgotten in his hand. She felt a need to bring him back. "You just love her," she said, because it was the best advice she had at the moment.

He lifted his eyes to hers before he looked quickly away. "So sometimes love *is* necessary?"

"It is for children," she answered, and she knew it was true. Her family loved her, and that love was the only thing that had kept her going. She'd give love to her children, whether she felt it toward her husband or not. Through the years, she could learn to love him or at least respect him and that was close enough.

Their discussion became much less personal after that, thank goodness. And as a result, by afternoon, the office was finished. All books put away, all crates emptied.

Katie sighed with pleasure when the last item, a picture of Julia, was placed on the mantel. "Done, at last."

John grunted. "But we should've stopped hours ago. Now I'm afraid it's going to turn dark while you're walking home."

Katie glanced toward the window. The sun was setting and by the time she made her hour's walk home, it would no doubt be dark. "I'll be fine. I walk in the dark all the time." She tried to act nonchalant. Normally the night wouldn't frighten her, but lately she'd been hearing something in the woods. She'd just be sure to carry her stick.

And she did carry it, all the way home and even while she ran the last bit after a growl interrupted the quiet of the forest.

Chapter Thirteen

Katie turned the frying chicken in the skillet one more time before she drained the boiled potatoes and added a glob of butter. Freddie should be arriving anytime now and even though he didn't seem to eat much, Grandpa's appetite always picked up whenever there was company.

"Did you bake a cake, Katie girl?" Pa ambled into the kitchen to steal a taste of the potatoes as Katie mashed.

"No, I didn't have any sugar."

"I thought the doc was payin' you so you could get sugar and such."

"He's going to pay me. He just hasn't yet." She twisted the masher into the buttery white potatoes, knowing she didn't need to add salt. Grandma had been through earlier, taking care of that necessity.

"If he ain't goin' to pay you, there's no reason for you to be traipsin' off to his office so much."

"He's going to pay me," she repeated, fighting the urge to rap Pa's knuckles with the masher.

"I still think you oughta quit. There's things here what needs done."

Her anger flared. "I'm doing my chores."

Pa snorted. "Still ain't right, you being around him so much. He ain't married, right?"

Grinding the masher into the potatoes, she moved the bowl away from Pa's reach. If he was going to insist on irritating her, at least she didn't have to let him taste the potatoes. "He's a widower."

"No wife around?"

"No, but John's a good man, and he's never been anything but respectful to me."

"You call him John?"

Katie felt her face heat. "Of course not. I call him 'Dr. Keffer,' and he calls me 'Miss Napier.' He's always a gentleman."

Thank goodness, Freddie arrived and Pa forgot about John as he hurried to the front room. It took most of dinner before Katie's temper calmed enough for her to join in the conversation. She hoped Freddie didn't think her sullen behavior was on his account. He'd obviously gone to a great deal of trouble to get ready for this evening.

He must have spent half the day and half a jar of pomade to get his wild hair to lie down against his head like it did. He didn't say much except "Mighty fine meal, Katie," which he said no less than fifteen times, and each time he did, Pa commented on what a fine young man he was.

Katie suspected he *was* a fine young man, but when it came time to sit and chat after dinner, Pa had him out the door to chop firewood before she could talk to him at all.

"Pa," Katie complained as they headed toward the door, "he's a guest."

"He don't mind, and we got to see if he's work brittle." He yelled to Freddie, "Do you mind helpin' out, boy?"

"No, sir, Mr. Napier," was Freddie's reply, and Katie wished she'd rapped Pa over the head with her potato masher. Maybe it would've knocked some sense into him.

The chopping session lasted until dark and until Freddie mashed his thumb between two logs. But Katie had to give him credit. He didn't complain while she bandaged the bloodied nail, despite the fact that it had to be hurting something fierce.

"I'm sorry Pa had you doing that," she said, tying the bandage in place while they sat at the kitchen table.

"Oh, it's all right," he said, but for the first time since she'd known him, his face was white instead of red. Most of his curls had sprung free of the pomade, and the glisten of moisture across his upper lip caused her to suspect he was close to passing out.

"Would you like to sit a spell on the front porch?" she asked, figuring the least she could do was spare him from an evening of visiting with her family, especially Pa. He was liable to have the boy putting shingles on the roof if she didn't do something now.

"I'd like that," he said, the color returning to his face. She led him from the kitchen to the front door, where they put on their coats and stepped onto the darkened porch.

Katie took a seat in her questioning rocker, as she was beginning to think of it, while Freddie took the rocker beside her. She realized he hadn't been heavy enough to creak a single board.

"Freddie?"

"Yes'm?"

"Why do you want to marry me?" Maybe she shouldn't have asked him so bluntly. His chair quit rocking, and she wasn't sure, but she thought he swallowed his tongue. "Freddie?"

"Uh."

Oh dear. Was he about to swoon?

"I . . ." he started again, and Katie felt guilty for putting him in such a spot, but before she could let him off the hook, he answered her question. "You're a fine cook."

Him too? She was going to start burning her meals from now on.

"And," he continued. "I've always been sweet on you, Katie."

She smiled. Finally someone who had actual feelings for her. "You have?"

Her response must have given him courage because she could see his head nodding in the dark. "Yes'm, I sure have."

"I think that's important."

Freddie didn't respond. He just bid her good night and walked off her porch to his waiting horse.

Katie watched him ride away, thinking that life truly was full of surprises. Who'd have thought that poor Freddie would manage to top the other two after all?

John looked at his dismantled library and cringed. The days he'd spent categorizing and sorting all his prized books had been disheveled and disorganized in a matter of moments. Maybe not moments, but it had been much easier to undo his work than it had been to do it. He hoped this mess would last long enough to get the locals switched to him for their medicinal needs.

The slight guilt he felt dispelled quickly when he reminded himself that Katie would be busy with a new husband soon and would probably enjoy the reprieve from tending to others. Unfortunately, the guilt was replaced with another feeling he didn't care to investigate just now.

He bounded down the steps to answer the door chime, slightly perturbed to discover that Mrs. Adkins and Julia had beaten him to it.

"Hi, Katie," Julia squealed, hugging Katie's skirts before she'd even made it into the hallway.

Katie laughed and handed her coat to Mrs. Adkins, who also seemed pleased as punch to see her.

"Would you like some tea, Katie?" Mrs. Adkins asked.

"No, thank you. It's actually warm out today."

Julia tugged impatiently on Katie's sleeve. "Can we take a walk, then?"

Katie stooped down to Julia's level. "I'm not sure. I'll have to see what your pa wants me to do."

"I think a walk would be fine," John interrupted from the stairs. The longer it took them to straighten up his library, the less likely he'd need to destroy another part of his home. "Maybe we can go to Frank's store later, if Mrs. Adkins has anything she'd like us to pick up."

Mrs. Adkins grinned, and said, "I think I can find a few things," before she took Julia's hand and led her to the kitchen.

Katie turned toward John, her face still shining with a beautiful smile, and his mouth suddenly went dry. Her gaze dropped to the floor, and the pink tinge to her cheeks told him he must have been staring. He hadn't meant to. Wouldn't have, in fact, if she hadn't looked so damned radiant.

"I'm hoping you could help me with my library," he blurted, trying to fill the embarrassing silence. "I haven't had a chance, and as you know, I'm not very good at organizing." He turned and headed up the stairs, hoping she'd followed.

Her light laughter behind him confirmed that she had. "I think you may be good at it, just not very fast."

He smiled, because he knew she couldn't see him, and because he couldn't stop it anyway, and led her into the upstairs library. The mess was impressive if he'd say so himself.

"Oh. My."

He turned back to see Katie frozen at the door. "This is going to take a while," she muttered, and he certainly hoped so. It was one of his best disasters.

Katie spent several minutes walking from pile to pile, her slender hand coming to her lips every once in a while, her head shaking from side to side as though she didn't know where to start. He might have overdone it.

"Maybe if we sort the fiction from the nonfiction

first?" he offered, afraid if he didn't, she would scream and run from the room.

"Yes." She forced a frightened smile, causing him to chuckle in response.

"Don't tell me you're faint of heart?"

"Of course not, but . . ." She turned in a small circle to survey the room. "Where will we sort them to?"

He looked around the room as well, noticing that in his haste to empty the shelves, he'd failed to leave any space on the floor for resorting. That was going to add to the time it took to fix this mess. Brilliant.

He shrugged. "I guess that will need to be our first job."

Sighing, she nodded, then began moving books. Being as tiny as she was, she could only move a few at a time. Being as sneaky as he was, he did the same. Even at that, the little woman was quite a worker, and she was making way too much progress.

Time to slow her down. "How's it coming with the fiancé choosing?"

She stopped carrying and frowned. "Not well, I'm afraid."

"What's wrong?"

She turned toward him, her brows still furrowed. "I can't seem to make a decision. They all have good points and bad ones, and I don't know what to do."

"I'm sure you'll figure it out eventually."

"Would you help me?"

Help her? Damn. "How could I possibly help you do that?"

She sat on a stack of books. "I've been thinking that

maybe I need to make a list of what's important in a husband. Then I could use that to sort them out."

"Sounds like a good plan." And not one he needed to help with.

"But I'm not sure what a good husband should be like. I've never had one."

"Neither have I," he noted, hoping she'd leave him out of this.

"No, but you've been married. What's important in that relationship?"

What's important in a marriage? Love? Trust? Sex? Hell, he couldn't point out that one. "I think that changes according to the individual. You'll have to decide for yourself what's important." Then again, stopping to make a list would take up considerable time. He knew he was going to regret this. "But I think making a list is a good idea. I'll help any way I can."

He sauntered downstairs to his office to retrieve some paper and pen and ink. A return saunter ate up a little more time, but his sauntering might have backfired. By the time he made it back to the library, she all but had a spot cleared on the floor for sorting books.

"I have some paper." He handed her his supplies, so she couldn't clean anymore, then proceeded clearing the top of the desk in the room. The fact that he cleared it by moving the books to the spot she'd just made only added to his satisfaction.

"Now." He pulled a chair up to the desk and motioned for her to sit. "Shall we begin?"

Katie wrote the names of her fiancés down the side of the paper: Randy, Harold, and Freddie.

"I'm not sure where to start."

He shrugged and scooted another chair up to the opposite side of the desk to face her. "I guess you should start with what you think you want in a husband."

Tapping the pen against her chin, she stared off for a second to think. "He'd have to be smart. Not too smart, but I don't want a man who can't think or cipher."

"Intelligence seems like a good quality."

She nodded and wrote it on her list. He'd hoped by giving her the task of actually writing the list, it would take a little longer, but her quick and fluid writing dispelled that hope.

"How about money?" he asked.

"I want him to be willing to work, but he doesn't have to be rich, just not too poor. I want my kids to have things if they need them."

"So not too smart. Not too dumb. Not too rich and not too poor?"

She frowned. "I'm not doing very well, am I?"

"Not too."

"Oh."

"But maybe if you keep going, you'll be able to narrow it down a bit."

Nodding in agreement, she looked off again before she said, "I think he should be handsome."

He remembered her telling him he was handsome, and his heart picked up a beat. "And why should that matter?"

"If I'm going to look at a man for the next fifty years, I want to enjoy it."

"Fair enough. Does it matter if he's too handsome?"

Her cheek dented with its dimple as she responded to his teasing. "A man can't be too handsome."

"Ah. Just too dumb?"

"Some of them are."

He chuckled. "I think I've met a few of those, myself."

"Then you understand my concern." She studied her paper again; then with a raising of her pen in an unspoken aha, she added, "He has to be kind. I won't tolerate a man who isn't kind to me or my children."

"Nor should you."

"And he should love me."

"I thought you said love wasn't important."

"I said I didn't have to love him. I didn't say anything about the other way around."

John laughed and Katie's eyes shone.

"Is that all you need on your list?"

"No," she answered, suddenly turning serious.

"What's missing?"

"He has to be a good kisser."

Kisser? His eyes riveted to her mouth as he thought of kissing her full, soft lips. Her tongue darted out to moisten the lower one, and he felt it in his gut . . . or maybe a little lower. Would she like his kiss? He suspected he would like hers. Clearing his throat, he attempted to jerk his mind back from its sidetrack. "Why would that matter?"

She blushed, and he realized what a stupid question he'd asked. "I want children," she murmured, writing the last item on her list. "I imagine some kissing would be expected."

"Yes, well." He searched for the perfect comeback.

Finding none, he simply said, "Now that you have your list, maybe we should get back to work. You can always add more to it later."

Katie knew exactly what she would be adding to her list later. When her husband looked at her the way John had, it had to do things to her insides the way John did. Those warm bubbles stayed in her insides until they stopped for lunch, and Julia bounced into the library ready for her walk.

They hadn't accomplished much. Between her list making and John's snail pace, very few books had been sorted and none had been put away. It was odd really, how a man as big as John could have no more strength than he did. She carried stacks of books as big as the ones he carried, if not bigger. Maybe he had a bad back like Pa.

"Mrs. Adkins told me what she wants from Mr. Davis's store," Julia said, her coat already buttoned under her chin, "but she said I couldn't tell you until we get there."

"Oh," Katie said, raising her brows. "Then we'd better hurry in case it's something important for dinner."

Julia's excitement was contagious and by the time they'd put on their coats and headed toward the store, there were smiles on each face. Julia grabbed Katie's hand, then John's, forming a human link that allowed her to lift her feet occasionally and dangle between them to avoid water puddles. Of course there were no water puddles, but one can't be too careful at the age of five.

"Oh, look!" Julia squealed, as a butterfly flittered

past. She pulled Katie's and John's hands together instructing them to "Hold my spot" as she chased after the elusive insect.

Their pace slowed considerably. John's large hand engulfed Katie's, and she suspected he was as uncomfortable with this as she was. Should she pull away? She didn't want to, but they weren't courting, and what would her fiancés say if they heard about this? Maybe if she loosened her grip, he could release her hand if he chose.

He didn't.

Instead he tightened his hold as they followed Julia down the street. Katie could feel her face heating and just when his thumb rubbed a small circle on the back of her hand, Julia bounded back to reclaim her spot. Her bounding didn't stop until they were inside Frank's store, and it was finally time to share Mrs. Adkins's secret instructions.

Frank leaned over the counter to hear the little messenger better. "And what is it you need, Miss Julia?"

She beamed and announced, "Three peppermint sticks, please."

"Peppermint?" John asked.

Julia nodded her head with utmost seriousness. "And she said we weren't to come back until we'd 'et 'em clear gone."

Chapter Fourteen

In the two days since she'd seen John, Katie had done a lot of thinking. As a result, she decided she needed to quit thinking so much about John. It was interfering with her decisions concerning her fiancés, and it wasn't helping get her chores done either.

Of course not thinking about him was going to be tough, especially today since she was heading into town to work for him. She'd just have to think about his library and Julia, and what she was planning to fix for supper, and why he had looked at her lips like he wanted to taste them, and how he had continued to hold her hand when she'd given him the opportunity to turn loose.

Shoot. There she was, thinking about him again.

The crunching of dried leaves snapped her attention away from John and into the woods. Another snap and a low growl sent her heart into her throat. Clutching her stick in front of her, she scanned the forest for a sign of whatever was lurking. Just when she had about convinced herself her imagination was running wild, a large wolf appeared from behind a boulder. The hair around its neck stood on end as it lowered its massive head and growled. With a curl of its lips, the beast bared huge fangs, snarling as it walked toward her.

Heart pounding, she gripped her stick firmly and faced the animal, praying it had no companions. She turned slowly, not breaking eye contact as it circled. Her only chance was going to be timing her swing to connect with its head if it attacked. She didn't have to wait long. The beast released a feral roar and lunged toward her throat. Swinging with all her might, she slammed her stick into the side of the huge head, sending the attacker whimpering off into the woods.

She turned and ran down the path, stick clutched in her hand, but in her haste she fell, banging her knee painfully against a rock. Scrambling to her feet, she continued her escape until she emerged from the woods onto the road that led to town, where she finally allowed herself the luxury of breathing. Gasping, she dropped onto a log beside the road, her eyes searching behind her in case the creature had followed.

Her palms stung, and a quick glance showed them bleeding from her fall. But at least it wasn't her throat. With shaking legs, she got to her feet and forced herself to walk the remaining distance to John's house.

"My God, what happened?" John exclaimed when he answered the door. Katie stood before him, muddy and bleeding, her shaking hand clutching a stick.

"I was attacked by—by a wolf."

His heart dropped and without further thought, he scooped her into his arms and hurried her into his office. "Did it bite you?" He set her in a chair and began unbuttoning her coat.

"No," she muttered, her voice shaky. "I fell when I was running away."

He pulled her coat down her arm, but had to stop when he encountered her stick. "Katie?" She looked up at him, her breathing still labored, a large tear rolling down her cheek. "You can let go of the stick now."

Forcing her fingers to relax, she let the stick fall to the floor with a clatter, and John saw her bloody palm.

"Hell," he said. "Where else are you hurt?"

"Um . . ." She paused, and he could tell she was forcing her mind to work. "I think my knee might be bleeding."

Quickly, he removed her coat, then crossed the room to retrieve bandages and salve for her wounds. He returned and knelt in front of her. "Which knee?" he asked, scooting her skirts up her legs.

She pointed to the right one, but she didn't really need to. The blood seeping through her torn stocking was a dead giveaway. He started to pull the stocking down, stopping himself when he realized he'd need to go well up her thigh to loosen the garter.

"Can you pull down your stocking?"

Nodding, she asked, "Would you turn around?"

He wanted to remind her he was a doctor, but then, if he was only a doctor, the thought of touching her thigh wouldn't have rattled him like it did.

He stood and walked to a washstand to get some water while the rustle of fabrics and a tiny gasp told him she'd pulled the stocking away from her injury.

"I'm finished." Her voice sounded more like hers now that the shock was diminishing.

He took a deep breath and faced her. She'd tucked her skirt around her other leg, leaving only the injured one exposed, her stocking dangling around her ankle and above a very worn boot. How on earth did she walk in those things?

Dragging a footstool over in front of her, he sat and began washing the blood from her knee. "Tell me what happened."

He'd intended to keep her talking so she wouldn't dwell on the fact that he was digging bits of rock and soil from her leg. But as she told of her attack, he found he was the one in need of distraction. The image of a large wolf, ripping her open on the trail, left his hand shaking.

"Do you think you killed it?" he asked, as he carefully wrapped a bandage around her knee.

"No. I don't think I hit it hard enough."

He raked his hand down her calf, telling himself he was only checking for injury until he came to the dangling stocking. "I'm afraid your stocking is ruined."

"I can mend it." She lowered her skirt off her thigh to cover her leg and for a second he felt like a lecherous animal. She was injured, and he was thinking about how smooth her calf felt in his palm. He hoped in her shaken state, she hadn't been aware.

"Let me see your hands."

Rolling her palms upward, he took her hands in his, so small, so delicate. The scrapes weren't as bad as the knee, but they still needed to be tended. A careful washing and some salve left him with the last of his tasks. Placing his finger under her chin, he lifted it so he could examine her face. A small abrasion marred the satin skin covering her cheekbone.

"Is my face hurt too?"

"A little. Can't you feel it?"

She shook her head, a wan smile lifting her lips. "The knee hurts too much to feel anything else, I guess."

"Your knee took quite a hit. You're going to have to keep salve on it so it won't get infected."

She nodded slightly, raising her eyes to look at him while he laid his hand against her face to clean her cheek. The silky softness was like touching a porcelain doll. And before he could stop the impulse, his thumb stroked across her face, painfully close to her lips, which parted, drawing him toward them just as Mrs. Adkins walked into the room.

"I heard Katie come in and thought she'd like some tea." She set a tray on his desk, then faced Katie with a gasp. "Good Lord, Katie! What happened?"

"She fell," John answered, dropping his hand as though it were on fire. He dabbed a bit of salve on her cheek, then did his best to act as though he hadn't almost kissed Katie.

Katie told Mrs. Adkins about the attack while John put away his supplies, trying to sort through his feelings. The ringing of his door chime interrupted both his musings and Mrs. Adkins's fussing, as the old woman hurried to answer the door.

A thin woman in a tattered coat stepped hesitantly into his office, dragging a young child behind her.

"Hi, Polly," Katie said, obviously recognizing the visitors.

Polly smiled at Katie. "They said you was here and could maybe take a look at my boy." She ushered the lad to Katie's chair and rolled up his sleeve. A putrid bandage, saturated with blood and who knew what else, was wrapped around his lower arm.

"Billy cut his arm on the fence a few days ago, and I think it's corrupted."

John stepped over to take a look, but Polly didn't seem too pleased with that possibility. She pulled Billy closer to her side. "Katie can fix this."

Katie raised her injured hands. "Right now, I'm laid up myself. You need to let Dr. Keffer tend to Billy."

Polly frowned and glanced at John.

"I assure you I'm qualified to deal with this," he said. "May I take a look?"

She looked back at Katie, who nodded her encouragement, before reluctantly leading Billy across the room to John.

Billy reached out his arm as though he was sure John was going to rip it off at the shoulder. And from the looks of the wound, the boy might have been better off. The filthy bandage had only managed to hold the infection in, and God only knew what treatment the mother had applied to the injury.

Based on the smell . . . "What is this?" John asked.

"Sheep dung."

Sheep dung. The woman had smeared sheep dung on an open wound and wondered why it was infected.

"My ma always used it, and it works fine."

There was no sense in trying to explain to her about bacteria. Many people still didn't believe in Pasteur's germ theory, but those who didn't needed to look at this boy's arm.

"This time, I think we should try another approach." He motioned for the mother to take a seat and allow Billy to sit on her lap.

"We're going to have to clean this out, Billy, and it's going to hurt some. Can you be a brave young man?"

Billy's lip trembled slightly as he nodded his head. John fetched a clean bowl of water and some supplies while Katie distracted the child with the tale of her falling. She'd omitted the part about the wolf and soon had the boy laughing instead at her clumsiness.

Cleaning the wound as gently as possible, John liberally applied a coat of antiseptic salve and rewrapped Billy's arm with a clean bandage. He had to admire the little fellow. He'd only winced a couple of times during the procedure. John handed the mother some clean bandages and a jar of the salve.

"I'll need to see him again in a couple of days. Make sure you clean this twice a day and only put this salve and clean bandages on it when you're finished."

Polly dropped her gaze to the supplies, then swallowed. "I cain't pay you with money."

"That's all right," John answered, trying to figure out how to save the woman's pride enough to get her to return. Billy could easily lose his arm, if not his life, if she didn't.

"Polly makes the best blackberry jam in the area." Katie's comment brought a smile to Polly's face.

"I do make good jam. Do you like blackberry jam, Doctor?"

John smiled. "Absolutely."

"I'll bring you some when I bring the boy back." Polly ushered her son out of the house, leaving the of-

fice quiet once more. Katie had known how to ease
Polly's discomfort.

Jam.

Who'd have thought of that?

"Thank you," he said to Katie.

"No need to thank me."

But there was. This had been his first patient, and if
the child's arm didn't fall off, she would tell her friends
and soon others would follow. Of course, it appeared
as though his larder would be filled as opposed to his
bank account, but he didn't need money anyway.

He'd been born filthy rich. He'd gone into medicine for the challenge and because it'd irritated his
grandfather to no end. Now suddenly he'd found another reason. If he hadn't intervened, Billy would've
died from infection. Might still, but at least his chances
were far better now. He could make a difference with
these people.

And get a lot of jam.

"Dr. Keffer?" Katie's question brought him back
from his newfound insights. "I need to fix my stocking
so I can walk around without falling over it."

He looked at her, sitting in the chair, the autumn
sun shining through the window behind her illumi-
nating her like the angel she had just proven herself to
be. "I'll go tell Mrs. Adkins we're ready for lunch."

Katie's pace declined only slightly as they worked in
the library after lunch, but John didn't miss the way
she watched the time. He'd suggested they quit early,
in deference to her injury, but she insisted she felt fine.

Then sometime during the afternoon it hit him. She was afraid to walk home.

"I'm going to walk you home," he blurted as soon as he realized her concern. It never dawned on him that she would've assumed otherwise.

"Oh, you don't have to . . ." She paused during her attempted refusal and looked up at him with relief. "But I'd appreciate that."

"How long docs it take?"

"About an hour."

An hour? She walked an hour to get to town? "Why don't you bring a wagon?"

"We don't have one." She immediately began sorting books again, and he suspected she wasn't willing to discuss the topic anymore.

"If it takes an hour, we should probably get on our way."

Katie nodded, standing stiffly to her feet. He wished he had a wagon, but they hadn't needed one, living in town. He could offer her the guest room for the night, but it wouldn't be proper, and her family would be worried sick if she didn't return tonight. An hour of walking with a sore knee appeared to be Katie's only option.

"I'll meet you downstairs," he said, leaving the library and heading straight for his den. After retrieving his revolver, holster, and a handful of shells from a locked box on the mantel, he joined Katie by the door.

She'd already pulled on her coat, her stick clutched firmly in her bandaged hand. Her eyes immediately landed on the gun strapped to his hip. "You have a gun?"

"I think under the circumstances, it's a good idea."

"He's a big wolf."

"I'm a good shot." Did he just wink at her? Surely not. He hadn't winked at a woman since college; of course, that was also the last time he'd done any target shooting. Hopefully that skill hadn't been forgotten either.

The first part of the journey was easy enough. Down the street a few blocks until a wagon road took over for the brick. Then the road split again, heading for the forest and the hills. John kept his eyes and ears open as they walked through the trees, deeper and deeper into the wild.

"How much land does your family own?" he asked when the conversation stilled. She was frightened, and talking was the best way he knew to deal with that.

"Not much. Only about three hundred acres."

"Does your father farm?"

"Used to. But he hurt his back, so his farming has been cut back a bit. He mostly just grows beans and potatoes now. Enough for us to eat."

John couldn't imagine living on beans and potatoes. "Is that all you eat?"

She laughed. "No, Dr. Keffer, we have chickens and a cow, and I get a lot of things from the people I treat."

"Like jam?"

"Like jam. I also sell eggs in town so I can buy flour and the like."

"Ah," he said, nodding as though he understood. But he didn't. He'd always left that sort of thing up to his servants, never worrying about where the food came from. In New York, it simply came from the kitchen. He'd never even purchased food until taking over for Mrs. Adkins in order to meet people at Frank's store. It was like falling into another world, and the farther he walked into the forest, the further away his old world seemed.

Katie suddenly started looking around, nervously. "This is where he attacked me this morning."

John removed his gun from his holster. "Which direction did he come from?"

She pointed to a large boulder situated in front of a rock cliff. John took a step toward what appeared to be a den area, but made it no more than a few feet before the animal growled and lunged at him from the darkness.

John fired three shots into the massive beast, dropping it just six feet in front of him.

"Is it dead?" Katie asked.

With any luck at all, but at the moment he was still too shaken to speak. Gun in hand, he walked close enough to the creature to nudge its side with his boot. When the animal didn't respond by ripping off his leg, he released a pent-up breath. "Yeah, I think he's dead."

She cautiously stepped up beside him.

"Is this your attacker?" he asked, hoping like hell it was.

"Is there a welt on his head where I walloped him?"

John leaned closer to look and sure enough, a mark from Katie's stick slashed across the wolf's head. "That looks like your handiwork."

She visibly relaxed, then looked up at him with a smile. "Thank you."

Pride did strange things to a man. Though he'd

never considered himself to be the type to slay drag-
ons, the look in this damsel's eyes had him rethinking
that stand. "My pleasure." And it was.

"I think I can make it from here, if you want to go
on home."

He holstered his gun. "I'd feel better if I walked you
the rest of the way. Wolves usually hunt in packs, don't
they?"

He hadn't intended to frighten her, but he had no
intention of letting her walk alone either. Katie only
nodded her response and they left the wolf to head on
toward the Napiers' home. It seemed like every time
they came to a fork in the road, Katie took the one less
traveled. Finally the road followed a stream until she
left even that to pick her steps atop several large stones
crossing the water. On the other side, a dirt path me-
andered up the side of a hill to an old log cabin.

Curling smoke rolled from the stone chimney and
over the moss-covered roof. A large wooden porch
spread across the front of the house, closer inspection
revealing a need to watch his step. Several of the boards
on the porch appeared rotted to the point of collaps-
ing. Rot-ation of that sort could be dangerous.

A large coonhound lay by the front door, the only
sign of life being a thumping of its tail against the floor
when Katie stooped to scratch his ear. "Don't worry
about Ol' Blue. He won't hurt you."

The only worry John had had about Ol' Blue was
the possibility he might be dead, but the responding
thump of his tail when John also scratched his ear confirmed that the dog was indeed alive.

John followed Katie into the cabin where her grandfather and father sat by the fire, apparently doing nothing more than staring into the flames. A tiny old woman rocked near the hearth, her sharp eyes homing in on John as soon as he stepped into the room.

"Who's he?" she asked, and John knew immediately he was about to meet the grandmother Katie had talked about.

"This is Dr. Keffer, Grandma. He walked me home."

"Why?" Pa had stood and was now ambling toward the door, his expression showing disapproval of the situation.

John felt his anger rise. "Because she was attacked by a wolf this morning, and I didn't want her walking back alone."

"A wolf?" Grandpa jumped to his feet. Finally someone who was concerned about Katie. "Does that mean you ain't fixin' supper?"

"Would you like to know if she was injured?" John knew his tone was sarcastic, but the dragon slayer in him was coming to the surface again.

"I'm fine," Katie said, pulling off her coat. "I just fell down when I ran away."

Pa snorted. "I seen you was fine. That's why I wasn't worried."

"I knew you shouldn't be going in there," Grandma said, as though to say, *I told you so*.

"And you ain't going back tomorrow," Pa added.

"I'm fine," Katie repeated, but the limp in her walk made John wonder. "Dr. Keffer killed the wolf, so there's no reason why I can't continue to work for him."

Grandma harrumphed. It was an impressive harrumph for such a tiny woman. "I can think of plenty of reasons why you shouldn't be working there." She raised her cane in a gesture John could only describe as threatening. "Randy, for one, wouldn't want you workin' there."

"Who gives a fig about Randy?" Grandpa asked. "Harold's the one we need to worry about."

Grandma harrumphed again, but before she had a chance to argue back, Pa stepped in. "She's going to marry Freddie. He's a good boy." He turned and pointed his finger at John. "She ain't got no reason to be workin' for you no more. Thank you for killin' the wolf and walkin' her home, but you can go now. She's got supper to fix."

Enough was enough. John took a deep breath in an attempt calm his temper, but it was too late. "Katie is a fine woman, and she can work for me any time she chooses, for as long as she chooses." With that, he pointed his finger back at her pa. "If you had any sense of decency at all, you'd realize she's had a hell of a day and you'd fix your own damn supper!"

He jerked open the door and stormed into the yard, hoping the wolf had a buddy. He had a strong need to strangle something right now.

"Dr. Keffer?" The sound of Katie's voice stopped his storming. He turned slowly back to face her, preparing for the anger she was sure to throw at him. It wasn't his place to raise his voice at her family like he had. But instead of anger, she seemed . . . pleased?

"I'll be at work tomorrow."

"If you need to take a day off because of your knee—"

She stopped him. "I'll be there tomorrow."

And he knew she would.

Chapter Fifteen

Where on earth John had found such an old mule was anybody's guess. The wagon it was attached to wasn't much better. Katie walked down the path from her cabin trying her best not to limp, but her knee had stiffened considerably during the night and hadn't had a chance to loosen up yet.

Finding John waiting by the creek with a wagon was like finding a shiny new dollar lying on the road. Only it wasn't new or shiny, just found. "I wasn't aware you had a wagon, Dr. Keffer."

"I didn't until this morning." He gestured toward the mule. "Meet Lightning."

Katie giggled. "Lightning?"

"I didn't name him," he said with a slow shake of his head. "My purpose just seems to be trying to control the beast."

Katie studied the mule a little more closely as John climbed from the wagon to help her to the seat. Large floppy ears drooping halfway down its head matched nicely with the eyes, half closed in sleep. Bony legs—at least there were four of them—held up a substantial potbelly, but the same could not be said for its back. The swayed spine of the animal made Katie wonder how it hadn't folded in two while pulling the wagon.

She climbed into the seat, unable to hide her grin. "Thank you for coming to get me."

"Don't thank me yet. We may have to let Lightning ride part of the way while *we* pull the wagon. At this point, I'm not sure if the mule pulls the wagon or the wagon pushes the mule."

Watching Lightning amble down the road, Katie had to agree with his assessment. "I hope he didn't cost too much."

"Actually, he's just rented. I'm going to the stables today to see if I can find a more energetic animal."

As though knowing he was being discussed, Lightning snorted and flipped his tail at the flies hovering over his rump, most choosing to ignore his feeble attempt to dislodge them.

They rode in silence for a few minutes before John finally said, "I'm sorry I yelled at your family last night."

"They had it coming."

"Yeah," he said, flipping the reins against the mule's back, as though it would make a difference, "but it still wasn't my place."

No, it wasn't, but he was the first person who'd ever come to her defense who wasn't a member of her family. Odd how it hadn't made her mad. "They didn't mean anything by it. They're just not used to me going off on my own like this."

"Do they expect you to stay there forever?"

Katie hadn't thought about it before. Did they? Or maybe more importantly, did she? "I don't know." Which coincidently was the correct answer to both questions.

"Do you mind if I ask what *you* want?" John asked, with another flip of the reins.

"From what?"

"Life."

What *did* she want from life? "I want what everyone wants, I suppose."

"And what would that be?"

The answer seemed too obvious to state. "I want to be happy."

He mulled over her answer for several moments before he asked, "And what would make you happy?"

"A healthy family, a warm home, and food on the table."

The wagon wobbled over a rough place in the road, making noises that caused Katie to hold her breath for fear it would fall apart. She clutched the side of the seat to stay upright as he encouraged Lightning to keep going, her answer to his question still hanging.

But he'd opened the discussion, and it seemed only right he participate. "What would make you happy, Dr. Keffer?"

"What makes you think I'm not?"

The empty eyes, the distant stares, the reluctant smiles . . . "Nothing."

Her tone must have said more than her response because he replied, "I'm not being fair, am I?"

"Not too."

"Happiness would be simple for me, Miss Napier. All I need to be happy is to forget."

She turned to face him. He kept his eyes forward, though she knew he had to be aware she was looking at him. Dare she ask? "What do you need to forget?"

"How to be sad."

He'd intended his answer to be a joke, but it hit too close to the mark for any real humor to seep in. It came out, instead, ambiguous, perhaps cryptic, and even though part of him wanted to tell her everything, a bigger part didn't want her to know. He was here to start a new life. If she knew about his failure, the past would always be his present. And the respect in Katie's eyes would fade.

"Why are you sad?" she asked.

Now he'd done it. He couldn't blame her for asking, having all but teased her with his answer. "I'm a widower. My daughter has no mother, and sometimes it gets very lonely." With a shrug and a forced smile, he added, "But then, I'm no different than many others, and this conversation has gotten maudlin. How are things going with your fiancés?"

Instead of immediately grabbing the segue, as he'd hoped, Katie remained silent for a few plop-plops of the mule's hooves against the dirt road before finally answering his question. She entertained him with stories of her suitors, which led to stories of her family, which led to even more stories of some of the locals he'd met. By the time they'd arrived at his home, he realized that most of the time he was with Katie he forgot how to be sad.

"If you don't mind going on up to the library," he said, helping Katie from the wagon, "I have some errands to run."

After waiting until Katie was inside, he bounded into the wagon to rush off for his tasks. Unfortunately, Lightning had other plans, so John settled for a plop-

plop to the stables, where he learned that Lightning *was* the most energetic animal they had.

Another plop-plop had him at the telegraph office, where he sent a message to his shoemaker in New York. He'd made a point to notice the length of Katie's foot against the floorboards in his office. He'd measured the distance as soon as she'd left, and he hoped that would be enough information for a new pair of boots. Next stop was Frank's store.

"Mornin', Doc," Frank said as soon as the door quit jingling.

"Good morning, Frank." John walked up to the wooden counter. "I need a pair of woolen stockings."

Frank nodded and pulled a box of stockings from the shelf to place on the counter. "These ought to fit," he said, lifting a pair of men's stockings from the box.

"Actually, I need women's stockings."

Frank raised his brows. "How big is she?"

John held his hand out to indicate Katie's height.

Frank nodded and returned the men's socks to the shelf. "Is she portly?" he asked, his back to John as he read the boxes.

"Slender as a reed."

"Is she pretty?"

"Beautiful." John tried to bite back the word as soon as he realized it'd slipped out. Frank turned to face him with a knowing grin and a box of stockings.

"These should fit Katie just fine."

There was no sense in trying to deny it. "She fell and tore hers and winter's coming."

"Yep," Frank said, wrapping the stockings in paper.

"It was my fault."

"Uh-huh."

"Not that she fell, I mean, I didn't trip her, but she was coming to work for me when she fell." The more he talked, the more Frank's grin spread across his face and the more ridiculous John felt. Clamping his mouth shut, he paid Frank and left the store with his stockings and a few chuckles from the men around the stove. Luckily, none of them were Katie's fiancés. Yet.

If it weren't for the need of flour, buttons, and such, Katie would gladly work for John without any more payment than the permission to borrow his books. Here she sat in the middle of hundreds of leather-bound, embossed volumes, none of which she'd read before. With the exception of the one currently clutched to her breasts.

Romeo and Juliet. With golden lettering on a tooled-leather cover, she wouldn't have been surprised if it were autographed by Shakespeare himself. Fighting the guilt of taking a short break, she looked around the room with satisfaction. She'd accomplished quite a bit in John's absence, though it would hurt his feelings if she pointed it out to him. Sometimes, it was almost as if he got in her way on purpose.

A little break wouldn't hurt anything. Flipping open the book, she rushed immediately to her favorite scene. The first kiss of Romeo and Juliet always made her head swim and her heart patter.

"What're you reading?" John stepped into the room, carrying a package and surprising Katie with his sudden question.

"Oh! I, um . . ." She gestured to the pile of books she'd already sorted. "I found this when going through the stack by the window and I—"

John interrupted her. "It's all right, Miss Napier. You're welcome to read anything in my library." Glancing nervously at the package in his hand, he handed it toward her. "I hope these will fit."

She set the book on his desk and reached for the parcel. Tugging at the string, she unwrapped the paper feeling foolish for the flutters in her stomach. A fine pair of woolen stockings, beautifully white and softer than anything she'd ever owned, lay inside the paper.

"I—I can't accept these." Though she wanted to so badly.

"I know it's not proper, but I feel it's my fault yours were ruined."

Folding the paper back over the hose, she reached them toward him. "I fell running from a wolf. A wolf *you* killed, I might add. You don't owe me anything."

"Please, Miss Napier. No one need know I gave these to you, and it would make me feel much better about your injury. If you hadn't been coming to work for me, you wouldn't have been attacked."

"I walk to town all the time—"

"What's the harm?"

She didn't know. She dropped her gaze to the package still clutched in her hands, convinced *something* had to be wrong with accepting them.

He must have sensed her hesitation. "Keep them for now, and if later you decide you don't want them . . . I'll do my best to convince you otherwise."

She hadn't expected him to add that, but before she

could respond, he reached behind her to the book she'd been reading.

"*Romeo and Juliet?*"

She immediately regretted not closing the book. She regretted it even more when he began reading. "'If I profane with my unworthiest hand this holy shrine, the gentle fine is this: My lips, two blushing pilgrims, ready stand to smooth that rough touch with a tender kiss.'"

Katie's face heated. John stood so closely to her, her skirts brushed against his pants leg. And he was talking about kisses. Not just any kisses. Romeo's kisses.

"Come now, Miss Napier. Something tells me you know Juliet's next line." He sounded playful, teasing her about her knowledge of the scene.

She swallowed, determined not to make more of this than what it was. A challenge. That's all. Little did he know this was her favorite scene, and she knew it by heart. "'Good pilgrim, you do wrong your hand too much, which mannerly devotion shows in this: For saints have hands that pilgrims' hands do touch, and palm to palm is holy palmers' kiss.'" She raised her open hand, palm toward him in a manner she'd imagined the actors doing onstage.

She was expecting his surprise with her knowledge of the scene. She wasn't expecting him to place his palm against hers, and the warmth of his hand threatened to upstage Shakespeare when he said, "'Have not saints lips, and holy palmers too?'"

Heart pounding in her ears, she fought to ignore his touch and focus on her lines. "'Ay, pilgrim, lips that they must use in prayer.'"

Still holding the book in one hand, he lifted his eyes to recite the rest without taking his gaze from hers. "'O, then, dear saint, let lips do what hands do.'" Slowly, he moved his fingers until they threaded between hers, and her mouth went dry. "'They pray, grant thou, lest faith turn to despair.'"

"'Saints do not move,'" she said, her voice now barely above a whisper, "'though grant for prayers' sake.'"

"'Then move not, while my prayer's effect I take.'" His gaze dropped to her mouth. "'Thus from my lips,'" he whispered, leaning to within an inch of her mouth, "'by yours, my sin is purged.'"

She felt his last words as he brushed them across her lips as softly as a butterfly's wings.

"Daddy?" Julia said, twirling into the room. "Mrs. Adkins said it's time for you to come to lunch." She twirled back out, unaware of what she had interrupted.

But Katie was aware and based on the look on John's face, not only was he aware, but he was as surprised as she was. "We'll be right there," he answered, stepping back so quickly he bumped into the desk.

They both stood in silence, staring at the door, unable to speak until John finally said, "You're quite an actress," then smiled as though what had happened hadn't happened. "Maybe you've missed your calling."

Attempting a smile of her own, Katie replied, "You're not bad yourself," before she hurried from the room and to their awaiting lunch, which John ate with blazing speed before he excused himself to do a "little weeding" in the garden.

Grateful, though not fooled, Katie allowed herself to relax as soon as the door closed behind him.

"Katie?" Julia asked, poking at her potatoes as though to make sure they were dead. "Did you know my mommy?"

So much for relaxing. "No, sweetheart, I didn't."

Julia twisted her mouth in deep thought, her mind obviously trying to figure out how to approach her next statement. "Mommy went to heaven."

"I know."

Large blue eyes rolled up to Katie, a touch of fear in their depths. "Are you going to go to heaven too?"

"I hope to someday, but not for a good, good long time yet."

Julia smiled, then directed her attention back to her lunch. It didn't last long, though, before she laid down her fork and folded her hands on her lap. "I don't remember my mommy very much," she said, as though confessing a great sin.

Katie scooted her chair closer to Julia and wrapped her arm around her tiny shoulders.

"I was little when she went to heaven." As if she weren't little now.

"That's all right," Katie said, rubbing her shoulder. "I'm sure your mommy knows you love her."

Julia nodded, though not with great conviction. "My nanny told me she got run over by a carriage. I wasn't there, but Daddy was, and he held her while she went to sleep."

"I'm sure he helped your mommy feel better." Katie hoped her voice didn't choke with tears. The image of John holding his wife in his arms while she died burned into her brain. It explained his sadness, but not his feelings of guilt.

"Julia?" Mrs. Adkins stepped into the kitchen. "Time for your nap."

Julia hopped off the chair and took two steps before turning back to give Katie a hug. "Don't go to heaven too soon," she muttered against Katie's neck.

Katie returned the hug, tears spilling despite her best efforts. "I'll work on that."

Julia hurried from the room, leaving Katie wiping her cheek as she walked over to the sink to look out the window. It was a warm day for fall. The sun shone through the leafless trees, casting spiky shadows on the grass, still green despite the light frost of a few nights before. John was kneeling over the remains of a flower bed, the sleeves of his white shirt rolled up as he pulled at weeds.

She suspected he didn't have much experience with gardening, as one of the weeds he pulled up looked suspiciously like thyme. But that was all right. It went well with the sage and fennel already on the ground beside him. She was debating whether she should go outside to tell him when suddenly he jumped to his feet. Spinning from the garden, he swatted at his back.

She hurried to the door. "What's wrong?" she yelled.

"Bee!" he answered. "I think it's in my shirt."

Crossing the yard quickly, she lifted the back of his shirt to find the attacking insect, still on his back, stinger embedded.

"Hold still," she instructed, flicking the bee away. "Is that the only one?"

"Yeah," he responded, teeth gritted. "Did you get the stinger?"

"I think so. Come inside and let me look closer."

Unbuttoning his shirt as he walked, he entered the kitchen and spun a chair around backward to straddle as she examined his back. He faced the back of the chair, his chin resting on his arms folded across the top.

Katie leaned closer to look at the angry welt. At least the stinger itself was gone. "I'll make a paste." She crossed the kitchen and began rummaging through the cupboard for Mrs. Adkins's baking soda.

"I wouldn't have thought the bees would still be out," he said, while she mixed a soda and water paste.

"It's been warm the last few days. I guess they're getting ready for winter." She turned away from the sink to return to him and lost the ability to speak.

Shirt gone, he sat, straddling the chair, a lock of his dark hair brushing against his brow. Thickly muscled, with a smattering of dark hair that crossed his bare chest and narrowed to a line disappearing into the waistband of his trousers, he looked every bit the part of Romeo he had played earlier.

Averting her eyes immediately, she prayed he hadn't been aware of her staring as she hurried behind him to apply the paste. "This should help," she muttered, embarrassed that her voice had broken.

She rubbed the cool paste against the red, swelling sting, too conscious of the warm skin beneath her touch. She'd known his shoulders were broad, but she'd had no idea they were so firm or that touching them would affect her like it was. Allowing her gaze to travel down his body to his narrow waist, she noticed the fabric of his pants hugged his hips and thighs. And for a brief second, she wished the bee had stung him a little lower.

"Well," she said, needing to get her mind away from those thoughts, "that should do it, Dr. Keffer."

Before she could step away, he grabbed her wrist. "We know each other well enough now to be on a first-name basis, don't you think?"

Think? She was lucky she could breathe. "All right."

He grinned, and the breathing part became more of a challenge. Then he squeezed her wrist lightly and dropped it. "Thanks for the salve," he said, reaching for his shirt.

She forced her legs to take her to the sink as she mentally added another thing to her list. When her husband touched her, it had to do things to her like John's touch had done. She wasn't really sure what those things were, but she suspected they would come in handy when it came time for making babies.

Chapter Sixteen

The smell of wood smoke drifted across the church-yard, carried by the slight breeze that promised the cold temperatures were about to return. Right about now, Katie would have been grateful for a break from the heat. Her turn at stirring the apple butter paddle was about up, and the fire under the copper kettle needed choking down a bit.

"Freddie," Katie said, stopping him before he threw on another log, "we probably ought to let that fire die down a smidge or the apples are bound to stick."

"I'm sorry, Katie." He returned the log to the stack, then hurried back to take over the paddle. "I'll stir next, if'n you'd like to rest."

He picked up one end of the seven-foot-long paddle and set his rhythm to match hers. Back and forth he rocked with one end of the handle against his hip and the other fastened to the flat paddle that stirred the bubbling apple chunks in the pot. Stepping slowly, he followed the circular path around the fire that had been made from hours of walking and rocking by a host of apple butter makers.

Three large kettles were working today, though not as hard as the women making the apple butter. Katie and six others had peeled and quartered apples for two days in preparation for the church's yearly fall festival. Everyone in the area would attend the two-day event, and the money made from selling the apple butter would help with repairs on the church and parsonage.

Beautiful quilts, jams and jellies, and crocheted tablecloths and shawls were on display for sale and anything not sold would be saved for the Christmas bazaar.

Katie headed to the well to freshen up before the box lunches were to be auctioned. All three of her fiancés were there and rumors were already running rampant that Harold Crowley was prepared to pay as much as five dollars for the privilege of sharing her lunch.

Katie's fried chicken, potato salad, and gooseberry pie were good, but no lunch could be worth five dollars. Still, the thoughts of everyone watching while the bidding climbed made her face heat and her belly quiver.

All of Katie's family had come into town today, even Grandma, who'd spent most of the trip trying to convince Katie it was a perfect day to announce an engagement to Randy. Katie didn't argue. Didn't need to. Pa and Grandpa more than took care of that for her.

"I'm a-tellin' you," Grandpa said, pulling Harold to the side as soon as he arrived at the festival. "If you don't get to work on Katie, you're going to lose her."

"What do you mean, 'work' on her? I'm courtin' as best I know how."

"You might be." Grandpa nodded his encouragement. "But I'm warning you, Randy is romancin' her all the time."

Harold snorted. "That hothead don't scare me none." He folded his arms over his chest and stared across the yard toward the hothead, who luckily had no idea he was being discussed.

"If you ain't worried about him, you need to watch out for the other one."

"Freddie?" Harold said his name like it was a big joke and watching him stir the apple butter, Grandpa had to agree. Skinny and gangly, the boy didn't look like much of a threat. But just then the doc said something to Katie, and her face lit up.

Grandpa frowned. "I ain't too sure it's Freddie you need to worry about." He nodded his head in the doc's direction.

Harold scratched his chin while he studied the situation. "Is she engaged to him now too?"

"Nope. At least I don't think so, but you'd better give her your best shot."

"Doin' what?"

Grandpa thought for a moment, then said, "Use what you got to your advantage. Buy her gifts and such. And make sure you bid the highest on her box lunch."

Harold patted his shirt pocket and grinned. "No need to worry about that. I got it covered."

Grandma watched Grandpa slip away to talk to Harold and decided it was a perfect time to find Randy. Hooking her cane on her arm, she scurried across the

yard to the jams and jellies. Randy had already managed to get free tastes from several of the young girls
selling the preserves. Didn't surprise her none. She'd
give him all the jelly he wanted if she were just fifty
years younger.

"Randy?" She leaned on her cane and hobbled a
mite. If that didn't get his attention, she could always
wallop him with it. "Can I talk to you for a bit?"

Randy left the giggling girls and headed her way.
He sure looked fine today.

"What can I do for you Mrs. Cole?"

"Oh, pshaw." She fluttered her hand in a shooing
motion and smiled. "We're practically family. You can
call me Grandma."

He smiled, and she wished again she were fifty years
younger. Even forty would work.

"I come over here because I'm worried about Katie."

"Why?" He looked quickly to where Katie stood
talking to the doctor.

"That's why." Grandma pointed her cane toward
the two of them. "She's spending way too much time
with him, and if you ain't careful, he's goin' to marry
her himself."

Randy balled his fists and puffed out his chest. "I'll
whup him from here to Williamson if I have to."

"No, no, son. You can't do that. That would make
Katie madder'n a wet hen."

"Then what should I do?"

Grandma patted his arm. "You could charm the
skin off a snake. Use a little of that on Katie, and you'll
have her eating out of your hand in no time."

"I smile and wink at her and tell her she's pretty all the time. What else can I do?"

"Have you kissed her yet?"

Randy grinned and Grandma decided if the room were dark enough, twenty years younger would suffice. "No, ma'am. I tried once, but she said we didn't know each other well enough for that."

"When was that?"

"Oh, about two weeks ago, I'd guess."

Grandma nodded. "Been long enough. It's time to lay one on her."

Grandma didn't realize Pa had overheard her advice to Randy. He hiked up his britches and made a beeline to Freddie. The foolish kid was stirring apple butter while every eligible bachelor in the area was homing in on Katie. The apples could wait.

"Freddie?"

Freddie took his eyes from the kettle, but never lost his rhythm. "Yes, sir?"

Sir. Pa really liked this boy. "I come over here to warn you."

"About what? I ain't done nothing." Freddie looked scared to death, and Pa realized he needed to change his tone. Having him faint face-first in the churchyard wouldn't leave a good impression on Katie.

"I know you ain't done nothin'. That wasn't what I was talkin' about." He followed Freddie around the kettle as he rocked and stirred. "Look over yonder."

Freddie's gaze followed Pa's pointed finger to Katie and the doc, deep in conversation. "Do you think he's going to hurt Katie?"

Pa shook his head. "Worse than that. I'm afraid he's going to marry her."

"*Marry her?* Are they engaged now too?"

"Nope, not yet. But if you don't step it up a little, I think he's going to steal her away."

Freddie frowned, and his pace slowed down a mite. "What should I do?"

"She likes a man that works hard and can help with chores and such."

"I helped set up the kettles this morning, and I've been stirring apples and washing jars."

"That's good," Pa said with a nod, "but you probably should do some work around the cabin so she can see you'd be handy to have around." Pa patted him on the arm, then added, "Oh, and be sure to win her box lunch today. Got any money?"

Reaching into his pocket, Freddie pulled out two silver dollars. "Yup. And I'm prepared to spend every bit of it."

"Good." Pa nodded, not having the heart to tell Freddie he'd heard Harold was going to spend five. "Get on with your work, then. I'd help, but my back's been hurtin'."

Freddie didn't question it, but then, he was a good boy and smart enough to tell when a man was in pain.

"Thank you, Doc, for what you done for Billy." Polly smiled and handed John a jar of her famous jam.

Accepting her payment, he patted Billy's shoulder. "You're welcome. Glad I could help."

He *was* glad. Glad she'd trusted him enough to do what he'd said and glad that the boy's arm no longer looked like it was going to fall off, but mostly he was glad that several of the people at the fall festival had taken the time to speak with him. Of course he'd purchased two quilts, four jars of preserves, and a tablecloth. With all the money he'd spent, they *should* speak with him, but he didn't feel they did it out of gratitude. Most of them seemed genuinely pleased to see him.

He set Polly's preserves on the church steps with the rest of his newly purchased items and headed to the side yard. He'd seen Katie walk around to the well a few moments before, but he was busy checking Billy's arm. Everyone else was on the other side of the church, and she might need a hand carrying some water.

Rounding the corner of the little white church, he froze and stepped back. Randy was at the well with Katie. Determined to leave them alone, John attempted to return to the others, but his feet wouldn't move. Then his head leaned forward to peek around the corner. Just to check on her, of course.

Randy edged toward her, but Katie smiled instead of retreating, so maybe she wanted his advances. After all, he was one of her fiancés. It was none of John's business, and he should leave, but neither his feet nor his head was cooperating.

Cocking his head in the arrogant way John was beginning to despise, Randy leaned closer and kissed her. John's teeth clenched as he waited for Katie to slap him. Much to his surprise, she didn't. Randy evidently took that as permission to do more, but when he tried to pull her into his arms, she stepped to the side and giggled.

A pent-up breath escaped John as she walked away,

leaving Randy to follow, swaggering as if he'd just won a major victory.

"Little bastard," John grumbled, surprised the words slipped from his mouth. He shouldn't even care, but Katie needed to be more careful. Why hadn't she slapped him? Randy had flirted with every girl there today. Hadn't she seen that?

John returned to the side yard determined not to let Randy upset him. Katie was surely smart enough to recognize a lothario when she saw one. A crowd was gathering under the big oak tree near the back of the churchyard.

"It's getting time for lunch," Reverend Stoker said, "and that means it's time for the box lunch auction."

Cheers and laughter came from the group as everyone gathered around for the bidding. Several of the young ladies came to the center, carrying lunches they'd made especially for the auction. The eligible bachelors in the bunch stepped forward with much shoulder smacking and ribbing from their friends. Each boy had a lady in mind and each lady blushed in response.

John watched from a distance, having no intention of bidding on anything. What he'd just seen had taken his appetite anyway. Two or three of the lunches came and went without gaining much of his attention, but when Katie suddenly stepped into the forefront, his mind snapped to.

Freddie, Harold, and the little bastard worked their way to the front.

"What's my bid for this basket?" the preacher asked. "Katie's a mighty fine cook."

The crowd laughed and Freddie raised his hand. "I bid one dollar."

A few people applauded at the opening bid.

"I bid two dollars," Harold said, and another round of applause ensued.

"I bid three dollars!" Randy shouted with a wave of his hand, and everyone gasped as if like it were a fortune.

The hair stood on John's neck. He couldn't let Randy win this bid. Whoever bought the lunch also bought the right to share it with Katie, and after what he'd seen, there was no way he could let her eat alone with Randy.

"Fifty dollars," John blurted, and the group fell into a stunned silence.

Reverend Stoker's jaw dropped as everyone in the crowd turned to look at John. "Did—did you say fifty dollars?"

Evidently he'd overdone it. Katie's face was scarlet and most of the people around him appeared to have quit breathing. But he'd gotten in too deep to back out now. "Yes, sir, I did."

The preacher nodded. "Going once? Going twice? Sold to Dr. Ketter."

He definitely had overdone it. The pitiful round of applause couldn't mask the hum of discussion that quickly shot through the crowd. Hands covering mouths didn't slow down the tongues wagging behind them. Everyone in town knew she worked for him and now they were going to assume she did more with him than just work.

Katie dropped her gaze and walked with her boxed

lunch and scarlet face through the crowd to stand in front of him. "Where would you like to eat?" she asked, her voice soft and hesitant.

He wanted to apologize to her but not with all eyes and ears focused in their direction. Luckily another girl brought her basket to be auctioned and the attention diverted. Some.

"I'd like to speak with you in private," he said, motioning to the side yard away from the prying eyes of the crowd.

Katie simply nodded, still finding it difficult to form words. Fifty dollars for chicken. For the life of her, she couldn't figure out why he'd done it. Though from the look on his face, she had the feeling he already regretted it. Maybe he'd meant to say "five" and another zero slipped out before he could bring it back.

She followed him to the side yard, where the shadow of the church cooled the air considerably. Fading orange and yellow maple leaves shuffled about her skirts as they walked to a bench near the well. John motioned for her to sit before he hesitantly joined her.

"I'm sorry I embarrassed you," he said, averting his eyes.

Embarrassed? The most handsome man in town had done battle for her and won, and he thought she was embarrassed? She'd never been more flattered in her life.

"I wasn't embarrassed, just surprised." She laid her hand on his arm and waited until he lifted his eyes to hers. "Why did you do it?"

A myriad of emotions flickered through those green

eyes before he finally landed on one. "I couldn't let Randy win the bid after what I'd seen earlier."

She pulled her hand back to her lap and frowned. "Earlier?"

"I saw him kiss you. Are you sure that was wise?"

"I'm not a child, and he happens to be my fiancé."

"One of them."

She didn't like his tone. He was dangerously close to meddling. "Yes, he's *one* of them," she said, schooling her voice to sound calm. "But, lest you forget, kissing is on my list."

"Do you intend to kiss all of them?"

Now he was meddling. "What if I do?"

"You can't just go around kissing men without asking for trouble."

"I'm not just kissing any men," she said, voice rising, "only my fiancés. Besides, how am I supposed to choose if I don't compare them?"

"How are you supposed to compare them if you don't know what you're comparing?" he answered angrily.

Setting her box lunch on the bench, she stood and fumed down at him. "I'll have you know, I've been kissed before."

Not to be outdone, he stood and placed his hands on his hips. "By whom?"

Mimicking his pose, she squared off with hands on hips. "A lady doesn't kiss and tell."

"A lady doesn't kiss half the county either."

She gasped. "Who do you think you are? *My pa?*"

"You think I sound like your pa?"

"Worse! At least my pa knows I'm a woman, and I'm ready for a man."

"Ha!" He ran his hand threw his hair and took a step toward her. "You think you're ready for a man? You know nothing about men."

"I'd like to know what makes you so sure of that!"

Before Katie saw it coming, he grabbed her around the waist and jerked her against him. His lips crushed hers, and everything she thought she knew about kissing crumbled away. She didn't know kisses could melt her brain or flip her insides over. She didn't know they could make her never want to stop kissing, even to breathe.

And she didn't know how much she'd wanted to kiss him.

His intensity softened almost immediately as he worked his mouth against hers before sliding his hands to her shoulders and pulling away.

"I guess you were right," she whispered, still stunned. "I wasn't ready for that at all."

"I'm sorry," he muttered, stepping back. "I shouldn't have done that."

She would have explained to him that it was all right. That she was a grown woman and they'd done nothing wrong, but before she had the chance, he hurried away, leaving her alone with kiss-tender lips, a mild case of shock, and a fifty-dollar chicken.

Chapter Seventeen

John adjusted the diploma on his office wall for the first time in weeks. Oddly enough, it had actually tilted a little to the left, though that wasn't why it had garnered his attention. Unable to sleep, he had finally given up his attempt at four in the morning, and he'd been pacing ever since. It was either adjust the diploma or wear a hole in the rug.

Should he use the wagon to pick up Katie? He'd been doing that ever since the wolf attack, but thanks to his stupid impulsiveness, everything had changed. Never would he forget the look on her face when he'd kissed her. She had been so surprised. She would really swoon if she had any idea how many times he'd come close to kissing her before he actually had.

Of all the unbelievable, improbable events to happen at a church fall festival, kissing Katie had to be at the top of the list. Like a drunken buffoon, he'd plastered one on her. Only he hadn't been drunk at all.

He stopped pacing—unaware until that moment he'd been doing it again—and looked at the clock. A quarter to nine and Katie wasn't there. Maybe she'd decided she couldn't work for him anymore. He couldn't blame her. He'd been a cad, and a decent woman like Katie deserved better.

Damn, he was tired.

Dropping into a leather chair by the window, he stared at the cold fireplace. The room was chilled and a fire would be nice, but he deserved to freeze to death, so he leaned his head against the back of the chair, closing his eyes to await his fate.

"John?" Katie's voice pulled him back from that nebulous place between sleep and consciousness.

Slowly he opened his eyes, allowing his vision to clear. She stood above him, her cheeks pink from her walk in the brisk morning air, a curl or two escaping from her bun as she leaned to speak to him. She looked soft, and warm, and heaven help him, but he wanted to kiss her again.

Luckily his brain awoke before he did something to scare her away permanently. "Katie?" He bolted upright. "I didn't hear you come in." He hurried from the chair to the fireplace. "I didn't know if you were coming today. I would have built a fire." Shuffling through the kindling, he began stuffing wood shavings into the hearth as he rambled. "It's cold, and I should have picked you up, but I wasn't sure . . ." He quit talking because he wasn't sure of lots of things and trying to narrow it down could take a while.

"It's all right," she said, her voice breaking through the uncomfortable silence.

He turned to look at her and for a moment their gazes touched. She didn't say more, but she didn't need to. Her eyes told him it was all right, everything from the lack of fire to not picking her up, to the kiss.

All of it was all right.

And he wanted to kiss her again.

"Aren't we going to work in the library?" she asked, and he realized he was staring.

"Um, yes." He quickly averted his eyes to the fireplace.

"Then shouldn't you just build a fire up there?"

That was logical and rational and for some reason, totally beyond his grasp at the moment. "Of course." He stood and brushed his hands together, suddenly realizing she was still wearing her coat.

"May I take your coat?"

She smiled the way a woman smiles when a man is acting like an idiot, then unbuttoned her coat to hand to him. Awkward didn't begin to describe the way he felt. Should he apologize for kissing her? He'd already done that once and damn it all to hell, but he didn't really regret it. He *wanted* to regret it, or at least claim to. But a man didn't think about committing a crime again if he truly regretted it the first time.

That made an apology out of the question. If only he could act as calm and unflustered as she was. She walked out of the room toward the library as though he hadn't kissed a woman who was engaged, and engaged, and engaged.

He followed her up the steps, which left her hips at his eye level. Back and forth her brown skirts swayed as her bottom rocked with the motion of her steps. He'd bet that bottom would be firm and smooth in his hands.

Damn it! He closed his eyes hoping the adage "out of sight, out of mind" would kick in. Of course he couldn't be so lucky. Closing his eyes only allowed his mind to imagine what was out of sight. Would she wear pantaloons? He didn't remember seeing bloomers when he worked on her knee, but maybe they had scooted up her thigh.

Great. Now he was thinking about her thighs.

Thunk. His toe caught the edge of a step, causing him to stumble and forcing him to open his eyes.

"Are you all right?" She turned to ask him the question, which thankfully took his eyes away from her bottom. Unfortunately, he now stood at face level with the part of her bodice that swelled with her breasts.

She had breasts.

Two of them.

Surely he had noticed them before, but it was strange how everything had changed in an instant when he'd pulled her into his arms and laid one on her.

God help him, he was becoming a lunatic.

"I'm fine," he blurted, wishing that were true. But the truth was, things were stirring that hadn't stirred in a long time, and now was not the appropriate place to analyze them.

"Daddy!" Julia came running up the steps and for once he was glad she had the tendency to appear out of nowhere. Her widened eyes and flushed face jerked his focus away from Katie and her bottom. "What is it?"

"Mrs. Adkins fell off the back porch, and now she's crying."

With a quick sidestep, John raced around Julia, down the stairs, and through the house. He could hear Katie behind him talking to Julia as they also ran toward the back porch. By the time he reached her,

Mrs. Adkins was sitting in the yard, clutching her ankle, and was indeed crying.

"What happened?" he asked, gently lifting her foot.

"I just plain ol' missed that last step. I feel like such a fool." John handed her a handkerchief, which she wiped across her eyes.

Unlacing her boot, he carefully removed it to examine the damage. "Can you wiggle your foot?"

She did, but not without a wince and a gasp or two.

"Katie?" he said. "In my office, in the case with my supplies, are some splints and bandages. Could you bring me some?"

Katie nodded and hurried into the house while he continued to prod an ankle that was already swelling.

"Do you think it's broke?" Mrs. Adkins asked.

"No, but you're going to have to stay off of it for a while. Can your husband make you a crutch?"

She nodded, then clouded up again. "I'm sorry, Dr. Keffer."

"I wasn't aware you'd done this on purpose."

She rewarded him with a weak smile, then wiped her cheek. "Who's going to take care of you and Julia?"

John looked up at the porch where his daughter stood, a lone tear rolling down her cheek. "Would you like to come down and help me?"

Julia nodded vigorously, then clutched the porch rail as though she feared she'd take a tumble too. One careful step at a time, she made her way off the porch and to Mrs. Adkins's side.

"Are you going to be all right?" Julia asked, obviously still frightened.

Mrs. Adkins grabbed her hand. "I will, thanks to you. You done real good, fetching your daddy like that." Julia smiled and John realized he needed to give Mrs. Adkins a raise.

Katie returned with the bandages and helped hold the ankle while John placed the splints and wrapped the injury. They managed to get Mrs. Adkins to the front of his house and into the wagon. After quickly hitching the mule, he climbed into the seat and gathered the reins. "Do you mind watching Julia while I take Mrs. Adkins home?"

Katie ruffled Julia's hair and said, "Of course not." Which was exactly what he knew she'd say.

Lightning pulled the wagon into the street just as Julia asked Katie, "Is Mrs. Adkins going to die?"

"No, sweetie," Katie answered, "your daddy fixed her."

The pride John felt vanished in a flash when the last thing he heard his daughter ask was, "Then why didn't he fix Mommy?"

Katie knew John had heard Julia's question by the sudden slump in his shoulders. Sadness knifed through her. "Sometimes things just aren't meant to be," she replied, watching John drive away and wishing she could hold him instead.

But based on the way he'd acted this morning, a hug was the last thing he'd want. He was so nervous she was afraid if she touched him he'd faint. Of course it'd serve him right. He had that effect on her every time he touched her and sometimes just when he looked at her.

"Let's go inside and see if Mrs. Adkins had anything on the stove." Katie took Julia's hand and led her into the kitchen, hoping the distraction would keep her from thinking about the last time John had touched her. It'd been less than twenty-four hours ago and her lips still tingled.

"We hadn't started on lunch yet," Julia said with all seriousness. "I was going to make biscuits."

"You're good at that."

Julia beamed. "Mrs. Adkins said I make the best biscuits in the county."

Katie fought to contain her grin. Julia should be good at making biscuits. They'd had them every day for lunch ever since Katie had started working for John.

"Do you want me to make them for lunch?" Julia asked.

"If you would, please." Katie watched amazed as Julia dragged her chair around the kitchen, climbing to get a bowl and flour from the Hoosier. She then slid out the tin top to make more room before asking Katie if she'd get her the milk.

"Where's the springhouse?"

"I don't know," Julia answered, clearly puzzled by the question, "but the icebox is in the corner."

An icebox. John had an icebox. Katie followed Julia's pointing finger to the corner of the kitchen where a beautiful oak icebox stood waiting her inspection. Katie knew of people who had them, but had never had the opportunity to explore one before. After a quick examination of the brass hinges, she opened the door and stared in wonder at the dark interior.

Milk, eggs, cheese, and several jars of apple butter and preserves sat on the zinc shelves, cool as a cucumber. She almost giggled when she felt the temperature of the milk pitcher as she lifted it from the shelf.

An honest-to-goodness icebox.

Gracious, John was rich. The big house, library, and fifty-dollar chicken had been a clue, but the icebox really sent it home. Iceboxes didn't work without ice and that meant someone had to be paid to bring it in.

"Daddy!" Julia's excited greeting took Katie's mind away from iceboxes.

John ruffled Julia's hair in a way Katie'd never seen him do before.

"I'm making biscuits," Julia announced. She hurried back to her awaiting dough bowl so she could prove her point.

Smiling at his daughter, he removed his coat. "I'm sure you are."

"How's Mrs. Adkins?" Katie asked while John laid his coat across the back of a chair.

"She's fine, but I realized on the way home that I have a dilemma. I need to hire someone to fill in until Mrs. Adkins is back on her feet. Would you know anyone?"

"Katie will do it!" Julia jumped down from her stool and hurried to Katie's side. "Won't you, Katie? You already come three times a week. Can't you come every day?"

"Oh, uh . . ." Katie glanced up at John and wished she could read minds. His was obviously whirling, which was good since hers seemed to have shut down.

Would John want her around all day, every day? Would she want it?

"I'll teach you how to make biscuits," Julia added in an attempt to sweeten her request.

"Julia," John said, "Katie knows how to make biscuits, and I'm sure she doesn't have enough time to come here every day."

His tone caused Katie to stop just before blurting a refusal. He was hesitant, but almost wistful, like having her around appealed to him.

"I could come for a while," she said tentatively, watching his face for a reaction. "At least until Mrs. Adkins is well."

"Yeay!" Julia jumped up and down, clapping her hands as she jumped. "Maybe we can get a kitten!"

"A *kitten*?" John and Katie said in unison.

"Mrs. Adkins is allergic to cats, and I've always wanted a kitten."

Julia ran from the room, temporarily forgetting biscuits, apparently in the pursuit of a feline.

John frowned, staring at the doorway through which Julia had dashed. "I didn't know she's always wanted a cat."

"Given her age, this lifelong desire could've come about yesterday."

John chuckled, then glanced in Katie's direction, suddenly turning serious. "If you can't . . ."

"Oh, I can. But if you don't want . . ."

"I want," he answered quickly, and she had the feeling he wasn't talking about housekeepers.

Chapter Eighteen

Katie hurried Lightning along the wagon road as much as the mule could be hurried. She'd overslept this morning and by the time she'd fixed her family's breakfast and gotten on the road, the sun was already rising. John had insisted she use the wagon since she was now going to make the trip every day, but she wondered if she couldn't make better time if she just pulled it herself. Lightning didn't appear to like mornings.

"If you'll pick up the pace a little, I'll get you a carrot," she said, attempting to bribe the lumbering animal. But either Lightning didn't like carrots or he didn't speak English because the only acknowledgment of her offer was a lackluster snort as he plodded down the road.

By the time she made it to John's, the sun had fully risen, and she was scrambling. She rushed in through the kitchen door and began stoking the cook stove before even removing her coat.

"Good morning." John's greeting from across the room startled her. She hadn't noticed him kneeling by the hearth. He always laid a fire in the kitchen hearth, usually while she fixed breakfast. Just another reminder of how late she was.

"Mornin'. I'm sorry I'm late." She pulled off her coat

as she scurried about for pans and eggs. "We had company last night and by the time he left and I finished my chores, I was late getting to bed. I'm afraid I overslept."

"Katie," John said, forcing her to stop her rambling and face him. "It's all right. You aren't that late, and we haven't starved to death." The twinkle of teasing in his eyes helped her relax a little. Maybe her being late wasn't the end of the world.

"Besides," he continued, "you're forgetting that you're doing me a big favor. Julia and I couldn't make it without your help. I'm very grateful."

He couldn't be nearly as grateful as Katie was. Since she'd started working for John, she'd saved over fifteen dollars. By the time Mrs. Adkins came back, she should have another fifteen at least. Thirty dollars would buy enough flour and sugar to last her family through the winter. Not to mention thread and yarn and if she were careful, she might even have money for new boots. Hers weren't going to make it much longer. The sole of the left one was already coming loose and though she'd be able to hold it together with some baling twine, the thought of walking through the snow in it already made her cold.

Julia ran into the kitchen to throw her arms around Katie's skirts in the hug that had become their morning tradition. Katie laughed and hugged her back before frying enough eggs for breakfast and a little extra bacon for later. Julia set the kitchen table as the crackling fire warmed the room.

"I was wondering," Katie said as she cleared the table after breakfast, "if you'd mind if I went to Rebecca

Fisher's today. Their barn got blown over in a twister this spring and there's a barn raising going on to help them out."

"Of course." John paused in obvious confusion before he asked, "What's a 'barn raising'?"

She guessed they didn't raise too many barns in New York City. "Paul's lumber just came back from the sawmill and as many men as can are coming to get the barn under roof. The womenfolk help with feeding them. There's supposed to be a pig roast this evening and maybe some square dancing if they can get it under roof by then."

"When do you need to leave?"

"As soon as I get breakfast cleaned up. I fixed some extra bacon for your lunch. I'll leave it in the icebox."

He nodded, but Katie could tell another question was on its way. "Do you think they'd want my help?"

She glanced at his suit trousers and crisp white shirt before giving what she hoped was a reassuring smile. "I'm sure they would."

He looked down at his clothes, then said, "I'll be right back." He didn't wait for her response before he headed out the front door.

Assuming he simply had an errand to run, she washed the dishes while Julia dried and chatted about the new kitty she wanted. "I want one with black and white and yellow and gray spots."

"How about blue?"

Julia wrinkled her brow. "Do they make blue kitties?"

"I don't know, but wishes are free so you might as well throw them around as much as you want."

Julia giggled. "In that case, I want a blue and purple and green kitty."

"With wings?"

That suggestion sent Julia into a spasm of giggles that continued while Katie heard the front door open and John rush up the stairs. In a few moments, her curiosity over John's unusual behavior was satisfied. He walked into the kitchen in a new pair of canvas work pants and a blue chambray shirt.

His excitement was palpable. "Ready?"

"Yes," Katie said, wondering if he had any idea what he was in for. "Let me get Julia's coat."

John hurried on to the wagon while Katie collected the things they'd need for the day. She handed John the basket of plates, glasses, and silverware to set in the back, not failing to notice the new hammer and saw on the floorboards beside his medical bag.

"I didn't know if there'd be enough tools," he said, setting her basket down and helping her up to the bench.

She covered the hard wooden seat with a folded quilt and reached for Julia, all the while fighting to control her grin. She hoped John's excitement held out at least until lunchtime.

The bustle of activity at Fishers' farm only escalated John's enthusiasm. It looked as though half the men in the county had shown up, all laughing and teasing one another as they carried lumber and raised walls. John grabbed his shiny new tools and headed toward the men, while Katie and Julia made way to the women sitting under the old shed roof near the new construction.

"Mornin', Katie." Rebecca sat in a rocker under the roof, her new baby sleeping in her arms.

"You're looking good, Rebecca. How's the little one?"

"We're both good thanks to you and the doc." She held the baby up for Katie to take. "Want to hold her?"

There was nothing Katie wanted more, with the exception of holding one of her own. She reached for the little bundle, as the women sitting on the bench beside Rebecca scooted to allow room.

Katie tucked down the blanket to look in awe at the tiny face, puckered in sleep.

"You need you one of them, Katie," Eunice Kopp said as she waddled over to stir one of the two bean pots simmering over a low-burning fire.

The other ladies giggled, and Katie flushed. "I think I ought to get a husband first."

Eunice returned to her seat with a huff and nodded toward the barn. "You won't find a finer one than that."

Katie tore her eyes away from the baby to look in the direction Eunice had indicated. Randy was lifting a beam over his head to the men working above him. He'd removed his shirt, leaving on only his undershirt despite the still cool air. His muscles bulged with the weight of his task and several of the younger girls giggled in agreement with Eunice's statement.

"Mornin', Katie," Randy yelled as though he knew she'd been watching.

"Mornin', Randy," she answered. Then he grinned

and she felt her cheeks heat. He finished shoving the beam up to the men before he flexed his arm muscle for her and winked.

She could have died. Probably would have in fact if the bundle in her arms hadn't picked that exact moment to wiggle and give the most adorable coo Katie had ever heard. Evidently Randy's appeal had no age limit.

Katie smiled at Rebecca. "Have you named her yet?"

"We have and if you ain't got no objections, we'd like to call her Katie Joanne, after you and the doc. If it hadn't been for you two, I don't think I'd have made it."

"Joanne?"

Rebecca grinned. "It's as close to John as I could think of without sounding like a boy's name. Do you think it's all right?"

Fighting back the tears, Katie looked down at her tiny namesake. "I think it's perfect."

About that time, little Miss Perfect decided she wasn't going to take all this attention lying down, and she let out a bawl that shook the shed roof. A chorus of cooing women responded, but Rebecca won out, taking baby Katie into her arms. "I think it's time for breakfast," she said, heading toward the cabin.

Several of the women went with her to start fixing corn bread for lunch, leaving Katie behind to watch the beans. She really wanted to watch John. She couldn't help noticing Randy was giving John a hard time, teasing him about his shiny hammer and asking every whipstitch if he needed to rest. But John didn't give in. If anything he worked harder than most of the men and by lunch, it was starting to show.

As soon as the women had the food ready, she filled a plate and went in search of him. She found him standing by the creek, hands on hips, sweat dripping from his brow. The sleeve of his new shirt had a tear, and his canvas pants were stained and soiled from top to bottom. He was staring off at nothing in particular, and she figured the only reason he was still standing up was that it would take too much energy to sit down.

"Would you like something to eat?"

He lifted his gaze from the ground and gave her a nod. Just one, but she suspected that was all he had left. Leading him to a fallen log by the creek, she took a seat, making sure to leave him the seat in front of a tree he could lean against. He did and it was a good two minutes before he finally reached for his plate.

"You know you don't have to stay all day if you don't want to," she said, taking a bite of beans.

His fork stopped halfway to his mouth as he turned to face her. "You don't think I can work like the rest of the men?"

"They were raised working like this. Were you?"

Not only was he not raised working like this, but he hadn't been aware that other people were. At least not since the Egyptians built the pyramids, but he wasn't about to admit that to Katie. Every limb of his body weighed five tons, and the damn fork weighed at least thirty and that was without the beans.

But he wasn't about to admit that to Katie either, so

he straightened his back—which hurt—and dug into the godforsaken beans.

"I can work as hard as any man," he said, wondering if he could talk her into chewing his lunch for him.

"I'm not saying you can't work hard. It's just that—"

"I'm fine."

And after lunch and its hour of rest, he was finer than he'd been earlier, finer and infinitely smarter. He worked slower and steadier through the rest of the afternoon, stopping periodically to bandage an injury. Most of which seemed to belong to Freddie. With a smashed thumb, torn nail, and a splinter the size of an oak tree, Freddie spent more time getting wrapped up than nailing boards.

The worst of his injuries, however, occurred when he managed to catch a board on the edge of the barn, bending one of his few unbandaged fingers backward.

"Do you think it's broke, Doc?"

John pressed on the crooked finger, its unnatural angle jutting out to the side. "I think it's just dislocated."

Freddie gulped. "Can you fix it?"

"Yup."

Usually popping the finger back in place before the patient realized what was coming was the best course of action. But when John grabbed Freddie's finger and jerked, the young man went from green to white to gray to the ground in a matter of seconds.

Katie ran across the yard to her inert fiancé. "Is he all right?"

Kneeling to check the pulse at Freddie's throat, John shrugged. "I guess I should have warned him."

Taking a small ax, he chipped a makeshift splint off one of the boards and wrapped Freddie's finger while Katie wiped a damp cloth across his brow. He was conscious now, but his hands resembled those of a mummy, which was fitting. Once they finished this pyramid, it would need an occupant anyway.

His latest injury required Freddie to sit out the rest of the afternoon, alleviating John's fear that he would run out of bandages before Freddie ran out of fingers. And by the time the sun sat behind the hill, the roof was finished, the pig was roasted, and John was exhilarated.

He'd made it.

He'd kept up with the other men, working like a borrowed mule. To make things better, as soon as Randy realized his teasing was getting nowhere, he ceased trying and by afternoon, the men were laughing and joking with John like he was one of them.

He was dirty and grubby and sore, and never felt better in his life. Dropping onto a bale of hay that had been brought into the barn for seats, he examined his work with pride. He recognized every board he'd nailed in place and every beam he'd help set.

"Tired?" Katie handed him a plate of pork, more of the beans, and a hunk of hot corn bread smothered in butter.

"A little. How's Freddie?" he asked, between bites. Ambrosia couldn't have tasted better.

Katie gestured across the barn where Freddie sat, holding a plate on his lap with bandaged fingers. A skinny young girl was feeding him and Freddie's face was red enough to light up the night.

John chuckled. "I'm glad she's feeding him. Maybe that way he won't poke himself in the eye with the fork."

Katie answered, grinning, "I swear, that boy could hurt himself on lint."

John's laugh stopped when Katie gently touched the back of his hand. "Looks like you got hurt too."

He glanced down at the dried blood on the gouge that crossed the back of his hand. "Just a scratch," he said. It'd hurt like a son of a bitch, but Katie would never know that either. Even though he liked the look of sympathy in her eyes.

"Y'all need to finish up, now," an old man shouted as he walked to the center of the barn.

John dragged his gaze away from Katie to the man. He carried a violin and was followed by a few other men with instruments John had never seen before.

"It's time to commence with the fun part o' the day," he said, tucking the violin into the crook of his arm.

John enjoyed the violin, but when the old-timer struck his with his bow, the sound that came out was nothing like John had ever heard before. Toes tapping and hands clapping, the crowd came to life with the strange music pouring from the strings.

"Old Pete is as good a fiddle player as you'll hear in this neck of the woods," Katie said, smiling and clapping with the rest of them.

Another man joined Old Pete with a round white instrument resembling a guitar. His fingers moved up and down the neck of the instrument with blazing speed. "What's that?"

"That's Ryan Stewart."

John smiled. "I meant the instrument."

"A banjo." Her smile was tinged with disbelief. "You've never seen a banjo?"

He shook his head.

"Then you've probably never seen a juice harp either."

Shaking his head again, he watched in fascination as another man joined the song. Only this one held a small object in his mouth, which he flipped at the side to make an odd twanging sound.

The last to join the crew had no instrument except his voice, which he used to shout, "Dancers, square your sets!"

"Do you square dance?" Katie asked John.

"No. I don't know how."

Before Katie could respond to John's confession, Randy rushed across the barn and grabbed her hand. "Come on, Katie. Let's show these folks how this is done!"

Katie laughed and followed Randy to the center where several other couples had already taken their places. The music kicked up a notch, if that was possible, and the shouting one began issuing orders in a language John had never heard before, but everyone else seemed to understand perfectly.

Sashay here, promenade there, and allemande in between, John watched as a whirlwind of skirts swept the new floor clean.

Laughing voices, clapping hands, and stomping feet

led John to surmise this was the way they tested their new barns. If the rafters held up after an evening of this, the barn was as solid as a rock.

One song ended and another began and the men, who had only moments before seemed too tired to walk, were now moving as if their pants were blazing.

But none in the group had Katie's spirit. Her face glowed and her smile sparkled as she laughed and twirled around the room. His enjoyment of her enjoyment was more than satisfying, but Katie had other plans. Before he knew what was happening, she was dragging him to the floor.

"I don't know how to do this," he protested, but it was too late.

"I'll show you!" she shouted, and then the twirling began.

She pulled him one way and then someone else pulled him another and by the time the dance was finished, he was surprised to learn he hadn't ended up in the creek.

He suspected that some of the pulling had been extraneous, especially when Randy had almost sent him into a pole, but even with that, he couldn't remember ever enjoying an evening more.

Until it was time for the wagon ride home.

John, Katie, and Grandma sat on the wagon bench, while the rest of Katie's family and Julia sat in the back. Rebecca had given Julia the ugliest yellow kitten John had ever seen, but Julia claimed it was exactly what she'd wanted, so it was cuddled inside her coat while she slept.

The cold night air was settling into John's overused

body and Grandma's conversation wasn't helping things any as they wobbled over the dirt road toward town.

"I swear, that Randy Kopp is the finest man I've ever laid eyes on. Don't you think so, Katie?"

"He's handsome enough," Katie answered.

"*Handsome?* He's more than just handsome! I don't think I've ever seen a man work so hard. Why, I think he single-handedly built most that barn today."

John gritted his teeth and hoped Lightning found a big enough hole in the road to bounce Grandma off the bench. As dark as it was, maybe John could pretend he didn't see her bounce away, and he could leave her behind as she sang Randy's praises to the night.

"All the men worked hard today," Katie replied, and the pitiful hole Lightning hit only managed to scoot Katie a little closer to his side.

The warmth of her leg, coupled with her response, helped soothe John's pride and keep his tongue in check. Maybe having Katie next to him was better than bouncing Grandma down the road anyway.

Tuning out Grandma's prattle, he concentrated on the mule's path down the road and allowed his mind to replay the day. Particularly the part where he'd decided it had been a great one. He was having trouble remembering that feeling since his muscles were setting up like stone.

"Do you want me to help put Julia to bed?" Katie asked, when they finally reached John's house.

"Nah," he answered, hoping he sounded better than he felt. He reached for his sleeping daughter from Katie's pa, who handed her over the edge of the wagon into John's arms.

"I'll see you tomorrow," he said to Katie. "But there's no reason to come until about noon. I imagine Julia will sleep in late."

Katie nodded, then drove the wagon and her family off into the night, while John struggled to make his legs move. Up the four thousand steps that led to his second floor, he carried his daughter, wondering when she'd gained so much weight. He removed her coat and shoes, deciding there was no harm in allowing her to sleep in her dress, with her kitten. She snuggled into her pillow without opening her eyes.

John eyed the floor beside her bed; tempting though it was, he decided he'd be better off to sleep in his bed. Unbuttoning his shirt as he walked down the hall, he managed to remove his shoes before finally falling face-first into his pillow.

No wonder the ancient Egyptians were all dead.

Chapter Nineteen

Lord have mercy, but Katie was tired. She'd been up half the night delivering Ida Thompson's ninth baby only to go straight to John's to fix lunch. After spending the day doing John and Julia's wash, she started their dinner, then headed back to her cabin. She was glad to have the use of John's wagon, but that required unhitching and bedding Lightning down in the shed each evening and rehitching him each morning.

To make matters worse, her family had turned into pigs—whiny, pouting pigs at that.

"Are we having eggs for dinner again?" Pa asked, acting as if that were all they'd had for the last ten years.

Katie plopped another egg into the hot grease of her skillet and cringed. "It's all I have time to fix. If you all would help around the cabin a little, maybe I'd be able to fix something else."

"It wasn't a problem until you started working for Doc." Grandpa came limping into the kitchen, evidently guilty of eavesdropping.

"It wasn't a problem for *you*. I was the one doing all the work." She couldn't believe she'd said that, but it was the gospel truth. It was also the last straw.

Untying her apron, she slammed it on the cupboard.

"Fix your own supper," she said, wishing she'd had the courage to add the word "damn" like John had done.

She stormed from the kitchen to the front porch and fresh air, realizing when she dropped into the rocker that she'd fried enough eggs for them. *She* was the one that wouldn't have anything to eat.

Her stomach growled when she thought of the beef roast with potatoes and carrots John and Julia were having for dinner. She didn't remember the last time she'd had a beef roast. If it weren't for the deer meat some of the people she doctored occasionally gave her, chicken was the only meat she'd ever get.

The cabin door squeaked loudly as Grandma came out to the porch, clutching her shawl around her shoulders. "Are you cold?"

"No," Katie answered. Anger had a way of keeping the chill away.

Grandma hobbled over to the other rocker and set it in motion before she began the speech Katie knew was coming.

"Things was much easier when you wasn't working in town."

Katie didn't bother with a response. It would save time just to wait until Grandma was finished, and Grandma was nowhere near making her point yet.

"I seen you with the doc at the barn raisin'. You fancy yourself in love with him, don't you?"

Katie stopped her rocker. In love with John? "Of course not."

Grandma's rocker didn't miss a beat. "That's good, 'cause you know that'd never work out."

Katie forced her legs to set her rocker back to rocking.

"He's not like us, Katie. He lives in a big fancy house and wears fancy store-bought clothes."

"That doesn't make him bad."

"No," Grandma agreed, "just different. You're a good woman, Katie, and you need to stick to your kind. Dr. Keffer will never fit in with your people, and you will never fit in with his. In his mind, you're just the hired help."

"I don't believe he thinks of me that way."

"He pays you, don't he?"

With that, Grandma left the porch and her point behind. And what a dandy point it was.

John placed the last of his Henry David Thoreau books on his library shelf with a grin of satisfaction. Now that Katie had taken over for Mrs. Adkins, there was no longer a need to leave his house in shambles. Another day should have his library restored to its original immaculate and boring state.

"Mornin'." He heard Katie's voice echo in the downstairs hallway, announcing her arrival, and not a moment too soon.

He'd done his best getting Julia ready for the day, but her hair had left him in a quandary. Every time he ran the brush through the curls, they seemed to expand until finally he gave up for fear they would gobble up his daughter completely. Katie would know what to do.

"Oh, Julia," Katie said as he walked down the stairs for the kitchen. "What has happened to your hair?"

"Daddy," Julia replied simply, leaving Katie to fill in the rest.

John chuckled, looking forward to the morning. A new development and one that never ceased to surprise him. He stepped into the kitchen, warmed at the sight of Katie attempting to tame Julia's curls.

"Good morning, Katie," he said, with a smile.

Katie looked up at him and for the first time since they'd met, a wall fell between them. "Good morning, Dr. Keffer."

"Doctor?"

She returned her attention immediately to Julia's hair. "I think that since I'm here so much now, that would be a little more appropriate, don't you?"

Hell no, he didn't. But getting to the bottom of this wasn't possible with Julia in the room. Luckily Julia took a nap right after lunch. If John could make it until then, he'd find out what was going on and fix it.

Was it the kiss? It didn't seem likely. That had happened more than a week ago, and they had been together every day since. Whatever had caused this change happened yesterday, and things that change that quickly can be changed back. He hoped.

Maybe she needed another kiss.

Maybe he needed to have his head examined.

Katie stoked the fire in the cook stove, then added a glob of bacon grease to the skillet, relieved when John left the kitchen. She'd thought long and hard about what Grandma had said, trying to decide if it was true.

Not that it mattered.

She already had three fiancés. Wasn't that enough?

But then again, he *had* kissed her. Of course he'd only done that once, and he'd done it out of anger. Though several times since then she'd gotten the distinct impression he wanted to kiss her again.

Maybe she needed another kiss.

Maybe she needed to have her head examined.

Katie started to add an egg to the hot skillet but stopped when the door chime jingled. Wiping her hands on her apron, she headed toward the front door only to find John had reached it first.

"John!" A beautiful woman in a fawn-colored traveling outfit rushed through the front door and into his arms.

Heart dropping, Katie stepped back. Unable to tear herself away, she watched from the end of the hallway as John returned the hug.

"Caroline?" he said, clearly surprised, but not disappointed, by the woman's arrival.

Caroline cupped John's face with her gloved hands. "It's so good to see you. I've worried myself sick ever since you left New York."

She lowered her hands and looked about her. "This house is lovely, but the town leaves much to be desired. There's nothing here, John. Why on earth won't you come home?"

Caroline didn't give John a chance to answer before she gestured toward the open door and front porch. "Oh! Would you mind paying the boy for bringing me here from Huntington? I thought sure you'd pick me up at the train station or send a coach." The tone of her voice was only slightly admonishing, and the look she gave John was teasing if not downright flirting.

"I didn't know you were coming."

"You didn't? I sent a letter. Didn't you receive it?"

John shook his head. "I'm sorry. I would have arranged to meet you had I known." He reached into his pocket and stepped onto the porch to pay whoever it was that had delivered Caroline to his door.

"Oh well," she said, with a flutter of her hand. "I'm here now and that's all that matters. Can you get your manservant to bring in my luggage?"

"I don't have a manservant," John said as he returned inside and closed the door. "I'll get your bags later."

She gasped. "How on earth do you survive without a servant?"

"Things are different here," he said, as though he'd been listening to Grandma too.

"Well, hopefully you won't be here much longer anyway." She flashed a brilliant smile that made her eyes glisten before she looped her arm through John's and said, "Where is your parlor? We have so much catching up to do." With that, she and John strode into the parlor and out of Katie's eyesight.

It was as though a whirlwind had swooshed into the house in perfectly tailored clothing with matching bonnet and gloves. Katie looked down at her brown calico day dress, her white apron smudged with this morning's breakfast. She didn't own a corset or a bustle, which no doubt had helped Caroline's figure look so perfect.

Absently, Katie patted her brown hair tucked into its simple braided bun and thought about the lush beauty of Caroline's upswept blonde curls. Even the way she spoke clearly placed her in John's world.

God had sent Katie a message. Had she been falling for John? Probably, but Caroline had snapped Katie out of her delusion faster than a slap in the face. And Caroline didn't even know Katie existed. By this time tomorrow, John wouldn't remember that fact either.

"Katie?" Julia tugged on her sleeve. "I set the table in the kitchen for breakfast."

Katie looked down at Julia and held back a tear. "We're going to need to set things up in the dining room."

"But we always eat breakfast in the kitchen."

Katie doubted Caroline had ever even seen a kitchen. "I suspect things are going to be different from now on."

"Why?"

"A friend of your pa's just came here from New York."

"*Really?*" Julia's face lit up with the news and, as usual, the excitement sent her to bouncing. "Who is it? Did you meet him?"

"No," Katie said, ushering Julia back into the kitchen. "It was a woman your pa called 'Caroline.'"

Suddenly the bounce stopped, and the light in Julia's face went out. "Aunt Caroline?"

"Well," Katie said cautiously, "I don't know if she's your aunt, but she was a beautiful woman with blonde hair."

"Oh." Julia walked over to the table and began collecting plates to carry to the dining room. Katie waited, hoping she'd explain her odd reaction and trying to decide if she should pry more out of her.

But Julia remained silent while she took three place

settings to the dining room, moping as she went. She returned to the kitchen and set a plate and silverware on the kitchen table. Katie knew that setting was for her.

Help eats in the kitchen.

Maybe that was what had Julia upset. It had Katie a little upset too, but it wasn't Julia's fault. It was just the way polite society did things.

Finally Katie could take no more of Julia's sadness. "Julia?"

Julia stopped and looked up at Katie as if her heart were breaking.

"Eating in the kitchen isn't that bad. I kind of like it out here."

Julia's lip pouted as a tear slipped out of the corner of her eye. "But I want to eat with Daddy."

"You are going to eat with Daddy."

Head shaking with the gravest expression, Julia wiped at her tear. "Aunt Caroline doesn't think children should eat at the big table. I always had to eat in the kitchen when we went to her house."

That changed things entirely. It was one thing to send the help to the kitchen, quite another to exclude Julia. "This isn't Aunt Caroline's house," Katie said with more bravado than she had a right. She was counting on John standing his ground, though based on his greeting of Caroline, Katie wasn't sure where he was going to stand.

Deciding to take a chance, she patted Julia on the head and said, "Why don't you go to the parlor and tell your pa and your Aunt Caroline it's time to come for breakfast?"

"But—"

"Then you," Katie interrupted, "are going to eat with your pa just like you always do."

After scooting Julia out the door, Katie dished up the gravy and eggs to carry to the dining room. John and his houseguest entered just as Katie set the food on the table.

"Katie?" John said, ushering Caroline in her direction. "I'd like you to meet Lois's sister, Caroline. She's just arrived from New York, and she's going to be staying for a while."

"Pleased to meet you," Katie said, wishing her apron weren't smudged.

But Caroline didn't look at her long enough to notice smudged aprons or even if Katie had an extra arm. She gave a quick nod, then turned her attention to John. Katie knew a dismissal when she saw one, and she wasted no time leaving the dining room, hesitating only for a second when she heard Caroline ask, "Really, John, don't you think Julie would be more comfortable in the kitchen where she could visit with the cook?"

Katie didn't hear John's reply, but since Julia didn't soon return to the kitchen, she assumed he'd defended his daughter's right to eat at the big table. She supposed she should be offended by Caroline referring to her as the cook, but considering she couldn't even get her own niece's name right, being called "cook" seemed like a mild offense.

Cleaning the kitchen with more zeal than usual, Katie failed to hear John enter the room until his voice startled her from behind. "Katie?"

She spun from the sink to face him, relieved that Caroline was not in company. "Yes?"

"Why didn't you eat with us?"

"I already ate." Which wasn't entirely a lie. She'd eaten many times in the last twenty-nine years.

"Oh," he said, apparently accepting her explanation. "Did you get enough?"

"Yes, but I'm afraid I'm faced with another dilemma that I need your help with."

"What's that?"

"I didn't receive Caroline's letter that she was coming, and I have no arrangements for her lodging. Not that it would matter, as there's no place else for her to stay anyway."

Katie nodded, wondering what he was trying to say, but decided to wait patiently until he got around to it.

"Anyway," he said again, "Caroline is a young, single woman and I'm a widower." He waited as though he thought she understood what he was talking about. He was wrong.

Sighing, he filled in the rest. "I'm afraid in order for her to stay here, I need a chaperone. Do you think you could move in until Caroline leaves?"

Katie felt her face flush. He didn't trust himself alone with the woman, and he thought Katie's presence would protect her.

"I'll pay you well," he added when Katie hesitated, and he couldn't have driven home Grandma's point more if he'd tried.

Packing up all her worldly possessions didn't take nearly as long as John evidently thought it would. He'd insisted she leave for home right after lunch as though it would take all afternoon to pack. Two everyday dresses, one Sunday dress, two pairs of stockings—one of which was still pristine white and in its tissue paper—a hairbrush, a coat, a cloak, and two chemises were all Katie had to her name. Considering some of the items were on her body, the bundle wrapped in her quilt wasn't very impressive.

She'd been given an assortment of quilts and shawls throughout the years, but had given most to her family. Besides, it wasn't like she was moving to John's for good. As soon as Mrs. Adkins returned, Katie would be coming home, bundle and all.

Leaving the way she had was probably cowardly. After packing, she'd fixed dinner and done her chores before finally announcing her new position and heading for the door. Grandma was livid, Grandpa just knew he was going to starve to death, and Pa still wasn't sure what was going on when she darted from the cabin, declaring she'd probably be back before Christmas.

It was exciting and daring and more than a little frightening. For the life of her, she couldn't remember ever sleeping in any bed other than the one she had in the loft of their log cabin.

Her fears vanished in a flash, however, when Julia greeted her with a fierce hug as soon as she stepped into the house.

"I'm glad you're back," she said to Katie's skirts.

"I wasn't gone all that long."

"It was long enough," Julia answered with a roll of her big blue eyes.

Before Katie had the chance to find out what Julia meant, John stepped into the foyer. "You're back." He flashed a smile and started for the door. "I'll get your things from the wagon."

"I have them," she blurted before he managed to open the door.

With a frown, he looked at the bundle clutched in her arms. "Is that all you brought?"

It was all she had, but he didn't need to know that. "It's plenty."

He chuckled. "Well, I must say, I've never known a woman to travel so lightly. I think Caroline brought half of New York with her."

"John?" Caroline called to him from the parlor.

He glanced over his shoulder. "Why don't you go on upstairs and get settled in while I check on Caroline? I'll be up in a minute."

Katie nodded, but it was a wasted gesture. John scurried to Caroline's bidding without waiting for Katie's response. She sighed and started up the stairs. Julia talked a mile a minute, which helped fill the emptiness John had left behind.

Julia followed Katie as she walked past the occupied bedrooms to the empty one at the end of the hall. She stepped into the room, immediately feeling overwhelmed. An ornately carved four-poster bed sat against the far wall. A walnut washstand, with its marble top, was next to the bed, a porcelain bowl and pitcher ready for use. Another walnut dresser had been placed across the room and a pair of velvet-covered chairs flanked a marble-topped table near the window. Thick oriental rugs covered most of the hardwood floor including the area in front of the hearth. A fire had been laid.

Katie sighed. She couldn't stay in here. It wasn't real, and staying in it might make her forget who she was. Turning from the room, she headed for the small chamber at the top of the back stairs leading to the kitchen.

No more than a quarter the size of the other room, this one had only a tiny bed, one wooden chair, and a trunk for her clothing. A scarred table with a plain pitcher and bowl sat next to the bed and would be a perfect spot for her brush. Much better.

"Daddy said you were going to stay in the front room," Julia said, bouncing on the little bed.

"I think I'd rather stay in here."

"Why?"

Because it was where she belonged. "It'll be easier to keep clean."

Katie assumed Julia accepted her explanation, but when she darted from the room and John appeared moments later, she assumed her assumption was wrong.

"Why are you moving in here?" he asked.

"It's plenty big enough." She continued to put away her things while she talked; that way she didn't have to look at him. Looking at him was hard today. It hurt, for some reason.

"Well, if this is what you want." He sounded forlorn, if not confused, as his footsteps told her he'd left the room. She still hadn't looked at him. At this point, she planned never to again.

Preparing dinner took most of the afternoon. Katie wanted it to be the best, and that called for chicken and dumplings. Julia added biscuits, of course, and buttery mashed potatoes and green beans finished the meal. Katie was proud. She might not own a corset, but she *could* cook.

John's sudden presence in the kitchen interrupted her while she dished up the meal. He wore a suit, complete with vest and a tie. She swallowed the hurt in her throat. "You're going somewhere?"

He frowned. "No." Then he glanced at his clothing. "Oh, Caroline likes to dress for dinner."

She nodded, absently wiping her hands on her apron. The smudgy one. "Well, you look fine." And he did, and she shouldn't have looked because now that she was, it was distracting.

John took a step toward her, his expression softening. "Katie, I need to talk to you."

"It'll have to wait," she said, grabbing a bowl off the counter and heading to the dining room. "I need to get dinner on before it gets cold."

Unfortunately the bowl she grabbed was empty, and it required a great deal of finagling on her part to make it appear intentional. But if there was one thing Katie knew, it was that men knew nothing about kitchens or bowls and as long as she acted like she knew what she was doing, he wouldn't question it.

Luckily, Caroline sashayed into the dining room and all of John's attention landed on the vision in green satin. Katie darted into the kitchen to fetch bowls that had food in them as Caroline's light laughter flittered in the air.

"John, you look so handsome tonight," Katie heard Caroline say when she returned with the dumplings.

John chuckled and made a return comment on Caroline's beauty that Katie tried her best to ignore. She helped Julia into her chair just as Caroline said, "What is *that*?"

Katie glanced up, looking for a mouse or possum or something that would've caused such a reaction of horror, then realized Caroline was referring to the dumplings. Katie flushed.

"Those," John said, placing a healthy portion on his plate, "are the best dumplings you'll ever eat."

"Oh." With a lift of her perfect eyebrow, Caroline placed a hand against her heart. "Well," she said, mockingly, "how quaint."

Katie headed back to the kitchen before the tear in the corner of her eye fell down her cheek, but not before she heard Caroline add, "I swear, John, I don't know how you've survived in such primitive conditions."

John dug into his dumplings, finding it difficult to understand his sister-in-law and her rules on conditions. He loved Katie's cooking. And her laughter and her company, which he was beginning to miss sorely. Where was she anyway?

He glanced toward the kitchen, anxiously awaiting her return, but when she failed to do so, he assumed she'd already eaten.

"Isn't that right, John?"

John jerked his attention back to Caroline, realizing with embarrassment he needed to comment on something she'd said, and he hadn't been listening.

So he said, "Absolutely," which must have been the perfect comment because she beamed in approval before continuing. Lois always said that Caroline was a wonderful dinner conversationalist, and he guessed she was. It was his fault he often had trouble staying focused.

But through the years he'd learned to nod and say, "interesting" and other such things that placated her until dessert.

"May I be excused? I want to talk to Katie." Julia's question interrupted Caroline's current story and the look of censure she gave his daughter seemed a bit extreme, but then, she wasn't used to being around children.

John nodded his permission, secretively envious of Julia's request. He wanted to talk to Katie too, and as soon as his sister-in-law was settled in for the evening, he intended to do just that.

Chapter Twenty

Katie unfolded her list, smoothing it out on the table-top in her room. It hadn't been updated since she'd first made it, and it was time to get serious. Dipping the pen in its inkwell, she added a chart to the bottom. She listed each of her fiancés down the side and across the top she placed the categories: intelligence, money, handsomeness, and kissing, making sure to leave an extra column for anything else she'd want to add.

Harold got two points for money, but handsomeness was not in his favor. Randy was handsome and a good kisser, but didn't have two nickels to rub together, and she wasn't sure about the intelligent part. Freddie was intelligent enough and seemed to have a little bit of money, but sorely lacked in looks and as for kissing? He hadn't given that a shot and Katie was afraid to suggest it.

"What'cha doing?" Julia walked into Katie's open room and plopped down beside her on the bed.

"I'm making a list."

"For what?"

"I'm getting married, and I need to decide which man I want."

"Is Daddy on your list?"

Katie hesitated at Julia's blunt question. "No."

"Why not?"

She swallowed. "Because he doesn't want to be."

"Oh." Julia wrinkled her brow, apparently thinking over Katie's response. And if Katie knew her well at all, she'd better get her sidetracked or else she'd run and ask her pa if he wanted to be on the list.

"Since you're here, do you think you could help me?"

"Sure!" Julia's face lit up at the prospect.

"I want to marry a man who'll be a good pa to my children. What do you think would make him a good pa?"

"Well," Julia started, as though she already had quite a list, "he has to like biscuits."

Katie smiled.

"And he has to like little girls."

"Of course."

"*And* he has to like you."

Katie laughed. It was a simple list, but probably better than Katie's.

Suddenly Julia's face sobered and her brow furrowed in earnest. "But the most important thing is that he has to be happy. Maybe your little girl will be able to make her daddy happy."

Katie pulled Julia into a hug, racking her brain for a way to explain something this complicated to a five-year-old child. "Sweetheart, you make your daddy happy."

Julia shook her head. "Only when you're around."

A movement by her open door caught Katie's eye while she fought desperately for something to say to the child. John stood in the hallway, his expression tortured, but clearly he had heard Julia. He stepped away before Katie could stop him, but she didn't know what she would have said to him anyway.

"Your pa misses your ma," she said to Julia, her eyes still riveted to the empty hall. "That's what makes him sad."

Julia sat back and wiped her cheek. "He wouldn't miss her so much if he'd just marry you."

"I already have three fiancés," Katie said, tweaking Julia's nose. "Isn't that enough?"

Smiling wanly, Julia said, "There's room at the top of your list for one more."

"Grown-ups have to do things their own way." She took Julia's hand, leading her to her bedroom for the night.

She'd hoped John would come tuck her in, but by the time she'd read Julia a story and put her to bed, the quiet house told her John had already retired. Maybe he couldn't bear to face his daughter just yet.

With a tired sigh, Katie left Julia's room and headed down the hallway, but before she made it to her room, a grumble from her stomach reminded her she'd missed dinner. Passing her door, she took the back stairs to the kitchen and the cold dumplings in the ice-box. They wouldn't be as good cold, but stoking the woodstove would take too long, and she was too tired to care about cold.

She almost dropped the bowl when she heard John say, "I suspected you hadn't eaten."

Spinning toward the kitchen hearth, she saw him sitting in a chair in the darkness. The embers of the fire barely glowed, but enough light filtered into the room to see his face and a bottle of whiskey sitting on the table in front of him.

"I wasn't hungry," she lied, setting the bowl on the counter.

He looked at her, something she felt more than saw, and a primal need flowed across the room. His fancy evening attire was gone now, his shirt hanging open as he studied her in the darkness.

"Thirsty?" He lifted his glass in an unspoken offer, then chuckled without humor before downing the contents in one gulp. "Of course not. The proper Miss Napier wouldn't drink whiskey, would she?"

"John, Julia didn't know what she was saying—"

"Back to 'John' now, are we?" He poured another glass of liquor, the bottle thumping loudly as he returned it to the table. "I prefer it that way, you know." Tipping his glass in a salute to her, he downed the contents once more.

She watched helplessly as he suffered, unable to think of the right things to say to ease some of his pain, but he filled the uncomfortable silence with something even worse.

"Do you know how my wife died?"

She swallowed. "She was hit by a carriage."

"No," he said, lifting his hand to correct her. "That's how she was injured. She died because of me."

"I don't believe that for one minute."

"Ah, but it's true." He set his glass on the table and leaned forward to rest his head in his hands.

She waited until he ran his hands back through his hair and sighed. "I had just graduated from Harvard Medical School. Top of my class. Everyone was proud as hell, except my grandfather, but no one can make him proud. Just isn't in him." He sat back in the chair and closed his eyes. "Lois and I went to the opera to celebrate my wondrous accomplishment. She was the proudest of all, you see."

Katie crossed the kitchen as he talked and sat in a chair near him. His voice had dropped as he recounted his tale as though he wasn't really talking to her anymore, just to the night.

"After the opera, we stepped out to talk with some friends. That's when it happened. I didn't even see it coming."

There was no emotion now when he spoke, only a deadly calm that pulled at her more than ranting ever could.

"By the time I got to her, she was lying in the street dying. And I couldn't do anything but stare at her. She was bleeding and gasping for air, and the great Harvard graduate froze."

Silence.

A slight hissing from the fire and the sound of his breathing filled the kitchen with sorrow.

"You're a man, John," she said, when she couldn't stand the quiet any longer. "If she was hurt that bad, your freezing for a few moments didn't make a difference. It was in God's hands."

He looked at her as though he'd only just remembered she was in the room. The corner of his mouth lifted. "Which is why I'm no longer on speaking terms with the old man."

"You blame God?"

"It's either Him or me. You pick."

He was sarcastic, combative, and raw, and it was all she could do not to pull him into her arms to soothe his pain. If only it were that simple.

"It was no one's fault."

He shook his head. "Doesn't work that way, Katie girl. It's always someone's fault, and since God has seniority, that makes it mine."

He reached for the whiskey, taking a swig without even bothering with the glass. She waited until he lowered the bottle before she stood and took it gently from his grasp.

"I think you've had enough."

He didn't argue or resist, just looked up at her as she stood before him. And why she laid her hand against his face, she'd never know, but her touch broke him loose somehow. He covered her hand with his and turned to press a kiss into her palm.

Something inside told her to run, but he stood and pulled her into his arms so quickly, there was no place to go.

"I need you, Katie," he murmured against her throat, kissing a trail to her jaw, then across her cheek until he found her mouth.

Desperately he kissed, pulling at her lips with his until she parted and his tongue swept her mouth. She could taste the whiskey and the need as he moved against her. His hands suddenly became as desperate as his mouth, one grasping her breast as the other cupped her bottom, pulling her tighter into his embrace.

Dizzying sensations assaulted her, clouding her thoughts and sinking her deeper into him. And the hand that had stroked her breast now fumbled with the buttons on her bodice. She knew she should stop him, but she couldn't. Somewhere along the way, his need had become hers. When his lips broke free from her mouth to find her breasts, she clutched his head closer instead of shoving him away. His mouth was warm, wet, and demanding as he suckled first one breast and then the other.

Never had she felt such sensations. Never had she dreamed they even existed, but she knew now she'd never forget. A cool breeze told her he was raising her skirts from the back until his hands grabbed her bottom, squeezing her through the thin fabric of her chemise. Her knees weakened, and a soft gasp slipped from her mouth.

Then suddenly he stopped. He dropped her skirts and buried his face against her breasts as though fighting to regain control. Finally he stood and hugged her against him, her damp flesh pressing his bared chest, his ragged breathing matching her own.

"I'm sorry, Katie," he whispered against the top of her head before he stepped back and wiped his hands down his face.

"I'm sorry," he repeated, leaving the kitchen with her feeling a lot of things, but sorry wasn't one of them.

Chapter Twenty-one

John's mother always said God watched over fools and children. If that was the case, God must be watching hard this morning because John had to have been the biggest fool to ever walk. His head thumped like a demon from the whiskey he'd consumed, and he deserved every nauseating throb. Unfortunately things were going to get worse before they got better.

He had to face Katie.

She was in the kitchen, if she hadn't run like hell, and he couldn't blame her if she had. He'd all but ravished her on the kitchen table, and now he had to face her . . . in front of his daughter . . . in the kitchen.

Hell.

He looked down at his wedding ring. He'd planned to wear it until the day he died, figuring he'd never want another woman, but last night had taught him otherwise. He'd wanted Katie. Fiercely, passionately, and shamelessly, he'd wanted her, so what had he done? He took. Without thought of her feelings or desires, he'd taken and would've taken it all if she hadn't gasped in surprise.

Bastards do that. Rogues, ne'er-do-wells, rakes, scoundrels, men of little or no morals take from women just because they want to. And he'd wanted to.

Still did.

Hell.

He headed to the kitchen. If he were an honorable man, he'd allow Katie to return home, but since he'd already established that he had no honor, he didn't think he'd bring up the option of leaving.

The smell of bacon frying rolled his stomach over twice before he entered the kitchen to face her wrath. He deserved no less.

"Morning, Katie," he said as soon as he checked to be sure they were alone.

She turned from the stove, her cheeks pink with embarrassment. "Mornin'."

Their gazes locked for a second before she dropped her eyes and turned back toward the stove.

"I . . . uh . . ." He took a deep breath and started again. "I need to apologize for last night."

She kept her back to him, but stopped moving. "No need," she muttered.

"Yes, there is a need." This was harder than he'd thought it would be. "I acted like an animal, and you don't deserve that. I'm sorry."

She nodded but kept her back to him, and it was killing him. He couldn't blame her for feeling humiliated—he'd stripped her to the waist—but it wasn't her fault.

Now was the time a decent man would offer to let her leave. "I—"

"John," she said firmly, then finally turned to face him. "It's all right."

He wanted to believe her. He also wanted to hold

her and kiss her, and all the emotions he'd felt the night before bubbled up in him again. Then she cracked an egg into the skillet and other things bubbled up, forcing him to run from the kitchen and humiliate himself in the yard.

"Where's Dr. Keffer?" Caroline asked when Katie set breakfast on the dining room table. She guessed Caroline assumed the help would refer to him by that title.

"John's taking a walk, I believe." It was ornery, but Katie couldn't help herself. Especially since John wasn't really walking. From what she'd seen out of the kitchen window, he was paying for his whiskey.

She'd paid last night. Based on his apology, he felt guilty for their encounter, but she had no guilt, only sadness. He hadn't meant to kiss her. She hadn't meant to want it, but she did, and now every time her future husband kissed her, she'd think of John. She'd remember his touch and the heat of his lips against her breasts and nothing would ever erase that feeling.

It was an accident for him. It was life changing for her.

She returned to the kitchen, surprised to find Julia sitting at the table, hugging her kitten. "Your breakfast is in the dining room."

"Can't I eat in here with you, Katie?"

"I thought you wanted to eat at the big table."

Julia sighed, theatrically. "I can't do it right."

"Eat?"

Julia nodded with equal theatrics, then proceeded to explain her eating problems. "I don't hold my fork right or put my napkin in the right place or talk when I'm supposed to." Rolling her blue eyes heavenward, she added, "It's too hard to eat in there."

Katie bit back a grin. She didn't want to eat in there either.

"Cook?" It was Caroline, and based on her tone, she wanted something.

Katie looked at Julia. Julia looked at Katie and both broke into laughter.

"Is there something you need?" Katie asked, finally forcing herself to return to the dining room.

"Yes," Caroline said, lifting her chin a haughty inch. "I want you to fix a picnic lunch for Dr. Keffer and me. I think he needs to get out into the fresh air."

"Please tell me you're joking," Caroline said, mouth gaping as she stared at Lightning and his carriage.

"About what?" John answered, knowing full well what Caroline was referring to.

"You expect me to ride in that?"

Lightning snorted as though her remark offended him, then proceeded to raise his tail and return the offense.

John shrugged. "It's either that or walk, and the stream I wanted to show you is quite some distance from here."

"Well," she said, tucking a blonde curl into her chignon, "if it means that much to you, I suppose I can manage." Then she smiled sweetly and held out her hand for him to help her climb into the seat.

He wasn't aware it had meant all that much to him. She was the one who'd insisted on a picnic and when he agreed to it, he thought it'd include Katie and Julia. But Caroline insisted they didn't want to go, so he hid his disappointment and hitched up the wagon.

He supposed he should feel sorry for Caroline. She bounced down the road with one hand holding on to her bonnet and the other gripping the seat as though convinced she was going to tumble over backward, and by the time they made it to the stream, "sweet" was no longer the word he would use to describe her smile. Come to think of it, even *smile* wasn't entirely accurate. Grimace? That was closer.

"Finally we're here," she said, reaching for John to lift her from the wagon. When he set her on the ground, she stumbled slightly, landing full against his chest.

"Oh," she giggled, looking up at him through lash-lowered eyes. "Thank goodness, you caught me." Then she gave a little squeeze to his arms as though testing his muscles. Was she flirting?

Releasing her, he grabbed the picnic basket and a quilt from behind the seat. Caroline flirting was an uncomfortable thought and not one he wanted to dwell on. "This way," he said, gesturing to a wooded area near the stream.

She tucked her arm through his and stepped cautiously through the tall grasses. A small waterfall poured from a spring in the side of a hill, cool droplets making a tinkling sound as they landed in a pool of water that flowed into the stream. Mosses and ferns grew in abundance around the spring and the fecund smell of the forest filled the air.

"What a lovely place," Caroline said as John flipped open the quilt to lie on the ground.

"Katie showed it to me."

"*Katie?* Oh yes. You mean the cook."

John opened the basketful of treats Katie had prepared, reluctantly admitting to himself she was the cook. But Caroline said it as though that made her beneath them. "She's a wonderful cook, but she's only doing this as a favor to me until my housekeeper returns."

Caroline joined John on the quilt, taking several minutes to adjust the folds of her gown and pat her hair, until finally giving him an expression that bordered on pity. "Really, John, do you think you should be on such friendly terms with the girl?"

"The *girl's* name is Katie, and we are friends, and I happen to like it that way."

She leaned toward him, placing her hand on his arm. "Please don't be angry with me. I'm just worried for you. You and I are both vulnerable right now." She lifted her hand to retrieve a handkerchief from her reticule and dabbed at the corner of one eye.

"I miss Lois terribly," she continued. "Such a dear sister, and it's only been two years since the unfortunate accident." She placed her hand back on his arm. "That's why I just had to come see you." She dabbed again at the same eye, making him wonder if she only cried from one eye at a time.

"I miss her too," he said, and he did miss her, but oddly enough, it didn't hurt as much to say it as it used to.

Caroline touched his wedding ring. "Don't you think it's time we both moved forward?"

At the angle she was leaning, any more forward motion would probably cause her to spill from the scooped neckline of her gown. Pulling his gaze away from her décolletage, he reached for the picnic basket.

"I am moving forward. That's why I moved here."

"There's a difference between moving forward and running away."

But sometimes the latter can cause the former, though at the moment, the last thing he wanted to do was point that out to Caroline. She was a little too smug with her earth-shattering revelation, and he decided to let her bask in it for a while longer.

A ring of the chime on the front door brought Katie quickly down the steps. It had taken forever to convince Julia that she wasn't too old for naps and even longer to convince the kitten. Today the kitten's name was Felicia. Yesterday it was Henry. Since it was still too young to determine whether it was male or female, Julia wasn't taking any chances. Katie didn't want to take any chances on the door chime waking either one of them.

"Afternoon, Katie," Harold said as soon as she jerked open the door.

"Harold." She pulled off her apron and patted her hair into her bun. "What a pleasant surprise."

He cleared his throat, then stretched to look around her into the house. "Is the doc home?"

"No. He's out for the moment. Are you ailing?"

"No, but I was hoping we could take a little walk. I ain't seen you much since you've been living here."

"Oh. Well, I'd love to take a walk with you, but Julia's upstairs asleep, and I can't leave her." She motioned to the chairs on the porch. "Maybe we could sit here for a spell and chat."

Harold frowned, which Katie was beginning to suspect was a natural state for him, and took the closest seat, leaving Katie to walk around him to the next chair.

They sat in silence for a few moments before Katie finally said, "How have you been lately?"

"Good," he answered, and she guessed she should be relieved. The last time she and Harold had had a private conversation, he'd shared his bowel problems.

"Well," she said, hoping he'd take the word as a cue that it was his turn to bring up a topic of conversation.

He didn't.

Luckily, John's carriage came wobbling down the street at about that time, delivering a topic of conversation to the doorstep.

"That's John's sister-in-law, Caroline," she said, nodding in their direction.

"Hmmph," was Harold's reply.

"She just came from New York City."

"Hmmph," again.

Katie had about had enough "hmmphing" to last her, but before she had to do something about it, John guided Lightning to the hitching rail in front of the porch and left the wagon to tie the mule before someone got hurt.

John glanced at the porch and gave a frown not too unlike Harold's.

"Afternoon, Doc," Harold said.

"Afternoon, Harold," John returned, helping Caroline down from the wagon.

She put her arm through John's and laughed lightly as though they shared some personal secret. Katie looked at Harold and smiled sweetly, wishing it'd been Randy who'd stopped by today instead of Harold. Randy was much prettier.

"Harold came by for a visit," she said, trying to sound excited. "Wasn't that nice of him?"

John continued to escort Caroline up the steps to the front door. He nodded in response to Katie's question, but didn't say any more on the subject.

"I was hoping I could get Katie to tell me what she'd like for her birthday," Harold said.

John stopped walking and immediately looked at Katie. "When's your birthday?"

"Thanksgiving," she answered, wondering why he was so interested.

"That's only a couple of weeks away."

"And we're hoping she'll let us know who she's going to marry by then."

Harold's statement snapped Caroline's attention to the conversation. To that point, she hadn't even made eye contact.

"Marry?" She smiled as though she and Katie were best friends. "Katie dear, you didn't tell me you were getting married."

Maybe that was because, up to that point, she didn't think Caroline dear, knew her name.

"I plan to."

"Who's the lucky man?" Caroline dear asked, beaming up at John as though it was the best news she'd heard in a while.

"I'm not sure just yet."

"Not sure?"

Katie's stomach sank. The last person she wanted to inform about her abundance of fiancés was Caroline dear.

"She has three fiancés," John said, and not with any of the sarcasm she would've used if the situation were reversed.

"Three?" Caroline threw her head back in a laugh that was borderline disrespectful. Of course, borderline for Caroline was an improvement.

"And is *this* one of them?"

Harold bristled at her implication but fortunately refrained from commenting.

"Yes," John answered. "This is Harold Crowley. Harold, please meet Caroline Humboldt."

"Afternoon," Harold said.

Caroline giggled behind her hand as she returned the greeting and led John into the house. Where was Randy Kopp when Katie needed him?

"So, Katie?" Harold asked, bringing her attention back to him. "What do you want for your birthday?"

"You don't have to get me anything, Harold."

"Now, don't be silly. A man has to get his girl something for her birthday."

She wasn't sure, but she thought he winked at her. Kind of hard to tell and compared to Randy's wink, it wasn't much, but she suspected he was flirting.

He was waiting for an answer, so she said, "Why don't you just surprise me?"

That seemed to placate him and for the next few minutes he thought out loud about what she might want as he watched her face for a reaction. A new skillet? Some spoons? A measuring cup?

"How about a new apron? A pretty white one with lace and fancy stitching?"

Katie smiled, but only because she realized if she didn't give him some reaction he was going to name everything in the kitchen. "That sounds nice."

Harold continued to speculate, then went from birthday gifts to all the things he would buy her once they were married. The man was going to have to build a new house just to hold all the kitchen utensils.

She nodded and smiled and tried to act pleased when he proceeded to tell her all his favorite foods and how he liked them fixed. Thank goodness. She probably wouldn't have slept that night if he hadn't.

"I best be getting home now," he finally said, standing, with an assortment of creaks, to his feet. And here all this time, she'd thought it was just her porch creaking.

"Nice of you to stop by," she said, waiting patiently for him to creak down the street before going into the house to check on Julia.

She heard it as soon as she entered the door. Music, and not a fiddle or juice harp or anyone singing. It was different from anything she'd heard before. Following the sound, she stepped quietly down the hallway, stopping just outside the parlor. She'd never looked in the large cabinet that sat against the wall. Didn't think it was her place to snoop in someone else's home, but now she kind of wished she had. The doors were propped open and inside was the biggest music box she'd ever seen.

And John and Caroline were dancing. She held his hand out to the side and had her other hand on his shoulder. His was at her waist as they stepped in circles around the room. Her skirt swayed and swooshed out with each turn as she glided around the room in his arms. Katie watched until the music stopped, then darted past the doorway before they could see her.

She forced herself to stay busy with dinner and Julia, not dwelling on the music box or the beautiful dance she'd seen. But as soon as everything was cleaned up and everyone had gone to bed, she headed to the parlor. Quickly lighting a lamp, she closed the door behind her and hurried across the room to open the cabinet.

Gramophone was written across the front, and after a moment of studying the instructions written inside, she started the music box. Beautiful sounds lilted into the room, sending Katie on a journey to lands she'd only imagined from reading her books. She closed her eyes and allowed the music to lift her to another place and another time. A handsome knight dismounted from his white horse, his armor shining, and his eyes on fire. He took her in his arms and swayed with her to the music, turning in circles, her satin skirts twirling about her like a princess.

"Would you like to learn the waltz?"

Gasping, Katie spun toward the door where John stood leaning against the frame. His tie and jacket were missing, his shirtsleeves rolled up to his forearms. The crisp white of his shirt exaggerated the darkness of his hair as he stood silently in the dim light of the room.

"I'm sorry," she muttered, rushing to shut down the

gramophone. "I shouldn't have done this without asking you."

"Katie. Stop."

She did, but she didn't turn to face him. It was too embarrassing.

"You can listen to it any time you want." He crossed the room and knelt beside her in front of the cabinet. "There are other records in here, though some of my best were broken on the trip from New York."

He dug through the cabinet and handed her a flat disc with grooves cut into the glass. "This one is by a man named Caruso."

She stared at the record, trying to see how something this flat could hold the sounds she'd heard.

"Someday, we'll listen to it." He placed the record back in the cabinet before taking her hand and pulling her to her feet. "But for right now, I think you need to learn the waltz."

"I don't, I mean, you don't need to teach me—"

"I believe I owe you a lesson. After all, you taught me how to square-dance."

"Not very well." She could have bitten her tongue. That wasn't exactly what she'd meant to say, but John chuckled and she decided not to amend her statement. He had a nice chuckle.

With a quick adjustment, he restarted the record to the beginning of the waltz music, then faced her, arms out. She stepped to him and placed her hands where she'd seen Caroline's earlier.

The corner of his mouth lifted, obviously pleased that she'd known what to do.

"It's really a simple dance," he said, folding his hand

over hers. "Just take three steps at a time and allow me to lead you around the room."

She nodded, because having him this close to her made speaking difficult, and then followed his lead.

"One, two, three," he counted, guiding her slowly around the room.

He only counted for a few moments before she fell into the rhythm and the music took over. She smiled as they floated, her eyes drifting shut and her steps taking her back to her magic kingdom. Only this time, she didn't have to imagine the knight. He was strong and warm, and with each turn, pulling her closer until finally he stopped moving.

She opened her eyes to gaze into the green ones searing into her in the faint light of the room. Neither spoke as he laid his hand against her cheek and the warmth rushed through her body. Were it not for the music, she knew her heartbeat would echo through the room, matched only by her breathing.

His eyes questioned her, asking for permission as though she had any power to refuse. He leaned toward her, taking forever to close the distance between their lips, and when he finally claimed hers, she thought she'd die.

Lord, how she wanted his touch.

Like nothing existed in the world except his kiss and embrace, everything else paling until it faded away. She slid her hands up his shoulders to the back of his neck, where she threaded them through his hair.

He nibbled and tugged at her mouth, slipping his tongue through parted teeth and stroking hers with passion as his hands rubbed her back. First, in small circles, then dropping lower and lower until he cupped her bottom and pulled her against him. A moan jumped from her mouth and into his, and the sound seemed to ignite him.

"Katie," he whispered, pulling back enough to press his lips against her throat, and the warmth in her body began pooling out of her control.

Lord, how she wanted his touch, only now she realized, with embarrassment, where she wanted it.

"John?" Caroline called from the hallway.

They froze for a second before jumping back from each other and quickly adjusting their clothing.

"John?" she said again, then walked into the room. "Oh." She glanced at each of them, looking at Katie as if she were a harlot. "I hope I'm not interrupting." Her implication was clear, and Katie had never been more embarrassed in her life.

"I was teaching Katie how to waltz." John pointed to the gramophone as though Caroline would have no idea where the music was coming from.

She smiled, far too sweetly, and walked to his side. "That's kind of you, but I doubt Katie's fiancés would approve of her spending time alone with you this late at night."

Her tone clearly indicated her disapproval, and Katie was still too rattled to defend herself—especially to Caroline. So she excused herself and hurried to her room, but as she lay in her bed, she realized with a jolt that she no longer wanted her future husband to touch her like John.

She wanted her future husband to *be* John.

Chapter Twenty-two

Katie had taken more time than usual preparing herself for church. To the point of even snipping a few strands of hair around her face, then dampening the tendrils so they curled. She loosened her bun a little, pleased with the effect, but when she stepped into the foyer and Caroline glided through, Katie felt as plain as a barn wren.

Caroline's soft yellow gown with matching gloves and bonnet made Katie's blue Sunday dress look like what it was—old, blue, and as plain as Katie herself. Suddenly she felt silly for cutting her hair.

"Katie?" John joined them in the foyer. "You've down something different with your hair."

"A little." Nervously, she reached up to adjust a curl.

"It looks nice." A soft twinkle in his eye and a subtle lift of his lip made her feel better.

"Thank you," she said, but Caroline made sure that was the last thing she said for the rest of the walk to church.

She managed to wedge herself between John and Katie and proceeded to chat the entire way about New York "this"s and New York "that"s. Only including Katie in the conversation to ask her questions like,

"What's your favorite wine, Katie?" Or "Don't you just love Monet?"

Katie wanted to trip her, but doing such a thing on the way to the Lord's house was probably a sin . . . at least on Sunday. So she controlled her urge as they walked to church, wondering whether a Monday tripping was as sinful.

"Oh," Caroline said, just when Katie thought she'd finally run out of words, "Ambassador Bashear sent his greetings. You remember the ambassador, don't you?"

John uttered a response, but Katie didn't hear what he said because Randy stepped beside her at the church steps. "Mornin', Katie," he said, smiling that smile of his and adding his ever-charming wink.

Katie's return greeting was cut short when Caroline tripped on the porch steps and fell into Randy's arms. Maybe the Lord had no trouble with a Sunday tripping after all.

"Oh my," Caroline uttered, pulling herself from Randy's arms. She blushed brightly, adjusting her hat.

"Are you all right, ma'am?" he asked.

"Yes, thank you."

"Caroline," John said, "this is Randy Kopp. One of Katie's fiancés."

"Pleased to meet you, Miss . . . ?"

"Humboldt," John supplied for Randy.

"Miss Humboldt," Randy said with a wink, and Caroline actually gasped in response. Not that Katie could blame her. Randy's first winks were always stunners.

Caroline lifted her chin and looked at Randy as though he were something she'd scrape off her shoe and then with a quick nod, she stepped past him into the tiny sanctuary of the church. Randy had definitely rattled her, though. In her flustered state, she'd left John and Katie together as she hurried down the aisle. Within a few feet, she stopped abruptly and spun back to face them.

"Where you would like to sit?" she asked, smiling at John, ignoring Katie.

He gestured toward one of the pews in the front, then guided Katie into the seat and sat beside her, leaving a place for Caroline next to him.

Julia wiggled around to sit on the other side of Katie, making sure to put as much distance as possible between her and her aunt. Caroline sat with her nose in the air and a look of sheer boredom on her perfectly schooled face. An air of total superiority hovered about her.

A quick hymn and a few announcements later, Reverend Stoker took the pulpit.

"Brothers and sisters," he said with jowls shaking, "we need to begin this service with a prayer."

After a prayer that lasted far too long and a hymn that was unrecognizable, the minister began his sermon. He went on and on about who shall sit on the throne of heaven, and then he slammed his fist on the pulpit to bring home his point. The consequence of which was beyond shocking.

John chewed on his lip in an effort to maintain his composure. Reverend Stoker should know better than to attempt to put the words "shall" and "sit" together in the same sentence. The first two times he'd gotten away with it, but the entanglement of the words in his third endeavor stunned the congregation into silence. Even Stoker turned red.

Caroline gasped, her pallor indicating she might actually swoon. John covered his grin with his hand, daring a glance at Katie only to see her sitting stoically and unaffected. The woman had an innate class that seemed to carry her through any situation with ease. Caroline could take lessons from Katie, though it wasn't her fault. She'd been raised in a sheltered cocoon and hadn't been given the opportunities to develop the strength Katie had.

Luckily for him, Katie had shared her strength. He owed her for that. Suddenly an idea popped into his head. It might not make up for the egregious liberties he'd taken with her, but it could be a start. He waited as patiently as possible for the service to end, and for their walk back home.

"Your birthday is in eleven days," he said to Katie once Caroline took a pause in her chatting long enough for him to change the subject.

"Yes," Katie said, clearly wondering what he was going to say.

"I'd like to throw you a party."

"A *party*?" Katie stopped walking and looked up at him as though he'd lost his mind. And maybe he had, but the more he thought about it, the more the idea appealed to him.

"As a thank-you for all you've done for me and Julia."

Slowly, she began walking again. "You don't owe me anything. You pay me well, remember?"

Why did that remark sound painful? "I could never pay you enough for what you've done for us. Wouldn't you enjoy a party?"

"I suppose," she muttered, avoiding eye contact.

"Of course you would, Katie dear," Caroline said. "It's a delightful idea, and would be a perfect opportunity to announce your engagement to all your friends."

John's gut knotted. "I don't think she's quite ready for that step. Are you, Katie?"

Katie wasn't even sure she was ready for the next step down the road. Why did John suddenly sound panicked at the thought of her announcing her engagement? Was he just afraid of losing his housekeeper, or was something else on his mind?

She'd love to ask him, but Caroline dear made it difficult to ask him anything. She was already rambling on about how the parlor could be emptied for dancing, and all the food they could serve, half of which Katie had never heard of, and then she focused on the engagement.

"It would be such a wonderful end to the evening. Just imagine, all your friends would be in attendance to share in your good news and excitement."

Chatter, chatter, chatter. Ramble, ramble, ramble. By the time they finally reached the house, Katie thought her head might burst. She hurried into the kitchen to fix Sunday dinner and managed to keep herself busy and away from Caroline for the rest of the day, thinking that in so doing, she could avoid the topic of her engagement. She was wrong.

"Katie?" Caroline knocked lightly on Katie's door, just as she was getting ready for bed. She wrapped a quilt around her nightgown and opened the door.

"May I come in and speak with you?"

Katie would rather have a beating, but Caroline didn't give her the option. "Of course."

Caroline sashayed into the room wearing an ivory satin dressing gown, her hair loose and flowing down her back in glossy waves. "I thought we could have a chat."

Katie pulled her quilt closer around her faded cotton nightgown and motioned to the bed, where Caroline continued her sashay across the room to sit on the edge. "I was wondering which fiancé you've selected. I promise I won't tell."

Katie chose to sit on her lone wooden chair to face Caroline dear. Her ivory satin didn't leave much room on the cot for another to sit. "I haven't really decided yet," Katie said.

"Haven't decided? You don't have much time to waste."

"I don't have to announce at the party."

"Yes, you do." Caroline's tone developed a slightly caustic edge before she plastered on a smile and giggled. "Oh, listen to me! I just don't want you to miss this perfect opportunity for an engagement party."

"I thought it was a birthday party."

Caroline chose to ignore that reminder. "Now, I've only met two of your fiancés, Mr. Crowley and the young man at church today. What was his name?"

"Randy Kopp."

"Oh yes," Caroline said, but the pink tint to her cheeks led Katie to believe she remembered Randy's name just fine.

"Is your other fiancé as handsome as Mr. Kopp?"

"No."

"Well then, that's the answer to your problem." For some reason Caroline seemed pleased as punch with her solution. She stood and headed to the door as though all Katie's issues were resolved.

"But there are other things a woman must consider when choosing a husband," Katie said, wondering why she bothered to tell Caroline anything.

Caroline turned back to face her and smiled. "Wealth is important, but I doubt any of them have much of that to speak of, and what woman wouldn't want a man as handsome as your Mr. Kopp?"

Caroline left Katie wondering if Grandma had acquired a new partner, but decided against it. Randy didn't need help turning a woman's head, regardless of her station in life, it seemed.

"John?" Caroline said from the other side of his door.

"One moment." Grabbing his dressing gown, he headed across the room and opened the door. "Is something wrong?"

Stepping into the light from his room, she turned to allow him full view of her dressing gown, complete with an astonishingly low-cut neckline, and then smiled. "Nothing's wrong. I just have some wonderful news. May I come in?"

His gaze raked across her breasts before he jerked his attention back to her face. He couldn't remember ever seeing her in something this revealing. "I don't think that would be proper."

Laughing lightly, she laid her hand against his arm. "It probably isn't, but I just can't wait until tomorrow to tell you. Besides, Katie is just down the hall."

Without giving him a chance to protest, she slipped past him into his room. Gliding to his bed, she sat on the edge, and if he didn't know better, he'd swear she posed.

He pulled his dressing gown closed and opened the door to its widest before taking a chair across the room. Caroline had something up her sleeve, and he shuddered to think what.

"What is this news?" he asked.

"Katie has finally selected her husband."

She beamed as though she actually cared about Katie, then folded her hands in front of her in a manner that caused her arms to shove her breasts up even more.

"Who?" he asked, with a sinking stomach.

"Randy Kopp."

That hothead? "What makes you think so?"

"She told me, but don't tell her I said so. I promised to keep her secret, but I knew you were dying to know." She flipped her hair back over her shoulder and leaned slightly toward him. "She decided to marry the most handsome one. Shocking, I know, but I suppose she felt that was the most important thing."

How could Katie decide such a thing? Randy? He was handsome, but John doubted he could outthink a pig. He shook his head in disbelief.

"I can't believe you're surprised," Caroline said, and

for a moment he'd forgotten she was in the room. "She said she wanted to marry him because he was the most handsome man she'd ever seen, and with all those muscles . . ." The way her voice trailed off, John wondered if Caroline wasn't considering the option herself.

She sighed as she walked across the room to kneel by his side. "I'm sorry, John. I know you thought highly of her, but a handsome man can turn even the most levelheaded woman to mush, sometimes. Someone with her breeding can't be expected to behave otherwise."

Looking down at her as she sat by his side, he felt his mind whirling. He'd known all along Katie was going to select a husband from her list, but hearing the decision had been made rattled him to his core. Standing, he offered his hand to help Caroline to her feet.

"Thank you for telling me," he said as he walked her to the door, closing it softly behind her. As much as he hated to admit it, Katie had the right to make this decision, unsettling as it was.

And he had the right to convince her otherwise.

Chapter Twenty-three

Maybe her new dress wasn't as fancy as Caroline's, but it was the prettiest Katie had ever owned. The deep green fabric had cost her plenty, and the hours spent working on it had left her tired, but the image staring back at Katie from the mirror made it all worthwhile. A real party dress, complete with lace and a daring neckline, lifted Katie's spirits higher than they'd been since Caroline arrived.

A quick pinch to her cheeks added color, and the curls around her face gave a soft touch, which pleased her. She smiled and took a calming breath, readying herself to leave her room to attend her party. Her party. She'd never had one of those before and just the thought of it made her giddy.

"Katie?" John called to her from outside her door.

She hurried to answer it, and her breath caught in her throat. He always looked handsome, but tonight he had outdone himself. His suit fit him like a glove, accentuating his strong physique, and the dark fabric of his jacket made his eyes almost glow. A whiff of bay rum tickled her senses and a smile curved the corner of his mouth. Suddenly she had images of his mouth on her body. Merciful heavens.

She swallowed. "Good evening."

John fought to remember why he had come to Katie's room. The vision standing before him knocked all thoughts from his head and half the wind from his body. Damn, she was beautiful. Where did she get that gown? The deep emerald color brought out her eyes, and the neckline brought out other things.

His eyes traveled quickly to her breasts, swelling above the neckline, before he forced them back to her face. Damn it if other things weren't swelling now.

"Did you want something?" she asked.

Of course he did, but what? Then he remembered his gift. "Yes, I wanted to give you your birthday gift before the other guests arrived."

"Oh." She smiled, her eyes sparkling even more. And he felt it throughout his entire body. Then she raised a brow, hidden slightly by a curl, and he realized he'd been staring at her like a nitwit.

"Here." He thrust his package at her, wondering how a man with his education and experience could be flummoxed by a mere brow.

She accepted his gift and walked to her bed to sit and open it. Hesitating for a moment, he followed her into the room, but took the chair across from her. His body was at a borderline mutiny, and he didn't trust himself to sit beside her just yet.

A tiny gasp brought his mind back from its lecherous thoughts to the beautiful woman who'd caused them. "Do you like them?" he asked.

Katie pulled the new boots from the wrapping paper and looked up at John with tears in her eyes. "I can't accept these."

"Why? Are they the wrong size?"

She shook her head. "They're too expensive."

"They weren't expensive at all," he lied. The boot maker in New York had charged him an arm and a leg to finish and ship the boots before Katie's party. Luckily, he had an extra arm and leg. "Besides, they're from Julia." Another lie, but he knew she wouldn't refuse a gift from Julia, and he couldn't bear the thought of her walking through the snow in her old boots.

The look in Katie's eye told him she didn't fall for his story, but she was grateful for it just the same. She could keep them if they were from Julia. "I'll be sure to thank her."

"Do you need help putting them on?"

She blushed, and he realized what a ridiculous question he'd asked. It wasn't his fault, though. All his blood had left his brain and pooled somewhere in his groin.

"I think I can manage."

He smiled. "You probably can."

Then she returned the smile, and he wished the rest of the world would go away. "I'll see you downstairs, then," he said, backing toward the hallway in an attempt to look debonair. It would have been more effective, however, if he hadn't bumped into the door on his way out.

Katie's soft laughter followed him into the hallway, but the warm feeling it gave him stopped abruptly when Caroline intercepted him at the top of the stairs.

"How lovely of you to escort me down to the party."

Was that what he'd done? "My pleasure," he said, adding to his recent list of lies. Though he probably wasn't being fair to Caroline. She was guilty of nothing more than not being Katie and that wasn't her fault, just her misfortune.

"Do you like my gown?"

Oops. John glanced at her obviously expensive, obviously French gown and smiled. "It's lovely." And he supposed it was.

By the time they reached the foot of the steps, the voices of several guests mingled in the air. Rebecca Fisher had been the first to arrive and had volunteered to greet guests so John could take Katie her gift. In his brief absence, many had come, all chatting and laughing as they ambled to the parlor.

Katie's family was there, all siding with their pick of her fiancés. Frank Davis, Reverend Stoker, Gloria Pennington, to name a few, were already examining the foods on the buffet table fixed by the cooks John had hired from Huntington.

The laughter and friendliness of the guests brought a smile to John's lips, but Caroline's grip on his arm tightened.

"Have you ever seen a bigger collection of hoydens in your life?" she whispered, looking up at him as though they shared a common bond. She tipped her head toward Rebecca. "Look at that dress. I wouldn't be caught dead in it."

John glanced at Rebecca and thought she looked remarkably well for a woman who'd just given birth to her fourth child a few weeks before. Her dress was plain but clean, and her face glowed with excitement. Actually, in many ways she was more attractive than Caroline.

But he couldn't tell her that so he said, "These people have no need for fancy gowns."

"Doc!" One of the men who'd helped at the barn raising smacked John on the shoulder before Caroline had a chance to respond to his comment. "This here's a real nice thing you done for Katie."

"She deserves it," John said, wishing he could remember the man's name. Luckily, Caroline had wandered off, and he didn't have to introduce them.

"She does indeed," he answered. "Ain't no woman finer than Katie." Suddenly the man looked past John's shoulder toward the hall and let out a low whistle. "Speak of the devil."

John turned to see Katie standing in the doorway. And for the second time that evening, she took his breath away. Unfortunately, she had the same effect on Randy, Harold, and Freddie. All three made a mad dash to her side, each vying for her attention like lovesick fools. He eyed the crowd for a second to determine if there was room for one more fool before Julia's tug on his sleeve diverted his attention.

"Daddy? Have you seen Harvey?"

"Harvey?"

"My kitten," she answered, bending over to look under the buffet table.

"I thought we determined the kitten was a girl."

"Today she is, but I want a boy kitten, and I think if I name her Harvey, she might change her mind."

There was a time he would've corrected her misconception, but he was finding it difficult to remember that time now, so instead he knelt to lift the tablecloth and look for Harvey.

* * *

Katie's heart warmed at the sight of John on his knees beside Julia. There was a time he would never have crawled on the floor in front of his guests, but she was finding it difficult to remember that time, and it was all she could do not to join them in their search for whatever they were searching for.

"Will you save a dance for me, Katie?"

Randy's question forced her to tear her eyes away from John. "Of course I will," she answered absently. Caroline had joined John at the table, her tinkling laughter carrying across the room.

"Who's the woman with Doc?" Grandma asked. Katie hadn't even noticed she'd crossed the room.

"That's his sister-in-law, Caroline."

"They look right purty together. Like they belong."

Katie knew what Grandma was doing, but it worked just the same. Caroline and John *did* look right together, like the perfect couple enjoying an evening with friends.

A warm hand on the small of her back dragged her attention away from the table once more. "I got you a birthday present," Randy said, then leaned over to whisper in her ear, "Later, I'll give it to you in private." He ended his message with a kiss on her cheek. She heated in response.

Every muscle in John's body tightened as he forced himself to stay where he was. Crossing the room and planting his fist in Randy's face would ruin Katie's party, but that little son of a bitch had just kissed her in front of everyone. Granted, it was on the cheek, but his hand was on her back and from John's vantage point, it appeared to be rubbing circles.

"Look, Daddy," Julia said, interrupting his homicidal thoughts as Randy stepped away from Katie to get some punch.

Julia beamed up at him as if it were Christmas morning. "We have friends."

And damn if she wasn't right.

Guest after guest greeted John and thanked him for inviting them, each smile genuine and open. Men teased about his blisters from the barn raising and women laughed about his fifty-dollar chicken, and for the first time in his life, he felt like he was part of a community. Imagine that.

"Is there any music around here, Doc?" Frank Davis asked.

"Absolutely," John answered, crossing the room to the gramophone. Several people partnered up in the center of the room, waiting for the music to begin, but when the soft waltz tune filled the air, all heads turned toward him in confusion.

"It's called a waltz," he said, and all heads nodded in unison as they looked at him as if he were from another planet. So much for community.

"It's really very simple." He searched the room for the perfect partner. "Katie?" he said, reaching his hand toward her. "Would you help me show everyone the waltz?"

She blushed prettily. "I'm really not very good at it."

"Nonsense. You're perfect." He hadn't intended that

to come out the way it did, but who could argue with the truth?

She stepped into his arms as the crowd cleared the center of the room. "Just follow my lead," he whispered, stepping into the music and out of reality.

Around the room they twirled, her skirts weaving about their legs as the music carried them away. Her cheeks flushed from the heat and excitement, her tenuous glances to his eyes causing his heart to skip. The soft scent of vanilla drifted from her, and it took all his willpower not to bury his face into her hair and inhale her essence.

Her hand on his shoulder seared through his jacket, and he remembered the feel of her fingers as she'd held his head against her breasts. His body responded for the thousandth time that evening, forcing him to drag his brain back to the present and away from its imaginings.

Then she looked up at him.

Her lips parted as her breathing picked up from the dance or maybe from his nearness. He could only hope. But as his gaze slid down the column of her throat to the valley rising and falling between her breasts, his step faltered.

She looked away with embarrassment and quit dancing. It was only then that he realized the music had stopped. A lone clap marked the beginning of a weak round of applause and a murmured response or two about the dance, jolting him back to the realization there were others in the room. Many others, and they were as embarrassed as he was. Should he say something?

He stepped back and bowed to Katie, trying to think of a way to salvage the situation, when suddenly the front door burst open.

"Doc!" A man rushed into the parlor carrying an unconscious woman in his arms. Blood poured from wounds on her head, soaking her dress in crimson. "Please help my wife," he pleaded. "She's been hit by a carriage."

Katie saw John's shock as soon as it crossed his face. All color drained from his cheeks, and his eyes locked on to a vision from the past.

"Of course," she said, stepping toward Ed Monroe. "Take Elsa across the hall to Dr. Keffer's office and put her on the examination table."

Ed left the room as the guests' confusion and noise filled the parlor. Katie grabbed John's arm and shook. "John," she said, squeezing until he turned to look at her. "She needs you."

"I can't," he whispered.

"Yes, you can and you will."

He rubbed his hand across his jaw as he stood staring at the doorway.

"We don't have time to think about this," she said, taking his hand. "You're not a new doctor, and that's not Lois."

Luckily, he followed as she led him out of the room. She wasn't big enough to pull him against his will. With each step she felt his strength return and by the time they made it to his office, John was back.

"Get the bandages and sutures from the cabinet," he said to Katie, pulling off his jacket and rolling up his shirtsleeves.

"Is she going to be all right, Doc?" Ed asked.

Katie glanced at John, catching his eyes for a second before he faced Ed again. "If I have anything to say about it, she will. But right now, I need you to leave the room. Miss Napier and I have work to do."

Ed nodded and left, pulling the door closed behind him. Rushing to John's side, Katie laid the supplies on a table beside Elsa.

He folded a bandage and placed it against the gash in her head. "Hold pressure on this while I check for other injuries."

Katie did as he'd requested, then watched in amazement as he ran his hands down her arms and legs, pressing and probing as he searched for broken bones. Then he pushed against Elsa's belly and sighed with relief.

"Anything broken?" Katie asked.

"I don't think so and there doesn't appear to be any internal bleeding. Hopefully, once we get this gash sewn on her head, it'll just be a matter of her waking up."

Lifting the bandage, Katie fought the urge to wince as the blood poured from the injury. But John's steady hands pulled the wound closed and sutured the damage with skill and gentleness. An hour later, the bleeding had stopped, and a bandage was in place, but Elsa still hadn't moved.

John pulled a chair beside Elsa and sat, his eyes glazed as he watched her.

"Do we let Ed come in?" Katie asked.

He continued to stare at Elsa and Katie knew what he was thinking.

"You've done all anyone could do," she said. "If she's going to die, there's nothing now that can be done to stop it. Ed has the right to be with her if that happens."

John looked at her, nodding silently in agreement. She crossed the room and opened the door. Ed rushed to Elsa's side and picked up her hand.

He looked at John in anguish. "Is she going to make it?"

"There's nothing more we can do," John said, slowly standing. "Now we just have to pray she wakes up."

John slid his chair to Ed and patted him on the shoulder before walking into the hallway. His knees no longer felt like they were about to buckle, but the memories that had surged through him earlier left a bitter taste in his mouth. He crossed the parlor to the banquette table and dipped a crystal cup into a bowl of punch. He'd never really liked the taste of punch, but Caroline had insisted that no birthday party was complete without it.

Taking a long drink, he turned to examine the now empty room. All the guests had gone home during the emergency, leaving piles of food and bowls of punch untouched.

"Rebecca put Julia to bed," Katie said, entering the room and crossing to the table. "I'll put some of this food in the icebox so it won't spoil."

He wanted to say something to her, but the words escaped him. This evening was supposed to be her celebration, but instead they'd been thrown into a nightmare. His nightmare, and Katie had been dragged right along with him. She lifted a platter of pastries and turned toward the door. That was when he noticed the blood.

"Your gown is ruined," he said.

"It's nothing. I'll get the stains out later."

But he knew those stains wouldn't come out without a torch. "I'll buy you a new gown."

"It's not important—"

"Doc!" Ed's shout interrupted her.

John's heart fell as he ran out of the parlor and across the hall, praying in earnest for the first time in years. Taking a fortifying breath at the entrance to his office, he paused for a second before pushing open the door and stepping inside.

Ed's smile knocked the wind out of him. "She's awake, Doc."

Elsa turned her head to look at him and gave him the weakest, most pathetic, most beautiful smile he'd seen in a long time. "I heard you're the one what sewed me up."

John smiled. "I had a little help."

"Very little," Katie said, moving to his side. "Dr. Keffer knew exactly what he was doing."

Ed lifted Elsa's hand to his lips, his eyes clouding with tears. "Thanks, Doc. I owe you one."

Nodding, John chose not to attempt to speak. Ed wasn't the only one choking on emotion at the moment.

"Can I take her home?"

Clearing his throat, John said, "I think she should probably sleep here tonight. You're welcome to stay with her. I'll be upstairs in case you need me."

John followed Katie out of the office and into the

now silent house. Caroline must have gone on to bed, and all the guests were long gone. Even Harvey was nowhere to be seen. The ticking of the grandfather clock made the only sound echoing in the hallway as they climbed the stairs.

He could see her new boots peeking from beneath her green skirts as she walked in front of him, and it seemed like a million years had passed since he'd given them to her.

Turning to face him at the top of the stairs, she whispered a soft, "Good night," then headed toward her room.

She had pulled him through his biggest nightmare, but somehow it only made him feel guiltier than ever. How come he had been able to save Ed's wife when he hadn't been able to save Lois? Why had he frozen when she had needed him most?

He stood for another million years in the empty hallway, staring at the soft light glowing from beneath Katie's door. He pushed away his dark thoughts by imagining her removing her gown and getting ready for bed. A knot built low in his gut, threatening to stop his heart. He needed to speak to her once more, to thank her for helping him before retiring for the night.

Closing the distance quickly, he stopped outside Katie's door, hoping he'd come up with a better excuse for seeing her again than just offering thanks. Katie was no fool. He swallowed and knocked.

"Yes?"

"May I come in? I need to speak with you."

She hesitated only briefly before saying, "Come in."

It wasn't too late to stop. If he just didn't need her so much he could tell her he'd speak with her in the morning or stay in the hallway. But instead, he opened the door to her tiny room. She sat on her bed, removing her hairpins, a brush lying on her lap. Long brown waves flowing down her shoulders to her waist, a soft smile parting her lips.

He stepped into the room . . . and closed the door.

Chapter Twenty-four

Katie didn't stand when John entered her room. She couldn't. His gaze riveted her to the bed as he stood staring at her. Neither spoke for the longest time, until finally he broke the silence. "Would you like me to help you with your hair?"

She'd been doing her hair for twenty-five years, but she didn't tell him that. Instead she nodded and scooted to make room for him on the edge of the bed. He sat beside her and began removing the rest of the pins from her bun. His fingers raked through the tresses, lightly touching the back of her neck as they combed.

"I wanted to thank you for helping me tonight," he said, his mouth so close she could feel his breath against her cheek. "I couldn't have done it without you."

"You didn't need me," she said, trying to sound calm despite the tremble in her voice.

He pulled a curl down her shoulder, allowing his fingers to trace its length over her breast to her waist. "That's where you're wrong," he whispered, closing his eyes.

John felt Katie's hands cup his face and when he opened his eyes, he knew he was no longer lost. Somehow this mountain healer had found him. She'd closed his wounds and opened his heart and now she owned his soul.

"Katie?"

"Shhh," she whispered, before she kissed him, her lips soft and timid as they pressed against his.

Pulling her into his arms, he claimed her kiss and made it his own, fighting down the passion that was building in him like a storm. "Tell me to leave, Katie," he murmured against her mouth. "This is your last chance."

But instead of taking her salvation, she untucked his shirt from his pants and ran her hands across the bare skin of his back. "I don't want you to go," she said between kisses, and he thanked God in heaven for that. He wasn't sure he had the willpower to leave even if she'd asked him to.

Then she sat back from him and began unbuttoning her bodice. He watched as she stood, the gown falling to her feet in a green pool, leaving her only in her chemise and the white stockings he'd given her, tied at the thighs with lengths of ribbon. Her hair flowed around her shoulders in a silky mass and he knew now what a goddess must look like.

Damn, he wanted her.

Like an all-consuming fire, he wanted to throw her onto the bed and drive into her until the need in him abated. But she was a virgin, a beautiful, sensual, enticing virgin who was looking at him as if he were the only man in the world.

Damn, he wanted her.

But he had to go slowly.

"I don't know what to do," she said, dropping her eyes.

He stood and removed his shirt, surprised when his legs didn't collapse. Stepping closer to her, he ran his hands down her chemise to her thighs, where the fabric stopped just above her garters. "May I look at you?"

She raised her gaze, nodding hesitantly, like she wasn't sure if he'd be pleased. Slowly, he lifted the chemise up her body, uncovering inch by inch the beautiful, soft skin of a goddess. She raised her arms to allow him to pull the garment over her head, her hair falling down her back in a curtain of silk.

He knelt in front of her, because that was what a man should do in the presence of a goddess and because his legs weren't as steady as they had been a few moments before. Wrapping his arms around her waist, he pulled her to him and buried his face into the smooth flesh of her belly.

Nibbling, he allowed his hands to stroke the rounded curves of her buttocks. Her fingers threaded through his hair as he kissed his way up her body to her mouth. Tongues dueling, hands exploring, they entwined with each other until falling onto the tiny bed. With a quick twist, he managed to land beneath her, her lithe body on his, her breasts perfect globes against his hard chest.

Katie looked down into the eyes of the man she loved, confused by her lack of fear. She should be terrified. She was about to give herself to a man who was not her husband, not even one of her fiancés, and yet there was no fear. No second thoughts, no doubts, just a longing and hunger like she'd never experienced before.

And there was the frustration. Deep, building, pulsating frustration that grew with every moment he toyed with her. Slowly he rolled with her on the bed until they faced each other, and his hands began caressing her once more. He fondled her breasts, pulling at the peaks while his tongue stroked hers. Then his mouth broke free and found the breasts his hands had awakened.

But the sensations tingling from her breasts were nothing compared to the shock waves that coursed through her body when his fingers glided between her legs. Gasping, she pinched her thighs together. What was he doing?

He lifted his head from her breasts and kissed her mouth before whispering, "Trust me, Katie."

And she did. She always had, and she always would. Slipping her hands behind his head, she kissed him and allowed his hands to do their will, trusting he knew what he was doing. Caressing, rubbing, stroking until the frustration built past bearing, and just when she thought she could take no more, he slid a finger inside her body and proved he knew what he was doing after all. The world exploded.

Luckily, he caught her cry with his mouth or she would've awakened the entire town. She was vaguely aware of him fumbling with his trousers, just before he rolled on top of her and positioned himself between her legs.

"Katie?" John said, waiting for her to open her eyes and look at him. "Are you ready for me?"

She smiled and nodded.

"It's going to hurt this first time, but I'll do what I can to make it easier for you."

She responded to his concern by placing her hand against his face and pulling him down for a kiss. Slowly he pressed into her until he felt the tight obstruction of her maidenhead.

"I'm sorry," he murmured into her mouth as he drove through the barrier and froze to give her time to adjust to him.

She gasped, but didn't cry out as Lois had done. She simply looked up at him and said, "Is it over?"

He laid his forehead against hers, fighting to maintain control. "Not close, but the pain should be leaving. Is it?"

She nodded and adjusted her hips. The movement took his control and threw it out the window. "Are you sure?" he said through gritted teeth.

She answered by kissing him and wrapping her legs around his waist. He needed no other encouragement. He wanted to go slowly, to take her to ecstasy with him, but the tight, hot body encasing him drove all noble intentions from his mind.

He took her as gently as his body would allow, but probably not as gently as he should have. A voice in his mind urged him to go easy, but the overriding desire won out. So he took with no finesse, with no restraints, and with no control until his body poured into hers, and he felt complete for the first time in years.

Carefully, he rolled off her and pulled her into his arms. "Did I hurt you?" he asked, as soon as he could speak again.

"No," she muttered against his neck, but knowing Katie, she wouldn't have told him if he'd ripped her in two.

He'd been a cad again. Taking more than he'd given, but he'd make it up to her. Once they were married, he'd worship her as the goddess she was and the next time they made love, there would be no pain, only pleasure. He'd see to it.

Brushing the hair back from her face, he intended to promise her he'd make her a happy bride, but the steady rise and fall of her breasts told him she was sleeping. She'd had a hell of a day and waking her at this point seemed cruel. He slipped from her bed, covering her before shutting off her lamp. He'd propose tomorrow as soon as he could find a moment alone with her. Until then, she deserved her rest.

"John?" Caroline stepped into his office and closed the door. "I need to speak with you. Do you have a minute?"

Not really, but she seemed genuinely distressed and Katie was too busy with breakfast for him to propose just yet, despite his eagerness. So instead of dodging Caroline's company he said, "Certainly," then motioned to a chair.

Caroline sat and pulled a handkerchief from her sleeve to dab at her crying eye. "I have something to tell you, and I just don't know where to start."

Sighing, John took a seat on the edge of his desk. "Take your time, and tell me what's bothering you."

"I'm afraid I've deceived you."

"How?"

She twisted the handkerchief in her hands before raising her eyes to look at him. "I didn't come to West Virginia just for a visit. I came here because Lois made me promise I would."

He frowned. "Lois?"

"Yes." She nodded as though it pained her to admit it. "After Julia was born she made me promise that if anything ever happened to her, you and I would marry and raise Julia together."

"She never said anything to me."

"Of course not. That's not something a woman would tell her husband. But she made me promise again the day before she died. It was almost like she knew her life was about to end."

"Why did you wait so long to tell me this?"

Pulling the handkerchief to her eyes, she sobbed into the fabric before lowering it to answer his question. "I guess I was afraid. I thought you needed time to mourn, and I wasn't sure if we'd suit. We weren't that close before, but now that we've spent this time together, I can see that we'd suit quite well."

Standing, John crossed the room to stare out the window at the cold November day, his mind racing in several directions at once. "We don't love each other," he finally said, trying to add sense to an otherwise insane conversation.

"Not yet, but that will come. Besides, it's the least we can do for Lois and Julia. Doesn't Julia deserve a mother?"

He started to tell her he'd found the perfect mother for his daughter, then remembered that he had to pry her away from her fiancé first. But he could do that.

Maybe. And Julia loved Katie almost as much as he did, if that was possible.

Didn't he deserve some happiness in this world?

Of course he did, or at least he thought so, until Caroline asked, "It was important to her that I help raise Julia. You know how much she loved her. Don't we owe it to Lois to grant her last wish?"

John's heart sank. He had failed Lois in life by not saving her when she needed him most. Was he to fail her again in death?

Chapter Twenty-five

A person can't fight fire with fire if they never get close to the flame. Katie patted a tendril of hair into her bun, determined to warm things up a little. Caroline had done her best to drive a wedge between Katie and John, but last night proved how ineffective she was.

"Julia," Katie said, adding the finishing touches to her gravy, "would you please set another plate at the table in the dining room? I'm going to eat with you and your pa this morning."

Julia raced from the kitchen as Katie finished dishing up the rest of breakfast. Katie carried the bowls to the table, fighting the nerves bubbling up in her belly. She hadn't seen John since they'd made love, but she'd been unable to think of anything else. John entered the dining room, barely glancing in her direction before taking a seat at the table. Caroline, on the other hand, came in glowing and talking a mile a minute.

"Good morning, Katie," Caroline said. "Are you joining us for breakfast? How lovely!"

Caroline sat beside John, reaching over to lay her hand on his. Katie's nervousness changed to dread. Slowly, she took her seat, fighting the urge to run. Something wasn't right.

"Good morning," Katie said in return. "You seem happy."

Caroline giggled. "Who wouldn't be?" She turned toward John. "Can I tell her, John?" Not waiting for his permission, she forged forward in typical Caroline manner. "Oh, how silly of me. I just can't hold it in any longer. John and I are getting married. Aren't you just thrilled for us?"

Caroline continued to babble, but Katie had no idea what she said from that point. Her brain shut down. Her heart stopped. All the blood in her body rushed to her ears, and the buzzing, whirling sound threatened to send her to the floor.

Swallowing, despite the cotton that suddenly filled her mouth, she looked at John, imploring him to explain. He closed his eyes as though he was in pain and when he finally opened them, he kept them focused on his plate. Obviously, he had no intention of explaining anything. He regretted what they'd done so much, he wouldn't even look at her.

Katie stood and walked from the room, not caring if she was being rude or if Caroline had finished her prattle. Her legs carried her to her room—thank goodness they were still working—where she rummaged through her trunk until she found her list. With a tearful dip of her pen in the inkwell, she marked John's name off the top. If only she could get him out of her heart as easily.

Maybe, if he weren't such a coward, John would've been able to look Katie in the eye, but he just couldn't yet. He hadn't even fully realized he'd agreed to any kind of engagement with Caroline. But the woman had a way of twisting everything he said, and her blurting of the news before he even had time to think made a mess of the situation. Katie must have felt devastated, but he couldn't talk to her with Caroline listening to their every word, if Caroline ever listened. For the last several moments, she hadn't quit talking long enough to breathe. He felt as though he had been caught up in a tornado.

He finally raised his gaze, surprised to learn that Katie was no longer in the room and Caroline's incessant chatting was directed toward him. "Beg pardon?"

"John, I swear, I think sometimes you don't listen to me at all. I asked if Christmas Eve would be a good time for the wedding. I thought we could have a small ceremony here, then plan a larger one when we return to New York."

"Ummm . . ." He didn't know where to start to get out of this nightmare.

"You could act a little more excited."

"It wasn't what I had planned."

"For a wedding?"

"For my life." He shouldn't have said that, probably. Caroline immediately bristled before attempting to look sympathetic, complete with a humble tip of her head.

"It wasn't what I'd planned either," she said, "but we're doing the right thing for Julia and for Lois."

"I suppose," he answered absently, which was an apt description for where his brain stayed for most of the morning. He absently ate breakfast before returning absently to his office, where he absently stared at some books, or was it the wall? It didn't matter. Absent stares have no purpose anyway.

Finally lunchtime rolled around, and he decided he needed to talk to Katie and pray that she understood why he was marrying Caroline. Then, with any luck at all, maybe he'd understand it himself.

Hesitantly, he walked to the kitchen only to find Mrs. Adkins making lunch.

"Mrs. Adkins?"

"Oh, hi, Dr. Keffer. My ankle's better now." She stuck out her booted foot and wiggled the ankle to prove her point. "So I come back to work. Katie said you was busy, so I didn't disturb you. I thought I'd just go ahead and start on lunch."

"Where's Katie?"

"She went on home. Said to tell you not to worry about her pay. She'd get it later."

He nodded, all his determination fizzling with amazing speed. "Oh," he said, because that was all he could come up with, and considering his current state of fizzle, it could have been worse.

The icy rain running down the back of Katie's neck fit nicely with her mood. Shifting her bundle of clothes to her other hip, she tromped over the muddy path to her cabin, determined not to cry. But that wasn't easy. She'd given herself to John wholeheartedly, sure he loved her as much as she loved him, but she'd been mistaken.

And it hurt.

Like nothing had ever hurt her in her life, his betrayal tore at her worse than the wolf ever could have.

With a quick stomp on the porch, she knocked the mud off her new boots and entered her cabin.

"Katie?" her grandma called from the kitchen. "Is that you?"

"Yes'm", she answered, heading straight for her bunk in the loft. The last thing she wanted to do was explain things to Grandma, or anyone else, for that matter.

"Are you home for good?" Pa asked as she climbed the steps.

For good had an ominous ring to it, adding to her depression and generally foul humor. She tossed her bundle on her cot before dropping beside it to feel properly sorry for herself.

For good. Was there really such a thing? Was this all the good she could expect in life? All she deserved?

"I'm home, Pa," she finally answered, "at least until I get married."

"Have you picked a beau, then?" Grandma asked, scurrying to stand beside Pa at the foot of the stairs.

"I'm marrying Randy." Her announcement jumped out with little thought, but the more she considered it, the better it sounded. Randy would give her hand some, healthy babies and that was all she'd ever wanted anyway. The fact that John hated him for living only made it that much sweeter.

It rained for two days and by the time the clouds emptied out, the temperature had dropped until the wet ground froze into frosty chunks. The last thing Katie wanted to do was head to town, but in her absence, Grandma had used the last of the flour and if they were going to eat, a trip to Frank's was Katie's only option. Besides, she needed to tell her fiancés that she'd made a decision. Chances were good she'd find Harold sitting around the stove, chatting with his friends.

"Mornin', Katie," Frank said when she stepped into the warm interior of his store. "How're you doin' today?"

She forced a smile, not too unlike the one John used to favor, and said, "I'm fine. I'm needin' some flour."

He nodded and proceeded to weigh out enough flour to fill a small sack while Katie turned toward the stove. Harold and Freddie were deep in discussion, raising their heads to look at her when she stepped around the fabrics.

"Katie," Harold said, walking toward her. "Me and Freddie was talking, and we think it's time for you to make your decision. I ain't getting any younger."

The jingle of Frank's door chime pulled Katie's attention to the newest customer to enter the store.

"Mornin' Katie," Randy said, smiling as he crossed the store to talk with her. "You're lookin' mighty pretty this mornin'."

She doubted it, but it was always nice to hear just the same. "Thank you." A twinge of nerves knotted her stomach. She supposed it was only fitting to inform him he was about to be married, but looking at him face-to-face while the other two watched made the duty uncomfortable at best. Then suddenly John and Caroline walked into the store, and her courage stepped up to the task.

"Glad I ran into y'all today." She could see John watching from the corner of her eye, Caroline hanging on his arm like a leech. "I've decided I want to marry Randy, if he's still willing."

"*Willin'?*" Randy hooted and slapped his thigh before grabbing Katie for a fierce hug. The hug didn't startle her as much as the kiss that followed, but the combination of the two left her embarrassed and totally rattled.

Harold's face flashed red enough to sizzle. "Wait a minute! Why would you want some hothead like him? He ain't got two nickels to rub together."

Freddie still hadn't said anything, but Katie got the distinct impression he was relieved to be off the hook. Randy, on the other hand, puffed up his chest and hooked his thumbs on his belt. "Well, apparently she ain't interested in rubbing nickels." He wrapped his arm around Katie's waist, tugging her against him while he grinned at Harold. "You lose."

Harold smacked his thigh and stormed away. "Come on, Freddie," he said over his shoulder. "Ain't no use trying to talk sense into her."

Freddie glanced down at the floor before gulping once and saying, "Good luck, Katie." Then he gave her a quick peck on the cheek before hurrying back to the stove.

Randy chuckled. "Well, at least Freddie is smart enough to realize the best man won. When do you want to tie the knot?" His smile sparkled and for a second, his excitement was contagious.

"The sooner the better." She tried her level best not to let her eyes drift toward John, but Caroline was dragging him across the store, too close to ignore.

Smiling as though Katie were her closest friend,

Caroline said, "I couldn't help but overhear. So it's official now? You and Mr. Kopp are getting married?"

With a lift of her chin, Katie looped her arm through Randy's and smiled. "Yes, it's official."

A strange glint in Caroline's eye made Katie wonder if she was pleased or jealous. Though why would Caroline be jealous? She was getting the man of her dreams.

"John," Caroline said, her tone admonishing, "aren't you going to congratulate them?"

Katie allowed herself to look at John for the first time since he'd walked into the store. A muscle in his jaw twitched as his eyes locked on to hers, making her knees weaken. He seemed angry and hurt, as though he had the right. He was the one who'd abandoned her, not the other way around. If anyone had the right to be hurt, it was Katie. And she did hurt, more than she'd thought humanly possible.

But she couldn't let him know that, so she lifted her chin and said, "Aren't you happy for us, Dr. Keffer?"

John's gaze narrowed slightly before he glanced toward Randy. "Congratulations, Mr. Kopp. It appears as though you've won the highly sought after prize."

Randy chuckled, his chest puffing with pride and a hint of a challenge. "I always do."

Katie fought the sick feeling that landed in her belly, as Randy's comment caused her earlier concerns to rear up. Randy had won his trophy calf after all. She guessed she shouldn't have expected that he'd fallen in love with her—she surely wasn't in love with him—but a reaction other than hubris would have been nice.

"Katie," John said, "I need to speak with you if you

have a moment. Could you stop by the house on your way out of town?"

She didn't want to, but she could and that was what he'd asked. "Yes. I'll be there shortly."

Giving a brief nod in parting, John escorted the leech from the fabrics as Katie released a pent-up breath.

Randy patted her hand, still hooked in the crook of his arm. "I've got to go, darlin'." He pecked a quick kiss on her cheek. "There's a lot of people who need to know there's a big wedding comin'."

She smiled as he hurried away, hoping her smile looked genuine and wishing she felt half the exuberance he did.

John paced across his office, never allowing his eyes to stray from the window facing the street. He didn't think Katie would refuse to stop by his house after she'd said she would, but he wasn't willing to take the chance. Seeing Katie with Randy ripped open the wound in his soul that he'd thought had finally healed.

Rubbing his wedding ring, he tried to convince himself that marrying Caroline was the right decision. Julia needed a mother, and Lois had always known what was best for their little girl. If she thought Caroline would raise their daughter right, who was he to argue? He certainly hadn't been the father Julia needed these last two years.

And now that Katie was marrying someone else—

The door chime clanged.

"I'll get it, Mrs. Adkins," he said, taking a deep

breath to bolster his courage as he hurried to the front door. Katie stood on the porch, cheeks pink from the cold, sadness in her gray eyes. He stepped back to allow her into the foyer and motioned for her to enter the parlor.

"Thank you for coming by." He followed her into the room, thinking how natural it felt for her to be there. "May I take your coat?"

"I won't be staying long," she said, and he missed her already. "What was it you needed to speak to me about?"

Stepping behind his desk, he opened the top drawer and pulled out an envelope. "I owe you the rest of your wages."

She hesitated for a second, a flash of hurt crossing her face, before she reached for the envelope. "Thank you," she muttered. He hoped she didn't look inside until she was home, else she'd surely return part of it. He'd more than doubled what he owed her, at least monetarily.

"I also owe you an explanation," he added.

Lifting her eyes from the envelope, she caught his gaze before quickly averting hers. "You owe me nothing."

"Please," he said, walking around the desk, "give me a moment."

She paused, then nodded and walked to a chair near the fire. Taking the one facing her, he tried to decide where to start. He probably should have decided that before now, but a part of him never expected her to actually stop by.

He took a deep breath. "The morning after we . . ."

He stopped. There was no delicate way to put what they'd done, and referring to it as making love would only add pain to an already painful situation.

So he started again. "The morning after the party, Caroline came to see me in my office. She told me something that changed . . ." He stopped again. Telling Katie he'd planned to marry her would serve no purpose either. She'd never said she wanted him, and even if she did, it was a moot issue now.

Another deep breath, followed by a sigh. This was harder than he'd expected. "She said Lois had told her that if anything ever happened to her, she wanted Caroline and me to marry and raise Julia together. It was her last wish."

He willed Katie to look at him, but she'd stared at the fire ever since sitting down as though the rambling he'd done had not been aloud.

"I'm sorry. If I'd known earlier, I never would have . . ." He ran his hand down his face, wishing the floor would open up and swallow him. "I never would've come to your room." It was a feeble apology for taking the woman's virginity, especially since he knew in his heart he wouldn't trade those moments with her for anything. They were what he'd live on for the rest of his life.

She continued to stare ahead for an eternity before finally turning toward him. Her eyes overbright with unshed tears, her pallor no longer pink but ashen, he regretted his desire for her to look at him. If pain had a face, he was gazing at it.

"I'm not a child, John."

"I didn't mean to imply—"

"And I don't appreciate you acting as though I didn't have any control over my life and my decisions." She stood and headed toward the door.

"I'm sorry, I—"

"We both picked fiancés according to our wants and needs," she said, her back to him as she strode across the room.

"Do you love him?"

Katie stopped, turning to face him, a defiant lift to her chin. "What woman wouldn't love a man as handsome as Randy Kopp?"

A knife entered his heart. "Is handsomeness a good enough reason for marriage?"

"Better than yours. At least my life isn't being ruled from a grave."

Chapter Twenty-six

"Why have you been moping around here like some-one killed your favorite hound?" Grandma said, carry-ing her cane into the kitchen. "You'd think that marrying a man like Randy Kopp would have you smilin' like a fool."

Katie had hoped that by keeping to herself in the week since she'd seen John, Grandma wouldn't ask questions. She should've known better.

"Hay fever," she said, wiping at the tear that just had to take that moment to roll down her cheek.

"I ain't never heard of no one having hay fever so late in the year," Grandma grumbled, adding a dash of salt to the gravy bubbling in the skillet. "Whatever it is, you need to snap out of it. Your wedding day ain't that far away. Christmas Eve is going to be here before you know it, and your groom is going to want a happy bride."

"Well then," Katie said, slapping the biscuit dough as though it were the one nagging her, "I'll be sure to perk myself up before the big day. I wouldn't want ev-eryone to be disappointed in me."

"Katie?" Grandpa yelled from the front room. "Doc's here to see you."

Katie froze. She hadn't spoken to John since he'd

explained his reasons for marrying Caroline. He deserved to be smacked with her skillet, but it was full of salty gravy at the moment. So instead, she jerked off her apron, smoothed her hair into her bun, and washed the flour from her hands. With a quick adjustment to her bodice, she took a calming breath and headed for the living room.

John stood just inside the door, coat still fastened, hat clutched in his hand. "Hello, Katie."

"John," she said by way of greeting, pleased her voice sounded composed. "Did you want a word with me?"

He nodded, then glanced at her family glowering at him as though they were ready to whup him if necessary. They would have to wait their turn.

"I would like to have a moment with you," he said, "but do you think we could go to the porch?"

"Yes," she said, crossing the room to get her coat. At least if they went to the porch, she was guaranteed to be the first in line for the whupping.

He waited while she put on her coat, then opened the door to step outside. Crossing to the edge of the porch, she forced herself to turn and face him. All the thousands of things she'd wanted to say to him suddenly flew out of her mind as she looked into his eyes. She'd missed them so much. "What was it you wanted to talk to me about?"

Reaching into the front of his coat, he pulled out a book. "I was packing things up for the move, and I came across this. I would like for you to have it."

He handed her the book.

Her book.

"*Romeo and Juliet*," she whispered, running her

hand across the leather binding. "Thank you," she said, noticing the warmth of his body still emanated from the book, and she'd bet if she lifted it to her nose, it would smell like him too.

"So," he said, filling the pause, "when are you and Randy getting married?"

"Christmas Eve."

"In the morning?"

She nodded.

"I'm getting married in the afternoon."

"Oh." It wasn't much by way of conversation, but at least she wasn't in tears.

They stood for a moment, their breaths leaving foggy wisps in the cold morning air. Until she said, "You're moving back to New York?"

"Yeah," he said, "Caroline wants to live there."

"At least now you won't have to mess up any more rooms in your home."

He lifted his brow, the corner of his mouth turning up slightly. "You knew?"

"I suspected."

"I should've known better than to try to fool you."

She wasn't so sure about that. He'd made a better fool out of her than most. "Why did you hire me?"

"So people would stop by to see me." He glanced away as though his answer embarrassed him. "I figured if you were there, they would trust me more."

"Oh." Here came those darned tears. She blinked them back. "It worked."

"Like a charm," he said, but with more sadness than pride. "Before I forget, Julia wanted me to ask you if you're coming to the Christmas Pageant. She said you helped make her wings and she wanted you to see her be an angel. There's going to be a little party at my house afterward for everyone who comes to the play."

"I don't know—"

"It means a lot to her," John added when Katie attempted to refuse.

But how could she refuse Julia? "I'll try."

"I also want you to keep Lightning and the wagon."

"I can't do that—"

"Just until after the wedding. I know you're going to make several trips into town, and I don't want you walking through the snow."

He waited for her response and when she gave none added, "Please."

She nodded and dropped her eyes, finding it difficult to look at him.

Another uncomfortable quiet engulfed the porch.

"Well," he finally said when the silence started screaming, "I guess I should be on my way."

Not trusting herself to speak, she simply raised her eyes. He took a step toward the stairs, then turned back to her. Laying his hand on the side of her face, he leaned into her, pressing a kiss against her cheek. "Good-bye, Katie," he whispered, then hurried away.

Or at least she thought he hurried away, but by the time his feet hit the ground, her tears blurred her vision beyond hope.

Lord have mercy. Grandma was walking to church and Katie wasn't. If that wasn't proof the world had turned upside down, nothing was. Grandpa glanced over at his wife, debating whether to ask why she'd suddenly decided not to die and to head to church instead. She hadn't been working very hard at dying lately and that meant all her energy was directed elsewhere.

Lord have mercy.

"All right," he finally said, deciding he might as well get it over with, "what's on your mind?"

"Katie ain't happy," Grandma said, stomping down the trail toward town with a breakneck pace.

"She don't seem to be," he answered, relieved he wasn't the reason for Grandma's current snit.

"A soon-to-be bride should be tickled to death, but she's as blue as I've ever seen her."

"Yup," Grandpa answered. Seemed a safe enough response. He glanced over at Gil, wondering if he had a thought in his head, but decided it didn't matter. When Grandma got like this, no one else's thoughts were needed anyway.

"We got to do something about it," she said.

Grandpa sighed. He hated to ask, but it did involve Katie. "What can we do?"

"I've been thinking about that. She ain't happy because she don't want to marry Randy. I can't understand it, but she's got her heart set on the doc."

"But he's marrying that other woman."

"Don't matter," Grandma said, and Grandpa gulped.

"What do you mean, 'it don't matter'?"

"As much as it pains me to admit it, Katie and Doc love each other. I seen it when they danced together at her party, and if you hadn't been eating everything on the table, you would've seen it too."

He'd seen it. Sort of. "I still don't know what we can do. The weddings are in three days."

Grandma grinned. "That's enough time to set this straight and still have two days to spare."

Lord have mercy.

Katie never dreamed that going to church would be so difficult. She'd managed to stay away from town ever since she'd left John's, sure she would break into tears if she saw him with Caroline again and maybe without. It would be too humiliating for others to know how much she hurt, especially since everyone thought she was happily engaged to Randy. Now if she could just continue that ruse.

She smiled and accepted everyone's best-wishes before the Christmas Pageant got under way. She was grateful when the angels began making their way into the sanctuary. Most were singing "Silent Night," though one or two must have taken singing lessons from Pa. They were on different notes, maybe even different songs. It was hard to tell.

"Cute little rascals, aren't they?" Randy whispered. For a second, she'd forgotten he was sitting beside her. It seemed odd to have him there, but since they were getting married in the morning, it would probably be odder if he weren't.

She smiled up at him and nodded. "About as cute as they can get."

Randy reached over and took her hand, folding it into his. She remembered John's hand engulfing hers and somehow found Randy's lacking. She glanced at him, hoping a glimpse of his blue eyes would erase the memories of certain green ones, but it didn't work. For the first time since she'd met Randy, he wasn't handsome or charming. He was just Randy. The sparkling blue eyes were just eyes and those darling dimples were now just dents in the man's cheeks.

Sigh. It was going to be a long wedding night.

A timid wave from Julia brought Katie's attention back to the stage and her favorite angel, who proceeded to point to her wings as though Katie didn't notice them tied to her back. They'd spent hours gluing chicken feathers to the paper cutouts, and the result was perfect. Beautiful white, feathery wings peeked around Julia's shoulders, though they tipped slightly to the left. But that wasn't Julia's fault. Billy was plucking feathers off on that side, and Katie prayed Julia wouldn't notice.

Mary and Joseph entered the stage, shifting Julia's attention. The little girl waved to someone on the other side of the church.

Dare she look? Katie allowed her gaze to flitter across the sanctuary to John, her heart jumping to her throat. So handsome in his suit, his hair combed perfectly and a slight smile lifting the corner of his mouth, he waved subtly at Julia. Before Katie could look away, he turned toward her and their gazes locked.

His mouth opened slightly as though he was going to say something, but before his lips moved, a loud smack drew attention back to the stage.

Julia had noticed Billy's plucking, and now he was wailing from a walloping. Served him right, but it managed to stop the play for a moment while Rebecca Fisher and Eunice Kopp hurried to the stage to calm the angels before someone else got hurt.

John contemplated rising to his feet to retrieve his

avenging angel, but decided to relax when the ladies got everything quickly back under control. Billy was moved to the other side of the angel chorus, and Julia's wings were straightened, though she continued to pout.

With a handful of retrieved feathers, Julia folded her arms across her chest and refused to sing the next two numbers. John tried not to grin at his daughter's spunk.

"She'll have to be punished as soon as we return home," Caroline muttered beside him. "She's ruined the entire pageant."

For a brief second, John imagined stuffing the detached feathers into Caroline's mouth. Not a smart thought for a bridegroom to hold on the night before his wedding. So he patted Caroline's hand. "She was protecting herself," he whispered, in an attempt to smooth over the incident.

"She was behaving like a hoyden," Caroline whispered back, "and the sooner we get her away from these people, the better."

Instead of explaining a few things to Caroline about *these people*, John focused on the rest of the play, not noticing until the end that his arms were folded across his chest not too unlike his daughter's. But at least he wasn't pouting. Much.

The last song rang out with jubilation, and then Julia bounced off the stage and straight to Katie's arms. John watched, wondering again how Katie could choose a man like Randy. That imbecile would never treat a woman like Katie right.

"Hard to believe, ain't it?" Harold Crowley stepped beside John in the aisle.

"What's that?" John responded, his eyes still fastened on Katie.

"That she'd pick that hotheaded whelp when she could've had a real man."

John started to make some humble comment, but before he had the chance, Harold snorted. "Yep, I'd have married her in a second."

"Hell, who wouldn't have?" John mumbled, temporarily forgetting he stood in the church aisle with his fiancée close behind.

Luckily, no one seemed to hear. Harold stormed off in his typical huff and Julia rushed to him for help with her wings. She insisted they be tied back on after they were removed to put on her coat. In the ensuing rewinging, John lost sight of Katie and, for a second, felt as though he'd lost much more.

His spirits lifted immediately, however, when he entered his home to find Katie among the guests in his parlor.

"Well," Caroline said sarcastically, "it's nice to see something return a smile to your face tonight."

He sighed, suddenly tired of her gibes. "I happen to like *these people*," he said, removing his coat and leaving Caroline standing in the foyer. Terribly rude, he knew, but Caroline would get over it. For now, he had to figure out a way to casually find his way to Katie.

He needed to talk to her.

He needed to make love to her.

He needed to stop those thoughts. They were foolish and would do nothing but cause pain. They were both marrying other people tomorrow. Of course, that didn't mean he couldn't enjoy a few moments with her before their lives took them in opposite directions. They could pass the time as any parting friends would, nothing more.

With feigned interest in the cookies on the buffet table, he crossed the room, closer to Katie's side. Randy handed her a cup of punch, then kissed her cheek.

John's gut knotted as his mind tortured him with images of what Randy would be doing to Katie this time tomorrow night. Luckily, laughter and a round of applause directed everyone's attention to the doorway of the parlor where Rebecca and Paul Fisher stood under a sprig of mistletoe. The couple exchanged a kiss, much to the delight of the children and the envy of John.

He wondered if they had any idea how lucky they were to be married to the one they loved.

"Daddy?" Julia tugged on his sleeve. She stood before him, Harvey clutched tightly to her chest. The cat's long body dangled almost to Julia's knees. She looked up at John, a tear perched precariously on the edge of her lashes. "Am I in trouble?"

He knelt to her level. "For what?"

"Smacking Billy."

John rubbed his chin, buying a second to think about his response. "It probably would've been better had you not done that in church."

"Aunt Caroline said I was wicked."

He started to say that Aunt Caroline was a witch, then bit back his words along with a hint of panic. She *wasn't* a witch. She was his fiancée and by this time to-morrow night she was going to be his wife—and Julia's mother. Some things were going to have to be sorted out and quickly, but theirs would be a marriage not unlike many of his friends'.

They would live in polite society with polite friends and have polite dinner parties.

And he would probably go crazy, albeit politely.

"You're not wicked," he said, suddenly remembering his daughter's need for validation. "You're the best little girl any daddy could ever want."

Julia threw her arms around his neck, Harvey and all, and hugged him fiercely before bouncing away to play with the other children. He stood, surprised by her reaction. Didn't she know how he felt? Then again, why should she? He'd been unaware of his feelings himself until recently. Until Katie.

Panic welled up again, threatening to choke the life from him. Now was not the time to have second thoughts and hearing Katie's voice just behind him was not helping things any, so he crossed the room to ask Rebecca about her new baby.

Katie had no idea how closely she was watching John until Caroline's voice spoke to her from nowhere. Only it wasn't from nowhere. It was from Caroline, and she was standing right in front of Katie. "Good evening, Katie. Are you excited about tomorrow?"

"Excited" wasn't the word she would have picked, but then again, most of her first picks hadn't been working out for her lately. "Of course. How about you?"

Caroline's smile froze on her face, and her eyes flickered to Katie's left. Randy had returned to her side with a cookie and a smile. He gave Katie the cookie and Caroline the smile. A strange look passed between them that caused Caroline to flush and forget that Katie was in the room. If she didn't know better, she'd bet Randy had forgotten that too, but Katie didn't care about that as much as she was grateful for the opportunity to excuse herself from their company.

Julia was standing across the room, and she looked like she could use another cookie. The fact that she was with her father was just a coincidence.

"Julia," Katie said, handing her the treat, "you were wonderful in the play tonight."

"Aunt Caroline thinks I was wicked for hitting Billy," Julia said.

Katie glanced up at John in time to see the muscle clench in his jaw, displeasure showing clearly on his face. "I'm sure that's not what she meant," Katie answered, but she knew to her bones it was exactly what Caroline had meant. How could John marry such a woman?

Her eyes begged an answer, but before he could give one, Julia giggled.

Katie tore her gaze from John's long enough to ask, "What's so funny?"

Julia pointed up to the sprig of dark green leaves with its little white berries, hanging just above their heads. "You and Daddy have to kiss now. You're under the mistletoe."

Katie looked up at John, waiting for him to make an excuse, but instead he stepped closer to her and slipped his hand behind her neck. The warmth of his touch threatened to destroy all her carefully built defenses. He leaned toward her, his breath brushing the side of her cheek, his eyes closing just before his mouth covered hers.

And the memories returned.

The memories of his touch, his taste, his heat and passion, all the things she'd fought to forget came back in an instant, flooding through her with bittersweet tenderness. He pulled hesitantly back, and in his eyes she saw the longing she felt. He started to say something, but before he had the opportunity, Randy jerked him away from her and shoved him into the foyer.

"You son of a bitch," Randy said, pointing his finger in John's face. "I've had about all I'm going to take of you goin' after my girl!"

"Randy," Katie pleaded, pulling on his arm. "It was just a friendly kiss under the mistletoe."

"His lips was on your lips. That ain't no friendly kiss." He turned toward Katie. "Get on back in the other room. I'm going to whup him."

John stepped toward him. "Don't talk to Katie that way."

Randy shook his fist at him. "What are you going to do about it?"

"You don't want to know," John said, anger flashing in his eyes.

"Stop it! Both of you," Katie said, but it was too late.

Randy jerked open the door. "Come on outside, unless you want me to whup you here in front of everyone."

John followed Randy outside, removing his jacket

as he stepped off the porch into the snowy night. Katie rushed onto the porch, followed by several of the guests who'd heard the commotion.

"Please, stop it!" she shouted, but insanity had already taken over and it had an audience. There was no turning back now. John was about to take a beating and the whole town was going to watch.

The two men circled each other, watching and waiting on the first strike until finally Randy took a swing at John and surprisingly missed. John timed his duck perfectly, rising to connect his fist soundly into Randy's jaw, sending him unceremoniously onto his rump and into the snow.

The shock of John's blow infuriated Randy. With a guttural roar, he scrambled to his feet, tackling John, and down they went, rolling in the snow, swinging fists and cursing shamelessly.

Katie quickly glanced around to make sure none of the children were witnessing this display of male foolishness before returning her attention to the men in the yard and the rather creative names they hurled at each other.

John threw a blow that snapped Randy's head to the side and brought a gasp from the woman standing beside Katie. Surprisingly, the woman was Caroline.

"John!" Caroline shouted. "Stop hitting Randy, right now!"

Stop hitting Randy? Since when did Caroline refer to Randy by his first name? And why wasn't she worrying about her own fiancé?

Katie frowned and looked over at Caroline, who

stood wringing her hands as though she was about to faint. "Shouldn't you be telling Randy to quit hitting John?"

Caroline sneered at Katie. "Randy is the one getting hurt. Besides, John deserves it after what you two did."

"It was just a Christmas kiss under the mistletoe." Katie knew it wasn't any such thing. Based on the glare Caroline threw at her, she knew it too. Katie didn't grin. She wanted to, but luckily Caroline stormed into the house before the grinning temptation won out.

Katie returned her attention to the fools in the snow, praying they wouldn't kill each other on the eve of their weddings.

Finally exhaustion won out and they parted, staggering to their feet to wipe mud and blood from their faces with the backs of battered hands.

"Had enough?" Randy asked, panting as he bent over to lean on his knees.

"Only if you have," John answered with a pant of his own. He stood with his hands on his hips, a lock of his hair falling over his eye and the cut at the corner of his brow, and it was all she could do not to run to him to tend to his wounds. But that was Caroline's job, regardless of the fact that she had disappeared.

"Huh," Frank Davis grunted next to Katie. "The doc done all right, didn't he?"

Katie didn't feel it would be appropriate to respond, despite the fact that she agreed with Frank. John had done more than all right. She had the feeling Randy had been the one to end up with the whupping.

Evidently, Randy did too. He stuck out his hand toward John. "Glad we got that settled, Doc."

John hesitated only a second before grabbing Randy's hand for a brief shake.

"Come on, everybody," Frank said. "Show's over." The guests on the porch followed Frank into the house, leaving Randy, John, and Katie outside.

Randy walked to the porch rail to get his coat just as Caroline returned.

"Randy?" she said, stepping down the steps, in her hand the sprig of mistletoe, which she lifted over his head. "I believe we owe them a kiss of our own."

Katie's jaw dropped. Randy pulled Caroline into his arms and kissed her like there was no tomorrow. Or at least like there were no weddings tomorrow.

When they finally separated, a frazzled Caroline entered the house without bidding John good night, and an equally rattled Randy walked away without speaking to Katie.

"I don't guess we have the right to get mad," Katie said, rubbing her arms against the cold of the night air.

John shrugged. "Caroline was just teaching me a lesson, well deserved."

"I guess Randy was doing the same thing."

John climbed the steps, stopping just in front of her. She clasped her hands tightly together to keep from touching his slightly swollen cheek or brushing the hair from his face.

"He's an idiot," he said. "I kissed you against your will. The same could not be said of our fiancés."

She didn't correct him as he stepped into the house. Whether he kissed her had nothing to do with Lois's dying wish or his determination to grant it. Based on his lack of concern over his fiancée kissing Randy, their marriage wouldn't be based on love anyway.

It would be based on guilt.

Chapter Twenty-seven

Dearest Randy,
*   I ain't been able to thank of nothing sept you*
ever since we met. Please meat me at Frank's store
at tin o clock this mornin. We need to talk. I'm a
feared we are both bout to make a mistake.
*   Yours truly,*
*   Caryline*

Grandma neatly folded the note, unable to contain her grin as she handed it to Billy. Randy had no reason to believe it wasn't real, and based on the kiss she'd witnessed through Doc's window, he'd take the bait like a hungry trout. "Now, remember what I told you?"

Billy nodded. "We're doing this for Katie."

"That's right," she said, patting the tyke on the head. "You run on to the Koppses' and give this to Randy, then let me know when he leaves."

Grandma watched Billy race down the street through the early morning snowflakes before she headed for Frank's store. Timing was everything.

"Is everything ready, Frank?" Grandma walked into his store and straight for the stove. The snow was falling in big fluffy flakes, and a few had managed to slip down the back of her coat. The fire felt good.

Frank walked from the back room, a grin plastered across his face. "It's just like we planned. You want to see?"

Leaving the warmth of the stove, Grandma followed Frank to the back room and chuckled. Frank had been busy. A pile of blankets in the corner, a small table with a lamp, and a basket with bread and cheese should keep the couple happy for their short confinement.

The distance from the stove caused Grandma to chill. "They're goin' to have to snuggle to keep warm."

"Yep." Frank's eyes twinkled. Who'd have thought he could be such an imp?

Now the challenge would be making it appear accidental.

"Did you fix the doorknob?" Grandma asked as she returned to her spot by the fire.

Frank grinned. "Observe." He pulled on the knob and sure enough, it came off in his hand. Had the door been closed, he would have been unable to leave the room without help. Excellent.

"Did you give her the note?" Grandpa helped himself to another one of Mrs. Adkins's cookies while he waited at Doc's kitchen table.

"Yep," Mrs. Adkins said, lowering her voice with a snicker. "I done just like you said."

"Did she believe it? What did she say?"

Mrs. Adkins snorted. "Miss Caroline don't talk to the likes of me, but she read the note, then blushed like a schoolgirl."

At the sound of the front door closing, Grandpa and

Mrs. Adkins hurried down the hall to look out the window. A well-bundled Caroline tromped through the snow in the direction of Frank's store.

Grandpa chuckled. "Things is goin' real good, so far." Glancing at his pocket watch, he smiled. "We got thirty minutes before we start on Doc. Time for more cookies."

Mrs. Adkins grinned. "I done started on Doc."

"Pa, can't you make Lightning go a little faster?" Katie asked. "I don't want to be late for my wedding."

"Now, Katie girl," Pa answered, "you know Randy ain't goin' nowhere."

"At the moment, neither is Lightning."

Katie was in a miff and even though Pa normally would have hated putting her there, this morning he was proud of it. Worked darned hard at it, in fact. Katie had ironed three of his shirts before he'd found the right one for the wedding. Then he spilled something on it. He dressed slow enough to grow moss and holding Lightning back wasn't easy. Well, maybe that part hadn't been hard, but he could've encouraged the mule a little more than he had.

He'd do his part to help make Katie happy, if she didn't kill him first.

"I hope Grandma and Grandpa have everything ready at the church." Katie pulled her scarf closer around her head and flipped up the collar of her coat to keep the snow from falling on her neck. "Are you sure you can't hurry this mule up?"

It took all Pa's willpower not to chuckle. "I think he don't like the snow. Don't worry." He paused to pat Katie's hand. "Your pa's got everything under control."

At the sound of the front door closing, John stepped to his bedroom window to peer out at the street. Caroline hurried through the snow, clutching her coat against her chest, her scarf barely covering her blonde curls. Odd she should run an errand when the wedding was only a few hours away. Maybe she needed to tend to something at the church.

John left his window to throw another log on the fire in his grate. He'd spent most of the morning in his room, coming to grips with his decision. He didn't love Caroline, never would. But most of the couples he knew were not love matches. That was why his marriage to Lois had been so special. He'd loved her.

Just like he loved Katie.

Why did he insist on torturing himself with these thoughts? He hurt badly enough without continually ripping open the wounds. Katie had chosen Randy. And in less than an hour, she was going to be his wife. The lucky little bastard had better realize what a prize he had truly won.

He walked to his washstand and splashed cold water on his bruised and battered face. His cheek was slightly swollen and a cut marked the edge of his brow. He only hoped Randy looked worse.

He retrieved his wedding suit from the back of a chair and removed his dressing gown. Mrs. Adkins had repaired the hem on his trousers and ironed his shirt just that morning. At least his clothes would look better than his face.

Quickly stepping into his trousers, he unfolded his shirt, not noticing the large scorched mark on the front until he faced the mirror to fasten the buttons.

"Hell," he grumbled, jerking off the shirt.

The expensive fabric of his hand-tailored shirt was ruined beyond repair. Mrs. Adkins must have left the iron sitting on the damned shirt while she fixed breakfast or plowed the garden. A mark like that couldn't happen quickly.

He opened his wardrobe to find another shirt, only to see it totally empty. No shirts, no trousers, no shoes. Nothing except a pair of socks that didn't match.

"Hell," he repeated, deciding it was an appropriate sentiment given the circumstances. He sat on the side of the bed to pull on his unmatched socks thinking the hem on his slacks didn't appear quite right. Standing, he looked at his reflection in the cheval mirror. One pant leg was shorter than the other by a good four inches.

"Mrs. Adkins!" he bellowed, leaving his room to cross the hallway and lean over the stair rail.

"Yes, Dr. Keffer?" She entered the downstairs hallway and looked up at him.

"My shirt is ruined, and I can't find another. Where are the rest of my clothes?"

She brought her hand to her mouth, her eyes widening. "I'm sorry. All your shirts are in the laundry. I thought you'd want them clean for your trip."

"Can you get one out?"

"No. They're all sopping wet."

"What about my slacks?"

She wrinkled her brow. "What about them?"

He moved so she could see his pants legs. "Notice anything unusual?"

She studied for a moment, turning her head first one way, then another, before she finally answered, "No."

"Great," he mumbled. Evidently he needed to get Mrs. Adkins a new pair of eyeglasses before he left for New York.

"Anything else?" she asked.

If he were a glutton for punishment, he'd ask about his other trousers. "No, thank you. I'll tend to it myself." He returned to his room to put on his shoes. At least there was a right one and a left one, even if they weren't from the same pair. They would go with the rest of his outfit perfectly.

Grandma darted behind the bolts of fabric in Frank's store as soon as she saw Randy heading across the street. She couldn't take the chance that seeing her would make him change his mind.

The jingle of the bell on Frank's door signaled Randy's arrival. "Mornin', Frank."

"Mornin', Randy. I was lookin' for you to get here. Miss Humboldt said you was to wait for her in the back room."

Randy grunted, then hurried past the stove to the storeroom. Frank caught Grandma's eyes and gave her a wink just before Caroline jingled the bell.

"Good mornin', Miss Humboldt," Frank said, as though this morning were no different than any other.

"Good morning," she answered nervously. "I was wondering if . . ." She paused for a moment to glance around the room.

Frank grinned. "Randy said you was to meet him in the storeroom. Said you was needin' to talk."

She nodded, then followed Frank to the backroom, where he motioned for her to enter before saying, "I'll close the door to give y'all some privacy." Frank carefully closed the door so the knob wouldn't fall off until someone attempted to open it, then returned to his counter.

"Well, Mable," he said, grinning as he put on his coat, "I think it's time you and me take a walk."

John's jacket barely covered the scorched mark on his shirt, but he seriously doubted anyone would notice. Unless he stood knee deep in a snowdrift, his legs were going to garner all the attention. His left leg looked normal enough. His black shoe peeked from beneath the hem of a trouser leg of appropriate length. A person wouldn't even notice the brown argyle sock hidden beneath the black dress slacks. But his right leg needed to be amputated. Brown shoe and blue sock stood on display thanks to the ankle-high hem of that pant leg.

Perhaps he could ask Mrs. Adkins if she had time to fix the hem or at least help him locate his mysteriously missing shoes. He hurried down the stairs, only pausing for a quick glance at his watch at the landing. Eleven thirty. Katie had been married for thirty minutes, and in another hour it would be John's turn.

"Mrs. Adkins?" he asked, entering the kitchen. "Have you seen my shoes?"

Mrs. Adkins jumped, then laid her paring knife on the counter beside the potatoes she'd been peeling. She wiped her brow with her wrist.

"Sorry if I startled you," he said, "but have you seen my shoes?"

She said, "Yes," then stood silently as though waiting for the next question.

He sighed. "Where are they?"

The expression she gave him bordered on pity. "They're on your feet, Dr. Keffer."

Before he could point out the obvious problem with the shoes on his feet, Mrs. Adkins asked a question of her own. "Have you seen Julia?"

"Come to think of it, I haven't seen her all morning."

"Oh dear." Mrs. Adkins began wringing her hands. "I thought she was with you. I ain't seen her since breakfast."

John hurried from the kitchen, a knot forming in his stomach. It wasn't like Julia to wonder off on her own.

"Julia!" he yelled, bounding up the steps, checking each bedroom on the second floor.

A quick search in the library also came up empty-handed.

"She's not up here, Mrs. Adkins," he shouted as he returned down the stairs.

"Do you suppose she went to see Katie get married?" Mrs. Adkins asked. "She was talking about her at breakfast."

"Possibly. You stay here in case she returns, and I'll head to the church." Quickly, he grabbed his coat from the hall closet and darted from the house.

"Do you think I'm going to get in trouble?" Julia asked, joining Mrs. Adkins in the hallway after John left.

"No, honey," she answered, giving her a hug. "We'll tell your pa it wasn't your idea. If all goes the way we planned, he's going to be too happy to get mad."

Where was Randy? Not that Katie was eager to be married, but getting left at the altar didn't set well with her either. If they didn't hurry, John and Caroline would be arriving and nothing would ruin her wedding day more than to see the man she truly loved marry someone else.

Katie sat in the back of the sanctuary, holding a spray of pine twigs and sumac berries. The pretty red bow tied around the bunch had been Grandma's idea. Katie had been unable to get excited about any of the arrangements for the wedding. Looked like that was just as well. At this rate, there wasn't going to be a wedding, a least not hers.

No one was in the sanctuary except Katie, Pa, and Reverend Stoker. Maybe everyone else had gotten snowed in.

Suddenly the door opened and Katie turned to see John enter. He knocked the snow from his shoulders as he walked toward her.

"Have you seen Julia?" he said, apparently not noticing she'd been jilted.

"No," she answered, standing. "Why would you think she'd be here?"

"Mrs. Adkins said she hadn't seen Julia since breakfast and that she'd been talking about you. I'd hoped she was here." His brows furrowed with worry. "I don't know where else to look. It's snowing so hard outside, I can't imagine her just taking off like that."

"You say you're looking for Julia?" Pa asked, coming toward them from the front of the church.

"Yes," John answered. "Have you seen her?"

"Yep, I seen her a little while ago. She said something about going to Frank's store to see his new litter of kittens."

Katie laid her bouquet on the pew and picked up her coat. "I'm going with you," she said, buttoning her buttons.

"What about your wedding?"

It was all she could do not to snort. "Randy didn't show up. I guess he didn't want to marry me as much as he thought he did."

"What a fool," John said, and she wasn't sure if he was referring to the marriage or the bride, but she didn't have time to ponder that. He grabbed her hand and led her out of the sanctuary and into the storm.

They tromped through the snow, the wind blowing icy flakes against their faces, making discussion impossible. Good. She didn't want to talk about being jilted anyway. Compared to the thought of Julia being out in this weather, her lack of groom seemed trivial.

Shuddering, Katie stomped the snow from her boots and followed John into Frank's warm store. "Julia?" she yelled. "Frank?"

No one answered, but the sound of something falling came from the back room. John ran to investigate.

"Look," he said, picking up the doorknob from the floor. "Sounds like someone is locked in here. *Julia?*"

He wiggled the doorknob back into the door, then shoved it open.

Caroline stood in the center of the room. Her perfect blonde curls in disarray, her perfect gown rumpled and fastened lopsided. A smile plastered on her perfect face. Red but perfect.

"J-John," she stammered. "Thank goodness you're here. We've been locked in here for hours."

"We?" John asked.

Katie looked to the corner of the room where a pile of blankets were as disheveled as Caroline. Randy stood on them, tucking in his shirt. "Mornin', Katie," he said, minus his wink.

Katie took a deep breath, surprised to find herself more relieved than angry. At least now she didn't have to marry him. "Have you seen Julia?" she asked, as though finding her fiancé with another woman was an everyday occurrence.

"No," he answered, glancing at Caroline.

"I haven't seen her either," Caroline answered.

John nodded his head, then directed Katie back into the store before he closed the door behind him and removed the knob.

"They'll be locked in again," Katie said.

John shrugged. "They can thank us later."

The front door jingled and Frank stepped inside. "Mercy," he said, shaking the snow from his hat. "It's a fierce storm out there."

"Have you seen Julia?" Katie asked, ignoring the thumping on the storeroom door.

Frank ignored it too. "I seen her just a little bit ago

heading to your house, Doc. She said she was going home for lunch."

"Thank heavens," John murmured, grabbing Katie's hand to leave Frank's. "You might want to let them out in another hour or two," he said over his shoulder as he led Katie back into the storm.

By the time they reached his house, her teeth were chattering.

"Julia?" John yelled. "Mrs. Adkins?"

No one answered. The house was silent except for the music coming from the gramophone in the parlor. Katie followed John into the room, surprised to find no one gathered around the blazing fire, or listening to the beautiful waltz.

The puzzled expression on his face matched her feelings exactly. Then the door closed behind them, the following *click* indicating it was now locked.

"Julia's fine," Grandma said through the door.

"Hi, Daddy. Hi, Katie," Julia said, to prove Grandma wasn't lying.

"Now," Grandma said, "you two might as well get comfortable 'cause you ain't getting out of there until you sort this mess and quit making everybody else miserable. In the meantime, we're all going to Frank's for eggnog and cookies."

Noises of shuffling, stamping feet, and murmuring voices followed.

"How many of them are out there anyway?" John's question brought a smile to Katie's lips.

"Sounds like the whole town." She turned to look at him, and his mouth suddenly went dry.

Lashes glistening from melted snowflakes, her cheeks flushed from the bite of the cold, she was the only woman he knew who could be more beautiful every time he laid eyes on her.

"Would you like to warm up by the fire?" It wasn't what he really wanted to ask, but it was a start.

She nodded, unbuttoning her damp coat as she crossed the room to the hearth. He followed closely behind, depositing his coat with hers on a chair. They stood in front of the flames, warming icy hands and staring ahead silently until he finally asked, "Now what do we do?"

Her dimple sank into her cheek with her grin, and a modicum of relief drifted over him. Maybe she no longer hated him.

"I'm not marrying Randy."

"You sure as hell aren't."

Turning toward him, a brow lifted with an unspoken challenge, she said, "What makes you think you have the right to say whom I marry?"

"Because I love you."

Katie's mouth dropped and as much as he wanted to kiss it, he didn't. There were things that needed to be said, and it was well past the time to say them.

"What about Lois's wish?" she asked.

He took her hands in his and lifted them to his lips before pulling off his wedding ring and laying it on a table. "Lois would have wanted what's best for Julia. And I'm sure if she'd had a chance to know you, she would have realized what a wonderful mother you'd be. I think Caroline might have seen it too if she hadn't been so blinded by her own ambitions." He pulled Katie into his arms. "She came here to marry me, and she wasn't expecting to find you in my life." Brushing a curl from the side of her face, he said, "Then again, neither was I."

He cupped her face. "I love you, Katie. I never thought I would ever love again, but I was wrong. I've been wrong about a lot of things. And I'd like to spend the rest of my life making it up to you. Please forgive me and tell me that you'll become my wife." He paused when she didn't answer, then added, "You do love me, don't you?"

She smiled, the twinkle returning to her eyes, the blood returning to his veins. "You know," she said, "my list didn't require that I be in love with my husband."

It wasn't like Katie to be coquettish, but the sly up-turn of her lips and her lash-lowered gaze made his heart swell. She loved him. She hadn't said it yet, but he knew it without a doubt. Everything was going to be all right after all.

He pulled her closer to him, nuzzling her hair with his mouth. She smelled good. She felt good, and he was sinking fast. Her closeness warmed him, chasing away a chill that had nothing to do with snow. He felt her hands glide up his arms until her fingers threaded through the hair at the nape of his neck and a tingle ran down his spine.

Pressing his cheek against her temple, he said, "There wasn't anything about loving your husband, but I specifically remember a kissing requirement." He moved his lips across her brow. She quivered and turned her face up toward him. And that was all the permission he needed.

"Katie," he whispered, claiming her mouth in a kiss that had tormented him for weeks.

Soft and sweet, he lost himself in the fullness of her lips and the warmth of her soul. Her tongue darted to meet his, and the waltz was replaced with music of their own making, its dance more primitive and much more enticing.

The heat of her body warmed his hands as he ran his fingers across her back and down to her hips. Seeking her flesh through the layers of gown and petticoats, he fought the desire to rip the fabrics from her body and take her on the floor. But he was determined not to overwhelm her again. This time, there would be no lovemaking unless she wanted it as badly as he did . . . if that was possible.

With more willpower than he realized he possessed, he pulled his mouth from hers long enough to whisper, "Do you love me, Katie?"

She looked up at him, eyes drunk with passion, breath ragged in her breasts. "Yes," she answered.

"Do you want me?"

"Yes," she whispered.

Taking a step back from her, he released his grip, lowering his hands to his side. "Then take me."

The passion in her eyes changed quickly to confusion, and then a slow understanding filled their depths. The corner of her mouth lifted, and it was all he could do not to grab her again. But he stood at her mercy, praying she had none.

She placed her hands against his chest, sliding them up his shirtfront until she could slip his jacket from his shoulders. It fell to the floor, unneeded and forgotten. Next came his shirt. Button by button, she opened the front, stopping halfway down to press a kiss against his chest, followed by a flick of her tongue. He balled his fists at his sides, forcing himself to remain still, but the twinkle in her eyes told him he was in trouble.

She finished with the buttons, then proceeded to pull the shirttail from his waistband, walking behind him as she did. With a gentle tug, she dragged his shirt from his body to join the jacket on the floor. He couldn't see her, but he felt her breath as she placed tender kisses on his back, her hands slipping around his waist to caress his belly above his trousers.

Torture.

Sublime, tantalizing, exquisite torture.

He closed his eyes, languishing in the feel of her hands as she stroked his belly and chest, her cheek pressed against his back. Then she pulled away. He waited, trusting she wasn't finished, and the sound of her dress falling to the floor behind him, rewarded him for his trust.

Katie scooted the pile of clothing away from their feet, still unable to believe she had the courage to undress a man. But it wasn't just any man. It was John, and she loved him more than she'd thought was humanly possible.

Slowly, she walked around in front of him, clad only in her chemise and white, woolen stockings. Her breasts puckered by the slight chill in the room and the powerful heat of his gaze. The green of his eyes intensified as he studied her mouth, her throat, her breasts.

Not even attempting to hide his desire, he licked his lips, and she felt it low in her stomach.

She knew there was more and she wanted all of it, but they had waited a long time for this, and she intended to savor it slowly. Taking his hand, she led him to a chair and motioned for him to sit. She remembered the first time she'd seen him bared to the waist, a bee sting marring his shoulder. She'd wanted to touch him then but dared not.

Things had changed.

With brazen abandon, she walked around him, dragging her hands across his chest and shoulders, marveling at the firm, hard flesh, kneading the muscles beneath her fingertips. Then with even more daring, she slid her hands down his waist to brush them against the swollen bulge in his lap.

He gasped. "Are you trying to kill me?" His voice was raspy and pained.

She smiled. "Yes," she whispered, next to his ear, ending with a kiss against his cheek.

He leaned his head back on the chair, closing his eyes with a groan. "Good."

Something about the way he said "good" made a shiver tingle through her body. It purred and rumbled, promising all sorts of things she was eager to explore. Stepping around in front of him, she settled across his lap. She was fully aware of the way her chemise slid indecently up her thigh. She crossed her legs to add to the effect.

She gently touched the bruise on his cheek. "Does it hurt?"

His eyes smoldered. "Like hell."

She leaned into him to place a kiss at the corner of his eye. "Is that better?"

His lips curved in a slow grin. "That's not where it hurts," he said, grabbing her hips and grinding her bottom into the bulge she'd teased earlier.

Catching her gasp with his kiss, he took the game out of her hands, and it was about time. Her chemise bunched up around her waist as he slid his hand beneath to clutch her breast. Molding, caressing, teasing, he lifted her with his hand as he kissed and nibbled down her throat.

But he didn't stop there.

His lips dampened the fabric of her chemise as they sought and found the pebbled tip of her breast. Stopping only for a moment, he pulled the chemise over her head and returned to his treasure.

She felt the fire pooling in her as the sizzling sensations started by his tongue rolled through her body in pulses of heat. He must have felt her need, for his hand released its grasp of her breast and slid between her legs. Slowly he grazed the skin at the top of her stockings, tracing his fingers along the edge of the garters, brushing against the warmth of her thighs.

But he didn't stop there.

As his mouth suckled her breasts, his fingers delved into the part of her that throbbed for his attention. Squirming, she moved impatiently against his hand. The anticipation built by the second, but before she could find relief, he set her off his lap and quickly unfastened his trousers.

She had just a moment to see the bulge she'd only felt. He grabbed her hips and pulled her back to his lap, guiding himself into her as she faced him. The split second of embarrassment she felt for straddling him was replaced with primal need.

Hard and hot, he filled her. "Love me, Katie," he ground out against her throat, his hands grabbing her hips and pulling her onto his body.

She did love him, but right now she needed him. She needed him to stop the torture and ease the throb. She needed him to return her to sanity and give her back control of her body.

"Love me, Katie," he murmured again, and somewhere through the haze, she realized what he meant.

She started slowly. Rocking her hips, squeezing him inside her as she rocked. Each movement deeper and faster than the one before, she gained intensity, digging her fingers into his hair and jerking his head back for a crushing kiss.

Then she took.

She took from his mouth. She took from his body and just when she thought she'd scream from the madness, her body gave back all she had taken with an explosion of shudders.

Shaking and gasping, she clung to him as he did his own exploding, crying out her name as though calling for a lifeline.

She sat, clinging onto his neck, until the shudders stopped and the world settled back onto its axis.

Then embarrassment seeped in. Naked, sprawled across his lap, one stocking down about her ankles and half her hairpins on the floor, she realized there was no delicate way to extricate herself.

She attempted to move, but his arms tightened

around her waist, stopping her where she was. "You're not going anywhere until we settle a few things," he said, his mouth buried somewhere in the hair beside her neck.

She liked the feel of his breath against her skin. "Like what?"

"Reverend Stoker is waiting at the church to perform a wedding."

She giggled. "Actually, he's waiting for two weddings."

"That doesn't seem like a kind thing to do to a man on Christmas Eve."

She wiggled a little, enjoying his quick intake of air. "Who do you think he should marry?"

Suddenly he stood, lifting her in his arms, where he turned and sat her in the chair. He knelt in front of her, stumbling slightly over the trousers still gathered around his ankles.

Placing a quick kiss on the one knee covered by her stocking, he raised her hand to his lips and said, "I love you, Katie Napier. Please end my torture by marrying me today." He kissed the back of her hand.

She smiled. "I'll marry you, but why does it have to be today?" Other than the fact that she couldn't wait another moment either.

"I have no intention of letting you have your clothes until we're married, and you might freeze to death in this weather."

"Shouldn't I have my clothes to go to the church?"

He frowned, pretending to ponder her question for a second before shrugging. "I suppose, but Reverend Stoker better talk fast."

"If he talks fast, he's liable to join us in moldy ha-tromony. Doesn't that worry you?"

He smiled, then kissed the other knee. "Not as long as you agree to mold with me."

And she thought she just might.

But based on the way John's kisses had moved to her thigh, Reverend Stoker might have to wait a tad longer. . . .

Epilogue

Katie tucked Johnny's blanket closer to his chin as she, John, and Julia walked to church. The autumn morning was warm and Katie couldn't fight the urge to show off her new little bundle for the first time.

"Do you need me to carry him?" John asked.

Katie smiled. He'd fussed over her constantly since she had given birth. "We're fine."

"If you need me to help carry him," Julia said, "I'm here too."

"Thank you, sweetheart," Katie said to Julia. "Johnny is lucky to have you for a big sister."

Grandma hurried across the yard to see the baby. Grandpa and Pa followed as quickly as they could, but now that Grandma was done with dying, keeping up with her was a challenge.

"Let me look at that great-grandson of mine," she said, lifting the blanket from his face. "I swear he gets more handsome every day."

"Hi, Grandpa!" Julia said, running to Pa for a hug.

"Hi, Julia girl." Katie's pa lifted her into his arms to carry her into church like a man who'd never had a back pain in his life.

Eunice Kopp waddled over to speak to Grandma. "Well, Mabel, I'm glad to see that you're no longer dyin'."

Grandma snorted. "I can't bother with that now that there's younguns to raise." She waited while Eunice waddled into the church before leaning toward Katie and whispering, "That woman is an idiot."

Katie controlled her grin until Grandma and Grandpa entered the sanctuary and Freddie came by to speak.

"Morning, Katie," he said without blushing, no doubt due to the lady on his arm. Mary Thomas had fed him at the barn raising when his bandaged fingers couldn't hold a fork, and lately the two had frequently been seen together in town. Katie wouldn't be surprised to hear of a wedding for them before long.

Two steps later, Randy Kopp sauntered over to pay his respects. "You're looking might purty today, Katie."

Katie glanced up at John, who simply shrugged and said, "No arguments here," as though Randy didn't bother him in the least. Though she did notice he had stepped closer and slipped his arm around her waist.

"I'm going to have to whup him again," John muttered, once Randy ambled away.

Katie laughed. "Not on my account."

They had finally settled into their pew to await the beginning of the service when she noticed Julia's coat was still tightly fastened all the way to her neck.

"Julia, do you need help with your coat?"

"No," she said, but Julia was terrible at keeping secrets and the look on her face said she had a big one.

That was when Katie noticed a wiggle in one of Julia's pockets and a fuzzy yellow head poked out to look at her.

"Julia!" Katie said, lowering her voice. "Do you have one of Harvey's kittens in your pocket?"

Julia bit her lip while she thought for a moment before shaking her head.

Katie pointed to the ball of fur. "Then what's that?"

"You asked if I had *one* of Harvey's kittens." Just then a second head poked from her pocket.

"You have *two*?"

Julia grinned sheepishly and reached into her other pocket for the third kitten. Unfortunately, Harvey had given birth to six of them. But before Katie could further investigate, Reverend Stoker took the pulpit and asked the congregation to bow their heads in prayer.

Katie leaned toward Julia and whispered, "Please tell me you don't have all of Harvey's kittens in your pockets."

"I don't," she whispered back. "Mrs. Adkins said these were ornery for climbing up her skirts this morning, and I figured they needed a good churchin'."

"I don't think the Lord's salvation works on kittens," she said, hoping to prevent Julia from bringing in everything from chickens to butterflies in the future. "They can't understand Reverend Stoker."

John leaned to whisper in Katie's ear, "I can't understand him either."

A laugh blurted out before Katie could clamp her hand over her mouth. Then John's shoulders shook. He rubbed his hand across his mouth in an attempt to stop a case of church giggles, but he wasn't having much success. Served him right since he'd started it in the first place.

At that moment, Johnny decided to inform the congregation that he was awake and hungry. His face wrinkled as he released an earsplitting squall that sent Katie and her son from the sanctuary amidst the smiles and chuckles of the rest of congregation.

John waited a few minutes before deciding to follow Katie out into the churchyard. He knew she was more than capable of nursing their son without his help, but it was difficult for him to let her out of his sight.

He found her, sitting on a bench near the well, facing the woods for privacy. The autumn leaves crunched under his feet, alerting her to his arrival. She turned to him, smiling and he felt it to his soul.

He said, "I love you, Katie," because the words were as natural to him as breathing.

She scooted to allow him room to sit beside her on the bench and watch their son nurse. "You know," she said, brushing her hand across the top of his tiny head, "I think I need to add something to my list."

He scrunched his brows. "What list?"

"The list I had for the perfect husband."

"What do you want to add?"

Her eyes twinkled as she leaned toward him for a kiss. "I think it's important that I love him after all."

☐ **YES!**

Sign me up for the Historical Romance Book Club and send my FREE BOOKS! If I choose to stay in the club, I will pay only $8.50* each month, a savings of $6.48!

NAME: _____

ADDRESS: _____

TELEPHONE: _____

EMAIL: _____

☐ I want to pay by credit card.

☐ VISA ☐ MasterCard ☐ DISCOVER

ACCOUNT #: _____

EXPIRATION DATE: _____

SIGNATURE: _____

Mail this page along with $2.00 shipping and handling to:
Historical Romance Book Club
PO Box 6640
Wayne, PA 19087
Or fax (must include credit card information) to:
610-995-9274
You can also sign up online at **www.dorchesterpub.com**.

*Plus $2.00 for shipping. Offer open to residents of the U.S. and Canada only.
Canadian residents please call 1-800-481-9191 for pricing information.
If under 18, a parent or guardian must sign. Terms, prices and conditions subject to
change. Subscription subject to acceptance. Dorchester Publishing reserves the right
to reject any order or cancel any subscription.